DOCTOR I DO

SHARON WOODS

FOR THE READERS WHO waited two years for this story. This one is for you.

CHAPTER 1

ALEX

"COME BACK TO BED," my one-night stand rasps out.

My head turns, following her voice. I smile when I spot the sultry redhead leaning up on her elbow, staring sleepily up at me. Her brown eyes are trying to pull me in. When my eyes drop to the blanket that's barely covering her breasts, I resist the temptation to lean over and pull it all the way down to expose her. Memories of the sex and fun we shared last night are enough, though.

"I gotta get to work," I say, shaking my head.

As soon as she leaves, I'll never call or see her again. It's just what I do. Even at the ripe age of thirty-two, I haven't been able to settle down. Nobody seems to hold my interest or has made me fall in love. On top of never growing attached to a woman, I'm too busy with work. Most women I meet at my age want to settle down and get married and have kids. And I'm not where I want to be in my career for that...well, not yet.

I spent so long in school to become a doctor that I've only been out a couple of years as a neurologist. I want to spend a couple more years developing my skills and traveling for conferences and courses. If I was married with kids, I'd feel guilty for leaving them. Being carefree and just having fun with no strings attached suits me.

"Work is so overrated," she mumbles cutely.

I chuckle. "Looks like you haven't found your dream job."

"But I found my dream man," she purrs and flutters her lashes, trying to tempt me to crawl back into bed.

I shake my head. "I'm not him, trust me." And I don't give her a chance to argue because it would be pointless. Instead, I walk to my bathroom to shower and get ready for work.

Afterwards, I step back into the bedroom to find her sitting on the edge of my unmade bed, bent over and putting on her shoes. I know I should feel guilty, because I'm practically kicking her out, but I don't...I feel numb.

"I wish I didn't have to leave," she whispers on my doorstep.

I peer down, wishing my heart or body would react, but the same empty feeling stays. I don't answer.

"Call me later," she says, waving as she walks off.

I remain silent, knowing I won't. I don't want to lead her on.

As she climbs into her car, I wonder if I'm broken. Will my future only consist of unfulfilling hook-ups? I thought there was meant to be a person for everyone.

I'm thinking that's not in the cards for me.

Flashing the light between the patient's eyes, I watch her pupils dilate under the brightness. I nod when I see everything's as it should be, turning off the light and putting it away. Once I leave the bedside, I order a range of tests and write up her notes and a new treatment plan.

As I sit at the nurse's desk, my phone rings. When I see my brother Mike's name, I answer immediately, as I've been waiting for the call that he and his wife had their baby. "Bro."

"Hey, Alex. Ah." He sounds out of breath, and it causes me to frown and sit up, closing the file.

"Yeah," I push.

"Alice and I had the baby," he says in a monotone voice.

"Congrats!" I bellow with a grin. But why the fuck does my brother not sound excited? A wave of worry hits me. "Are you okay?"

"I...uh...don't know. It was hectic."

"Is Alice, okay?" I ask.

"Yes. But me? Not so much. I'm traumatized."

I chuckle. My older brother has always been a drama queen. "I'm assuming birth was more intense than you thought."

"Yeah, watching your wife in pain fucking sucks," he chokes out.

I swallow hard, because I can't imagine having someone you feel so strongly about that you choke on your words. Staring down at the closed file, I say, "Let me finish up here, and I'll come right up. Did you need anything?"

He breathes heavily down the line. "Nah. I'm okay."

Doesn't sound like it, but I don't say that. "All right, see you soon. And, by the way, bro, I'm pumped for you. You're going to be an amazing dad."

"Thanks. Catch ya soon."

I hang up, but my phone buzzes again. Mom's name flashes on the screen. A small laugh escapes my lips as I answer. "Yes, Mom."

"Your brother and—"

"I know. I know." I chuckle, cutting her off. "I'm trying to finish work so I can head up."

Hearing the noises in the background, I can tell she's already upstairs.

"Okay, well, don't be too long," she says kindly. Mom is a retired doctor, so she knows how much we work. But she has been pushing for more of a work-life balance...well, more on me, because of my lack of a committed relationship. I can only hope she'll leave me alone now, being too busy in the new grandma role to worry about me.

"I gotta go. I'll finish some notes and talk to the patient, and then I'll be up, okay?"

"Okay, love, see you soon," she sings-songs.

I hang up and re-open the file. I scan the observations and other notes before picking up the file and heading into the patient's room to deliver the news. As I leave their room, it's with a heavy heart, knowing the prognosis doesn't seem bright, but being a neurologist, I barely get to deliver the good news. Maybe it's because of this job I've learned to switch off my feelings.

Yeah, that could be it.

I've had to toughen up.

I'm reading emails as I enter the hospital elevator, my stomach growling, reminding me I've only had coffee today. As I'm heading downstairs to grab something to eat along the way, the doors open, and a friendly face is revealed.

"Hi, Tahlia," I say with a lopsided grin.

Tahlia is Alice's best friend. As I take her in. I remember the last time I saw her. She was dressed up for Mike and Alice's wedding. Unlike today where she's dressed for comfort. Her blonde hair is tied up in a high ponytail. A few tendrils have fallen out. They now hang loose around the sides of her heart shaped face. She's staring back at me, with big glossy green eyes framed by dark lashes. She has the cutest button nose and pouty lips that are currently parting.

"Ale—" she tries to say, but the box of cupcakes she's holding fall from her grip.

I'm moving before I register what's happening, dropping to my knees to help with the mess.

"Great," Tahlia mumbles under her breath. She squats in her dark blue skinny jeans, that I see now have pale blue icing down the side, trying to pick up the cupcakes that have dropped on the floor. From this angle, I get an up-close view of her slim neck that leads down to her low cut shirt. Ample cleavage I have no right staring at but can't help wondering how good they'd feel in my hands. I force my gaze up with a smile.

"At least you look good in blue." I try to lighten her up, and that has her eyes meeting mine. On our knees, we're closer than I thought, and I suddenly feel like I'm in the desert, desperate for a trace of water. Am I in need of some sleep, or are sparks flying?

This is new.

She peers back down, her cheeks flushed, and I finish helping her pick up the scattered cupcake destruction, pushing any wayward thoughts aside. But the icing is stuck to the floor, making it a bit slippery, so I stand and say, "I'll grab some napkins. Hang on a sec."

I stride to the cafe and grab the napkins, and when I walk back she reaches out for them, but I shake my head. "Let me."

"I would fight you on it, but I'm certain my hands aren't working properly right now." She gives me a half smile before nibbling at her lip.

I wonder if she is nervous about her best friend who just had a baby, or if it's something else.

Me?

Do I make her nervous?

Don't be ridiculous...

After I wipe the floor clean and throw the napkins in the garbage, Tahlia looks up at me curiously. "Are you working today?"

"Yeah. Do my clothes give it away?"

She drops her gaze over me. When she finishes checking me out, her green eyes land on mine again. Her tongue slides across her bottom lip as she says back with a mischievous gleam in her eye. "Navy suits you."

My heart hammers. I'm glad she likes what she see's. I can't stop the smirk spreading on my lips, knowing I feel the same way. I like what I see. "Did you work today?"

She sighs, tucking a strand of hair behind her ear. "Yeah. Even though I think my parents were right. I should've stayed in college."

Her answer surprises me. "You could always go back. It's never too late."

"I could..."

"You don't want to?"

"No. Ah...Have you seen the baby yet?" she asks, changing the subject.

I shake my head. "No, I was going to grab something to eat and head up."

"I might need to get new cupcakes." She giggles, and it's the cutest, lightest laugh. I've heard it once before at Mike and Alice's wedding, but I've forgotten just how much I love it. Hearing it again makes me feel a way I'm not used to.

I peek down and see only one cupcake could be saved. And I don't dare tell her I didn't know it was a boy, since the blue icing gave it away.

"Did you get them from here?" I wouldn't object to one right now.

"No, I picked them up at a bakery by the coffee house where I work." Her eyes flick to me, and I swear she almost seems embarrassed.

"Let's grab something for you to take up there, but first, have you had a coffee or something to eat?" I ask.

"Maybe I shouldn't have a coffee. I'm already jumpy." I swallow the disappointment swirling in my gut. I want to spend more time with just her.

"But I might go for tea and something to eat. I've worked all day and have barely eaten anything," she adds, and I spring to life at the knowledge she'll sit down with me.

"Same. I'm living on coffee."

I don't miss the way her eyes flick to my body before moving away to the food counter, clutching her cupcake box to her chest. "I'll find something to take up after."

"Good idea, but maybe pop them in the garbage before you wear any more of them."

Her head turns quickly, and she pulls the box out, to see her white long-sleeve has a smear of blue across the middle.

"Oh, God. I'm getting worse by the second."

I smile. "Let me take the box and put it in the garbage so you can go to the bathroom and clean up. I'll grab you a drink and something to eat."

She sighs with relief. "Are you sure?"

"It would be my pleasure," I say with an honest smile, trying to tell her with my face that I'm here to help her.

I take the box from her, and try to ignore how my hands graze her soft ones. I've never been so distracted by a simple touch. Clearing my throat, I get my thoughts back on track.

"Order?"

"Oh, yeah. A hot chocolate and a cookie, please."

"As a doctor, that is the worst choice, but as a friend, I'll say I'll meet you over at one of those tables." I point toward the empty tables and chairs.

"Don't doctor me around. I just need to eat my feelings right now." She smirks, and a stupid grin settles on my face as I look at her. Spinning on her heel, she walks off, but in the opposite direction of the bathroom.

"T," I call out and she turns around, brow furrowed.

I lift a hand and point in the direction of where she needs to go. "That way."

A pained expression hits her face, and I read her lips. *"What is wrong with me today?"*

Her face is crimson, and she keeps it down and walks fast in the right direction. I turn and dump the box in the nearest bin and set out to get us drinks and food.

As I go to order her a cookie, I scan the different flavors, wondering which one she likes.

I peer over my shoulder catching sight of her. As if feeling my eyes on her she glances back. Our eyes hold momentarily before she turns and disappears into the bathroom. I stare dumbfounded at the door she just entered. My body is excited by her. And I've never been exhilarated by a woman. That revelation leaves me pondering. Who is Tahlia Adams other than beautiful?

Chapter 2

Tahlia

I'm so damn embarrassed, and I can't shake it. As I scrub my soiled top with hand soap and water, trying to get the blue icing out, I mutter to myself about how ditzy I seemed in front of Alex. When I saw him come out of the elevator, I was so shocked at the sight of him.

In my defense, it's the first time I've seen him in scrubs. He looked so sexy with the navy material hugging his broad chest that I fumbled and tipped the box.

He seems to unravel me unintentionally, but I need to remember he's eight years older, a playboy, and my friend's brother-in-law.

My mind goes back to the first time I met Alex, over a year and a half ago. I was on a night out with my friends at a club called Luxe, and he was dancing with Alice when I interrupted to tell her I wanted to leave. But as my eyes held Alex's bright blues, something inside of my chest jolted. And it happened again today.

That has to be why I'm clumsy and flustered today. It can't be the way his tall frame looked stupidly handsome.

His eyes framed beneath dark brows, brown hair tousled to perfection, his sharp jawline dusted with scruff, and when I dragged my gaze up to his throat. I froze. Even that part of him is sexy. How weird is that for me to think? But it is. When he swallowed, his Adam's apple bobbed, and I imagine for a second me leaning over to lick it...yeah, like I said, I'm losing my mind.

I don't like him, not like that, and I definitely couldn't fall for him.

I huff, annoyed that I can't stop thinking about him. I've already spent too long in here, so I give up when there's only a tiny bit of blue left and move to the hand dryer. Quickly, I dry it as much as I can, so I don't go out in a see-through top. I think I've managed to make a fool out of myself enough in front of Alex.

After I take a deep breath to calm the swarm of nerves in my belly, I head back out to find Alex.

I tell myself not to change subjects if he wants to discuss my job or college this time. I can talk about it. I chose this path. So, I shouldn't be embarrassed that I had no idea what I wanted to do when I finished school. Therefore, I studied what my parents wanted me to. But it didn't last long. I quit college after 2 years. I wanted to choose my future. Not have them tell me what to do. That's how I found myself working in a coffee house.

Recently, my grandfather passed, leaving me, a stake in the family business. But the condition to receive the inheritance isn't conceivable.

It isn't long before I spot him in the crowd of tables and walk up to him with a smile. I can't help but chuckle at the piles littered all over the table. Staring down at all the bags and bags of cookies, I tease him. "Are you hungry? I thought doctors ate healthily."

His face morphs with amusement, and he gives me one of his signature smirks that makes every woman drool. And I can't lie. I'm one of them, but I quickly push it away.

"I do. But, ah, I didn't know what flavor you liked, so I, um, ordered them all." His gaze drops and he looks around, as if embarrassed. It's such an odd look for such a confident man.

My mouth slacks and my heart thumps harder. He ordered me every flavor because he didn't know what I'd like.

Who does that?

He does, apparently.

My mouth opens, then closes, and I finally find my voice. "Wow, thanks. That's so kind of you," I say quietly and drag out a chair to sit. I'm in a state of shock. I can't remember the last time a man was nice to me. Especially one as hot as Alex.

"So, what is it?" he asks.

I glance up at him, still in la-la land, thinking about his sweet gesture.

"What's your favorite flavor?"

Ah, what type of cookie I like.

I answer with ease. "Chocolate chip."

He snaps his fingers and leans back into the chair. "I was gonna guess that."

I smile at his enthusiasm. I'm enjoying being around him like this. We've never had one-on-one time together; it's always been with our shared friends around.

He pushes one bag closer to me. "Here."

My gaze flicks to his, and he stares back with warm eyes. "This one is yours."

I smirk back and pick it up to peer inside. When I see the big chocolate chunks, my stomach growls. I pull it out without hesitation and take a big bite, instantly closing my eyes and moaning loudly, savoring the sugary taste on my tongue. When I open my eyes to grab my drink, I'm met with a fixed, heated gaze, thin lips and something swirling between us that feels a lot like sexual tension.

A piece of the cookie becomes lodged in my throat right at the moment he licks his lips, and I concentrate on swallowing it down, but my mouth is too dry. I grab my hot chocolate, and he reaches out, lips parting to speak, but it's too late. I've already taken a big sip, and it burns all the way down. I gasp, and wince screwing up my face as I hold back a swear but fail. "Fuck, that's hot."

"Sorry, I tried to warn you. They were hot to the touch when I carried them over," he says quietly.

I try to lighten the mood by joking. "Hence why you haven't had a sip of your coffee."

His face softens and a small lift in the corner of his lips lets me know it worked, and I watch as he opens one of the bags and takes out a cookie. Watching him chew is too mesmerizing, but I catch myself before my attraction takes over my face. I hope...

I look away to take a breath and focus on something else before I return to eating the rest of my cookie. This time, with no moaning.

"It's a decent cookie," he says, causing me to look back up at him as he wipes his mouth with a napkin.

"Yeah? When was the last time you ate a cookie?" I keep my gaze on his eyes and don't let them wander. No, my mind needs to stay away from the gutter. But I'm only human, and I can't help but sneak a glance over his body—just for a second.

A very long second...

"I can't remember, but it's a damn shame."

I scrunch up my now empty cookie bag, and then hold up my hot chocolate and ask, "Should we take these upstairs?"

"What's the rush? They aren't leaving today. Are you trying to run away from me, T?" His playful tone makes a laugh slip out of me.

I shake my head. "No rush. I just want to meet the baby and see how Alice is." It's half the truth, because I really do want to see them, but I also need to get away from Alex and his effortless sex appeal.

He stands. "Fair enough. These are too hot to drink anyway, so we can carry them up."

I raise a brow at him, surprised he is giving in to me so easily. Before I can say anything else, he continues.

"Well, maybe I should carry both, in case another accident arises." He winks at me, causing me to laugh loudly.

"No, I'm good. There'll be no more accidents for me." I pick up my drink and add, "Oh, but I need to grab some new cupcakes before we go."

"Nah, I got them already." He reaches down beside him and lifts a box to the table. I look at the box, and then back at him, at a total loss for words. He's a lot more thoughtful than I assumed he would be. I imagined him as a selfish and hard to talk to type of guy, but so far, he's been the complete opposite.

"How?" I ask, confused.

"Ordered and delivered them from a bakery nearby."

I must've been in the bathroom longer than I thought...

"Thanks."

He rubs his chin like he's pondering over something. "They're not the same cupcakes you had."

I shrug. Knowing I'm grateful for anything other than empty hands. 'That's okay. What do I owe you?" I grab my purse to pay for them.

"Don't be silly. They're my family too." He shakes it off like he's offended.

"But it's my gift."

"I won't tell them if you don't."

I blink, totally taken off guard by his kindness. "After my day so far, I don't have it in me to fight you."

He leans down, his breath hitting the side of my face and causing the hair on my neck to prickle at the closeness. "You wouldn't win anyway."

The walk to the elevator is almost painful. I'm taking steps with care in an attempt to not make a fool out of myself in front of him. Again.

There's a hint of sexual desire—totally coming from me—that's circling around us, one I'm finding very hard to ignore.

Once we arrive at the elevator, he presses the button, and we remain silent. His deep woodsy and caramel scent are so strong, I can almost taste it. It causes the tingle to spread between my thighs. Maybe the fact he showed me his tender side is making me sensitive. It's tricking my body into thinking what if he was naked and all I could inhale with every breath was him?

Yeah, no, dumb idea. I'll never give in to the temptation with him.

We step into the elevator, and I sag against the wall, grateful for the people inside, even though I stay standing beside him. It feels better knowing the people are barriers for my dirty mind today.

My mouth parts into an easy smile when I realize I'm about to see my friend. I push the tingling feeling for Alex away and replace it with pure happiness. "I can't want to see if he'll look like Alice or Mike."

"I bet he looks like Mike. It's a boy, after all, Tahlia." The way he says the word "boy," my heart drops, and I gasp, lifting my gaze to his humorous one.

"You didn't know, did you?" I ask with wide eyes.

He shakes his head, but the playful smile keeps me from feeling any worse than I do. And right now, I want to kick myself for being so stupid.

I drop my chin to look at the floor.

"Hey. I don't mind. I'm the shit brother who never asked when Mike called."

My head lifts, and my eyes hold his as he continues. "Don't beat yourself up, but maybe don't tell me his name." He winks, and I can't help but laugh.

The elevator doors open, and we exit, walking through the short corridor and straight up to the nurses' desk.

"Hi, Doctor Taylor." I watch as the nurse looks up at Alex with hearts in her eyes and a flush across her cheeks. Suddenly, I'm a little jealous.

"Hey. Can you tell us which room Mike's in?" he says without even a flicker of flirting to be deciphered, which I didn't expect. I've seen him flirt. Maybe because he's at work? Yeah, that's probably it. But secretly, I wouldn't mind if it was because of me.

"Sure." Ignoring me completely, she glances at a piece of paper, then up at Alex. "Room twelve," she answers sweetly.

"Thanks," he replies with a charming smile before pushing off.

He really could charm anyone.

I walk off in the direction of their room and knock on the door. Alex's shoes sound behind me, but I don't wait. I want to see my best friend and her baby.

"Come in," Mike's voice bellows from behind the door.

I hurry inside and beam as I see Alice holding her baby. Tears prickle behind my eyes as she smiles through puffy, tired eyes up at me.

I step straight over to her and hug her, whispering into her ear, "Congratulations," before sitting down in the nearby chair. "Tell me everything." I shuffle my butt to the edge of the chair to get even closer.

"I'm not going to scare you, but it was intense. The ring of fire is something I don't want to feel again anytime soon." She shudders, as if remembering it vividly.

I scrunch up my face, telling myself to not Google it, because it will probably turn me off from having kids in the future. And one day, I want a family of my own.

"I'll take your word for it," I say.

Her eyes drift to Alex and then back to me, and her brow raises.

"What?" My voice stays hushed so the guys can't hear.

Her eyes flick to Alex again before answering in a soft tone. "What's going on there?"

Swallowing, I reply flatly, trying to seem unaffected. "Nothing."

"Are you sure? He keeps looking over at you."

He does?

I can't help but peek over from the corner of my eye, and she's right. He stands in the back of the room with Mike, his hands inside his pockets and those blue eyes set straight on me.

He's not interested. They're probably just talking about the baby or my cupcake incident downstairs, not about me, specifically.

"I dropped the cupcakes for you downstairs and wore half of them. He's probably retelling Mike how much of a clumsy mess I am."

"No, you didn't," she says with a chuckle that causes the baby to cry.

"I did."

She cuddles him closer, cooing to soothe him, and I use the opportunity to get off the topic of Alex fast.

"How long was labor?" I ask, but instantly regret it. I don't really want to know how long my best friend was in pain.

"Twelve hours."

Yeah, that sounds awful.

"That's a really long time," I say with a wince.

She shrugs, and then asks me, "Did you want to hold Ethan?"

My mouth opens with a wide smile. "Do I? Of course, and by the way, I love his name."

"It's sweet, just like him," she says as she looks at Mike longingly, and I wonder what that would feel like. To be utterly consumed with a man who you can trust and love wholeheartedly.

She gently places Ethan into my arms and giggles.

I look up at her and frown. "What?" I ask in a rush, thinking I'm doing something wrong and hurting him somehow. I haven't got experience with babies.

"You won't hurt him, relax. You're so uptight."

It does feel uncomfortable to be sitting so straight, so I take a big breath and ease back into the chair, staring down at Ethan. Smiling, I think of what Alex said to me earlier, and I look over at him. I'm taken aback, as his tight expression is firmly focused on me. It's so intimate and unexpected, it causes my throat to tighten. I swallow so I can speak. "You're right, he looks like Mike."

Alex doesn't move or say anything, he just stands all hot and broody across the room, watching me. I feel like I'm on fire again.

"Told you," Mike says, and I tear my eyes to Mike and his bemused face looks directly at Alice.

I drag my eyes back to Ethan, but I still have Alex's gaze burning a hole through the side of my face.

CHAPTER 3

ALEX

I'VE GONE FROM WANTING to know what color panties and bra set she's wearing to watching her hold a baby. I've never been a family man, but there is something holding me tightly by the throat at watching her with Ethan. There is this new glow on her face, and when she locked eyes with me, there was a wave of peace shining in her eyes. Ethan stayed asleep, and once she eased back in the chair, I thought straight away she was a natural at this.

"How's the dad mobile?" I ask, but I'm unable to tear my gaze from Tahlia.

He grumbles and mutters, "It's okay, I guess…"

"You still sour because you had to give up Marty?" This time, I turn to him with a shit-eating grin. Alice nicknamed his Aston Martin "Marty," and he will never live it down. It's the fun side of Alice. She is so innocently sweet, ignoring anyone who laughed at her habit of naming cars. It's her thing and I kind of love it about her.

My gaze wanders back to the woman in the chair. After today, I probably won't see her again until Ethan's first birthday, and what a damn shame that is. I run my gaze over her and memorize every dip and curve in her delectable body.

"You should have seen how much I cried after Ethan was born."

My lips part. "Wh-what?" I stutter, shock transforming my expression.

His eyes focus on Alice, who stares back at him warmly. "She handled labor so well. Like, it's fucking traumatizing. And then, the next minute, they lifted a little piece of me and her onto her chest, and I bawled like a fucking baby. The feelings were so overwhelming."

"How come you felt like that?" I didn't mean for that question to leave my lips, but I'm curious about what made my hard-ass brother break down. It's not like him.

"I remember it all too well; it's so fresh in my mind. My chest was going to combust with pride. She's a warrior."

While he's all soft and sleep deprived and won't think anything about my questions, I ask what I'm dying to know. "How did you know she was the one?" I say it quietly, not wanting the girls to overhear.

His face breaks into a bright beam of glee. "She feels like home. Keeping me safe, warm, and loved."

Home?

What does that mean?

I don't ask, because I figure if I have to ask, then I've never felt it.

I remember last night, when I was with another meaningless hook-up, how numb and hollow I felt...definitely not a feeling of home.

I was cold, not warm.

There was no care or desire to hold on to them because I love her with every piece of me.

Yeah, no, that's not where I'm at. My life is to focus on my career, and when it's my time, I'm sure I'll know.

"Yeah, that makes sense."

The girls have stopped talking, and the room is now quiet. I'm still leaning back, watching Tahlia hold Ethan with fascination. "Why'd you ask? Are you seeing someone?" Mike asks.

Tahlia's head turns to us curiously, so I say loud enough for her to hear, so she knows, I can see her listening in.

"No, I'm just curious, that's all." I shrug, and he nods, and luckily doesn't push any further.

A knock sounds at the door, and it swings open.

"Where is this little man?"

I peer over and see Tahlia's roommate Maddison, and her friend Blake. Everyone says hi, including me, but I know it's my cue to leave. There are too many people in this room.

I turn to Mike, whose puzzled expression stares back at me. "I'll let you all catch up, and then I'll come back later for a hug."

Blake and Maddison take a seat directly next to Tahlia, and she stands immediately, handing over Ethan into Maddison's arms.

Mike rolls his lips, as if deliberating something. "You know what, I might grab a coffee from downstairs and let them be alone for a minute," he says.

I nod and wait as he crosses to the other side of Alice. She smiles lovingly as he whispers something and presses a soft kiss to her lips before rejoining me.

"Ready?" he asks.

I walk over to the group, Mike behind me.

Tahlia looks up, curiosity etched into her face.

"I'm going to leave you all to meet Ethan. Nice seeing you again T, Blake, and Maddy. I hope to see you again soon."

Blake winks. "I'll probably see you at Luxe this weekend."

"Maybe." I shrug, not knowing what I'll be doing. I have a membership that costs me a small fortune, and it's a good place to drink and unwind after work, so I might just be.

I give them a genuine smile, then look over at Alice. "I'll see you soon. Rest up and kick them out if they're annoying you." I wink.

As the group gasp, Maddison fires back, "Shut up, you."

I chuckle and take one last glance at Tahlia before giving her a smile, to which she gives me a wide one back. I dip my chin, and, for some reason, my chest feels heavy as I exit the room.

I swing my driver and hit the ball, watching as it sails into the air.

"Nice shot, son," my dad says proudly.

My lips part into a smug grin before watching it land on the green perfectly. Fuck yeah.

"Think you'll be going down, old man," I say as we walk back to the golf cart. I take my seat on the driver's side as he slips in beside me, holding on to the bar when I take off.

"I think I might be buying you beers today."

"You may have had a better chance if Mike was here," I tell him, taking a quick glance at his profile.

"Ha. You mean come in second instead of last?" He meets my stare.

"Exactly." Still grinning, I look ahead of me and put my foot down to go a little faster until we arrive at our golf balls. I park.

"Are you on call this weekend?" Dad asks, as we both step out of the cart.

He walks around to pull a driver out of his bag and walk up to his ball.

I stay silent as he makes his hit, and then I answer, "No, I'm off, so I'll catch up on a little paperwork, maybe watch the game, or go to Luxe, but really, nothing much."

He walks over to me, fit as the sixty-six-year-old he is, and comes to stand beside me. I keep my arms over my chest as his ball lands closer to the hole.

"Nice," I mutter.

"Is there someone you're meeting up with at Luxe?"

I tilt my head in the cart direction in silence, offering to get in the cart.

"Do you mean a woman?" I pull on the brim of my green hat, shielding the sun from my eyes. I'm pissed I forgot my sunglasses at home.

"Of course, I mean a woman."

I chuckle. "I'm just checking. But to answer your question, no, I'm just catching up with my friends, Ryan and Jackson."

"You know your mom kills my eardrums over you not settling down or bringing anyone to Sunday dinner."

I roll my eyes, picturing her talking my dad's ear off about my single life and how I need to settle down, as Mike and my sister Stephanie did.

"I can imagine her following you around the house, lecturing you. How I'm the last one and how disappointed she is."

I pinch my lips closed at the last part, hoping he didn't hear it, but it slipped out. It was supposed to stay in my head. But of course, I'm not lucky and the old bugger has the best hearing.

"She isn't disappointed; she just doesn't want you lonely or to never experience love."

Sitting in the parked cart, I don't make any moves to get out. I sit still, holding the wheel in my hands, and stare out at the lake the course backs onto. The trees, shrubs, and peacefulness are hard to beat out here. It's the best course to play at. I try to do this once a week with him now that he's semi-retired, but I've been so snowed under with work that I've missed a few weeks. I continue watching the lake, not wanting to face him when I talk about how I feel. It's not that easy to confess the hollowness, the empty sex, and the lack of connections I fill my life with.

"I don't believe I'll be lonely...but I don't know about love. I don't have much faith that it's out there for me."

"I think you will find the right person at the right time. Well, that's what I tell your mom anyway." He grabs my shoulder with his hand and squeezes. Not a tight one, just a dad offering his soft, reassuring squeeze.

I'm hoping he's right.

CHAPTER 4

TAHLIA

"HOW WAS WORK?" BLAKE asks, watching me grab some Doritos from the cupboard for us to graze on while we chat in my kitchen.

"Crap. I seriously hate my life right now," I mumble as I tear open the bag and pop one in my mouth. I'm hangry. I didn't get time for a break today.

"I get that. But quit." He grabs the bag off me to eat a chip, chewing it loudly.

"I can't. I don't wanna sit around all day. I need to keep busy. But this wasn't the life I thought I'd live."

"Why's that?" he asks with a slight frown.

I grab another chip and shake my head as I eat it before speaking.

"I rent, I'm single, and I hate my job, but I can't quit because I don't even know what to do instead. There's nothing I like other than styling clothes, and college isn't for me."

He turns to the fridge, grabbing the wine out to refill our glasses.

"You're only twenty-four. Calm the fuck down. Things will pan out the way they're meant to."

"I hope you're right," I mumble.

"I'm always right. Oh, and before I forget, your mom called, looking for you."

I roll my eyes. "I'll call her back."

"When?" he asks with a raised brow.

I sigh, knowing I'm not calling my parents back tonight. "Soon. I just need a second before dealing with people who have my life mapped out for me."

"Fair enough, babe. It's your life. I'm just the messenger," he says as he fills the glasses.

"Not too much, Blake." I hold my hand out. We've already had one glass of wine, and it doesn't take much alcohol for me to feel a buzz running through my body. Especially with the lack of food today.

"All right. All right. Keep your panties on," Blake replies with an eye roll.

I take the glass he offers me with a smile, and he lifts his to cheers with me. "To a good night."

"To a good night," Blake says.

We almost clink our glasses when we hear a screech. I jump from the surprise.

"Wait! I'm coming," Maddison adds, her heels clicking fast on the tile behind me. I spin and watch her approach. Gripping the counter with one hand, she grabs her glass with the other and holds it between us. "Cheers."

I flick my gaze from hers to Blake's, and we all say "Cheers," clinking our glasses together before taking a generous sip.

My phone rings. I put my glass down and run to my bedroom and pull it off the charger, seeing Alice's name on the screen. Answering the video call, I hold the phone out, smiling.

"Hi," I whisper, seeing Ethan in her arms. I head back to Maddison and Blake, turning around so we can all huddle together to talk to Alice.

"Where's that hottie of a husband of yours?" Blake asks.

Alice's eyes light up and it's like she just got married, not just had a baby. I've heard there's a new love for your husband when you have a child, seeing the way they dote on you and the baby and how you look at them with a newfound love. And she's definitely glowing, her cheeks flushing at the mention of Mike.

"He's gone home to shower and eat."

"I was going to say, I'm surprised he left your side," I tease.

"It wasn't easy. He took a lot of convincing," she says.

"You mean you offered him a blow job," Blake counters.

I suck in a breath and turn to Blake to narrow my eyes. "Little ears."

"Come on, T, lighten up; he's a baby."

"Not the point," I grumble, leaning back and grab my wine to take a sip.

"Wine? Where are you all off to?"

"Good old Luxe," Blake answers with enthusiasm. He's always the most excited to go compared to the rest of us. Don't get me wrong, it's the best place in town, and it doesn't have sleezy drunk men everywhere. It's filled with the most successful men and women around, so out of all the clubs, it's the place to be.

Alice's face pinches. I know there is a mix of happy and painful memories from Luxe. And I wonder if I'd rather be going out or be her, married with kids.

If I were Alice, I'd be right where she is, but I'm still trying to figure out my life and career, whereas she was a nurse and following her dreams. Me...well, I have no idea who Tahlia Adams is. That chapter is still to come.

"Well, come on, if I can't be there, show me what you're all wearing."

I show Maddison's and Blake's outfits off before facing it to me. As I tilt the phone, Alice grins at my tight white dress. White is risky, but it is one of my favorite colors to wear. I just don't know how much dancing I'll be doing in it.

"Of course, T outdoes us all by rocking something unusual and stylish. Bordering between slutty and sexy," Blake cuts in.

An easy smile plays on my lips. I do have style. Maddison requested I help her find an outfit tonight, so I loaned her my new black dress that has rhinestones on it, outlining her curves. I paired it with her own black peep-toe stilettos and a matching black bag. Blake chose his own colorful tropical shirt. I'd love to style him, but he flat-out refuses. He likes his unique look. And to me, that's what styling is about. A look you love and feel your best in.

"You all look amazing. T, you've heard me say this before, but you should be a stylist," she coos, before adding, "I'm not jealous, other than wanting wine, but I can't while I'm feeding. But soon, wine nights at my house."

"Oh, look at you, Momma. Already needing the booze," Blake teases.

"No, but I'm still young and want to be around my friends. I have zero desire to go to Luxe, but wine...yes, please."

"Why are you talking about wine?" Mike's voice can be heard in the background.

"Nothing, calm down." Alice rolls her eyes at us, but the lift in the corner of her lips lets us know she loves the bossy attitude Mike exudes. "I've gotta go feed Ethan."

"Okay. We should go call a taxi, so you guys have a good night. Thanks for calling. Miss you," I say, waving my hand at the camera.

"See you all soon."

We all say bye, and then I hang up and put the phone down on the counter.

"I ordered the cab," Maddison says.

"Thanks," I say picking up my drink, I take another sip.

"I can't believe she has a baby," Blake says.

"I know! She is a baby herself," Maddison replies.

"She's not a baby," I argue.

"No, I know, but she's still young. Are you saying you'd be down for a baby at this age?" Blake asks.

My face drops in horror, and I shake my head vigorously. "No way. I can't care for a child. I haven't got a house, or a stable career, or—"

"A man," Blake interjects.

"Exactly! No. I'm not ready. You two have more of a chance of settling down than me," I say.

They both turn toward each other and burst out laughing. And I can't help but join them.

Blake composes himself quickly to throw back his drink in one go before demanding, "Chug, girls."

My brows pull together, not understanding what's the rush.

"The cab's here," he says, answering my silent question.

I hold the glass up and see it's still half full. Bringing it to my lips, I drink it quickly. I shoudn't be drinking anymore tonight, I have work again tomorrow. I don't want to be hungover while dealing with my arrogant asshole of a boss. He is bad enough sober.

Putting the glass down, we grab our bags. We don't bother with coats, knowing it's always warm inside the club. We will only be cold for the few minutes lining up.

The drive isn't long, and when we arrive at Luxe, we join the line to get in.

Once we're inside, Maddison and Blake go straight for the bar.

"Wait. Not for me," I call out, grabbing Blakes arm to stop him.

"Come on," Blake pleads, clasping his hands together and fluttering his lashes.

I playfully hit his shoulder. "No, I'm pacing myself. I'll have one soon. I'm already warm from the first two drinks."

"Lightweight." Maddison laughs, and I nod.

They turn to the bar while I go looking for a free area for us to sit down. Spotting one in one of the very back corners, I turn and yell, "Blake."

He turns, and I point in the direction I'm going in. "Chairs."

I ease myself between all the hot suits and sleek dresses, and as I'm about to sit, I see a man sitting too. He's on a call. I'm about to speak when I realize who it is. At the sight of Alex, I'm gulping down air like I need the breath to speak.

He hangs up and tucks the phone into his pocket.

"What a nice surprise," his velvety voice says, pulling my gaze up to his amused face. He must've caught me checking him out. It's not my fault he wears a suit so well.

"Hi, Alex," I say, my head tilting to the side. If I was a smart woman, I'd think of a way to get up and leave and not see him for the rest of the night. But I'm not smart when it comes to Alex.

"I haven't seen you here for a while," he replies, his eyes dropping to my mouth.

"Yeah, I don't come as often as you, clearly," I tease, licking my glossy lips.

His smile broadens before his eyes meet mine and hold them. "Are you jealous?"

"What? No!" I scoff, pretending to be offended.

I'm not...right?

Even if there was a slight green-eyed monster, I would never let him know. His ego is as big as this room.

"You seem defensive."

"And you're being an ass," I say without thinking. My hand flies up to my mouth, unable to comprehend the fact I just said that to him.

He doesn't seem bothered at all. Instead, as I stare back, I see humor and a twinkle in his eye. He leans in. "I knew you'd be like this."

I want to ask what he means by that. Knew I'd be like what?

But as Blake and Maddison take their seat, there is no way I'm asking now. I pick up my drink and take a big sip, my dry mouth thankful for the cold liquid.

"What were you two talking about?" Maddison probes. Her eyes dance between me and Alex.

He eases back in his chair and my hand trembles, so I lower the glass, scared I'll break it with my nervous energy.

I glare at Alex and silently beg for him not to tell them, but of course, he doesn't listen.

"Tahlia called me an ass."

"I said you're *being* an ass," I fire back, clutching my hand into a fist and biting down on my finger. Dammit!

Blake and Maddison let out a roar of a laugh and I roll my eyes at their reaction.

"You're two are being ridiculous," I say, crossing my arms over my chest. But secretly, I'm pinching my lips together to prevent a smile from leaking through. Alex is watching me with a dark expression the whole time. I desperately want to ask what he's thinking.

Alex sits talking to Blake and Maddison, but I can't seem to find my voice right now.

My body is quivering with desire. I can't concentrate long enough to think. The way he keeps looking at me makes me worry about how much restraint I have to keep my hands to myself tonight.

"I better get back to my friends," he says. His smooth voice feels like a caress over my skin, and I bite down on my lip to stop from asking him to stay a bit longer.

Maybe it's better for me if there's distance between us. He doesn't remove his gaze from me, and for a minute, I think he won't go, but then he dips his chin and moves to join his two friends. Ryan and Jackson. They stand by the dancefloor clutching glasses filled with amber liquid as they talk. I didn't even notice them when he was here. Maybe because he clouds my thoughts.

I haven't been able to take my eyes off him since he walked off. My eyes linger over his tall, suited frame and admire how he holds himself with others.

He exumes sex and power.

All eyes are on him.

Including mine.

Annoyed at myself, I drag my gaze back to my friends, who wear curious expressions. Taking a deep breath, I sit back, expecting a lashing. But they look away. I don't miss the way Blake shakes his head before sipping his drink.

I turn to avoid Alex, so I swivel to watch the crowd on the dancefloor under the strobe lights. The club music is much louder than when we arrived, trying to get everyone on the dancefloor and away from the outer edges. I know soon we will be down there until our feet ache, and we want to collapse from exhaustion.

"Did you want another round of drinks?" I yell, cutting through their conversation.

"Yeah! Then let's dance!" Maddison shrieks, as if her voice wasn't loud enough. I can't help but giggle and nod. Rising to my feet, I speak when my bladder twinges.

"I need the bathroom before our next round," I confess.

"Same," Blake says loudly.

We all stand, and before I move a step, I peek over my shoulder at Alex and his friends. His back is to me, but I notice a few women are now talking to them, and a sigh slips from my lips. Just as I turn back around, he catches my eyes and holds my gaze. He scans me openly. As if he's undressing me with his eyes. My heart thumps louder in my ear at the attention. I give him a small smile before walking off. I need a moment alone to cool down. The sexual chemistry between us tonight is palpable.

Making my way through the crowd to the bathroom is a mission, but getting to the front of the bar afterward is almost impossible. I slide against bodies to get to the front, and once I order a round, we stand together, swaying to the new song.

As soon as Maddison finishes her drink, she shouts, "Let's go."

"Hang on, I'm not done." But as the words leave me, Blake tips his head back and drains his glass.

Dammit. Now I have to hurry.

I take a big sip, but wince from the taste of alcohol. This vodka cranberry is so strong, my stomach dry retches. I can't drink the rest, so I lower the glass and follow them out onto the dance floor.

It isn't long before I'm moving my hips to the beat, getting lost, and sweat beads trickle from my neck down my back. I grab my hair and bring it to one side, trying to cool off. The dance floor is crowded, and my feet keep getting stepped on every two minutes, but I'm lucky they're aching from dancing, so I can't feel them anyway.

The next song comes on, and it's slower, so I slow my hips to a rocking motion. A moment later, I hear a tear and a cool draft hits my legs, I know it's the back of my dress. Internally, I curse and squeeze my eyes closed. Why is my luck so bad lately? Who have I pissed off?

I reach down quickly and touch it, happy to find only a small tear. But I don't have long to dwell on it, because I'm met with surprise when I back into someone. I jolt, and I'm about to spin, but a warm hand snakes around my waist. It's causing my throat to constrict with the panic rising, and I'm about to tell him to remove it.

But then there's a warm breath against my neck as someone whispers in my ear, the panic transforming to a hum when I recognize the deep, velvety voice.

"It's me. I've got you, T. Dance with me." Alex's words tickle my neck, and his scent is even stronger and more intoxicating this close. Suddenly, I feel lightheaded, and it's not from the alcohol.

Did he know my dress ripped, and he's helping me cover myself?

The song changes to more of a R&B rhythm, and I feel the bass in my chest. His body slides behind me, closing the distance between us, so we are flush together. The movement causes all the air to leave my lungs.

"Grab onto me," he whispers against my neck, and I follow his direction without a second thought. I want to dance with him.

As soon as my hands grasp his forearms, I notice how thick and muscular they are, and then his soft hair adds some texture. I move my hands lower to intertwine with his. He accepts and then tightens his grip. A spark of electricity thrums through me. I rest my head against his powerful chest and brush my ass against his groin. Our hips move in a sensual rhythm, making my body tremble. There's a need between my thighs I've never felt before. Feeling his obvious erection against my lower back sends a dull throb into my sex, and I want more than anything for his hand to slide under my dress and inside my panties.

"What are you doing?" I ask as loudly as I can through my dry throat.

He steps back and spins me, and I stare up into his eyes as I'm pulled against his chest. They are heavy with lust, and it makes me feel desired, wanted...sexier than ever. His hands hold my hips, and he continues to dance, bringing me closer, our eyes locked on one another's. Both of us are breathing heavily, his breaths coasting over my face. When he moves his lips closer, I wonder if he's about to kiss me. I want him to. I even lick my lips in preparation.

"Dancing with you," he answers simply. His words pull me from my lust-filled haze, and my gaze moves from his perfectly shaped lips over his sloped nose and up to his dark, heated blues.

I stare back, at a loss.

He moves his face into my hair, his hot breath tickling my ear. "Does this feel good?"

I'm too transfixed with his face being so close to mine that I need to concentrate on breathing.

Yes, this feels good...a little too good.

Chapter 5

Alex

"T, honey, answer me." My voice is husky from the desire coursing through my veins. Our faces are dangerously close, I can hear her pant.

I'm so hard from Tahlia's sexy ass grinding against me. There's no way she didn't feel it.

I need a second to pull myself together. It seems she does too. Her mouth opens and closes. She's still trying to catch her breath.

The alcohol I consumed evaporated the moment I had her in my arms; the soft curves of her body fit perfectly against my hard ridges. I enjoy holding her, but spinning her and seeing those heavy, lust-filled eyes sent a thrill up my spine. I noticed the tear in her fitted white dress, and I know she wanted to leave, but I saw it as my opportunity to sweep in and cover her up. But the moment I held her, I wanted to dance with her. Enjoy the moment.

A smile erupts on her face, telling me this is a really good idea. Most of her blonde hair is to one side, but some pieces are cascading down her back. Dropping my gaze lower, the white fabric clings to her and enhances her lush, full ass that looks like a good handful. I'd love to get my hands of her curves and lift her up into my arms, but I don't want to scare her away, or worse, tear her dress further and expose her to other guys here. The thought makes my teeth clench, not wanting anyone to see her body, so instead, I keep my hands around her hips.

"Mm-hmm," is all she says.

Leaning toward her ear, so she can hear me, I'm hit with her strawberries and white chocolate scent, and it makes me swallow a groan from how perfect it is. It's everything her—sexy, sweet, warm, and Jesus, I want a taste.

"Where's your voice tonight? Are you enjoying this?" I ask again.

"No. I just...like this music," she says, highly amused.

"If you say so," I reply playfully.

I swallow at how close her face is to mine. She's so close I can almost taste her breath, and I wonder what those lips would be like to kiss. She's staring at me with come-fuck-me eyes, and even if it kills me, I don't give in.

"Of course, I'm enjoying this. I'm sure you can tell. But I'm surprised you can dance," she says with a teasing tone.

I cock a brow. "Really? Did you think I was that unco-ordinated?"

She peeks up at me, blinking, her thick black lashes standing out against her bright green eyes. They are drawing me in. "Yes, I didn't picture you to be good at dancing. I thought grinding would be the best hip action you could do." Her lips pinch together to prevent a smile, and she turns her head to stare out at the crowd.

"Why?" I tilt my head, only getting a view of her profile, as she refuses to look at me.

Her lips part and she mutters, "Because having a woman in front of you, directing you, is easy."

She has no idea how much restraint I have right now not to come inside my pants from the way her ass moves against me.

Taking a deep breath, I speak directly into her ear.

"I would love a woman to direct me and show me what she wants me to do with these hips." And I don't have to wonder if she gets my double meaning, because her eyes roll. I bet underneath her sweetness is a bold and sassy woman, yearning to be set free. She seems very close-lipped with me, and I can't help but be excited by that.

Maybe I'm different for her?

"Always a hook-up with you," she says in a clipped tone like the word "hook-up" is disgusting to her.

I'm about to argue, when Blake cuts in, yelling, "Look at you two, the picture-perfect couple."

As soon as those words leave his lips, Tahlia's warm body and presence slip away, and my body mourns the loss with a shudder. I don't turn to Blake or respond, as I'm too busy stopping myself from begging her to come back and dance with me. The way her arms are crossing under her chest, it pushes her breasts up and out of her dress, and my brain isn't working properly, too busy lost in dirty sex positions with my dick and her tits.

"No way," she yells back, but it lacks conviction.

And I can't be irritated, even though I know we shouldn't hook up for the sake of her heart. I'm sure I'd break it, and then Mike would lose his shit at me over it, because Alice would be upset, and no one upsets his wife.

"Imagine the hot babies," Blake says.

Yeah, no, that's drawing a line, even for me. "Sorry, bud. Not happening."

Maddison comes over with a fresh round of drinks. I look over at Tahlia, and she's wearing a hurt expression. Surely, not over the kid comment, or because I won't kiss her? No way, it must be something else. But before I can ask if she's okay, she turns away, telling Maddison she isn't drinking anymore tonight. When she faces me again, the hurt has gone, and her smile is back.

We dance for a little longer, and this time, I hate it. I'm not touching her at all, not even our fingers lacing together. I keep my gaze locked on her hips, watching them sway from side to side and moving to the beat of the music. We're all pushed closer together, and with each song, the crowd gets drunker. I take the opportunity to speak to her while everyone's distracted.

"Are my dance moves getting any better?"

Her eyes glow under the strobe lights and the little tilt of her head makes me grin.

"You're not bad. I'll give you that, Doctor."

My brow rises and my lips quirk. "Doctor?" I ask with mischief.

"Well, you are one, right?"

"Oh, the sass on you, T," Maddison says.

I flick my gaze to Maddison, wishing she didn't hear our chat, because Tahlia curls back away from me. All the humor gone. She's back to the quiet Tahlia I've seen when I've been around her with Mike and Alice. But at the hospital and tonight, she's flirted with me, and I have to admit, I like her relaxed and flirty.

"What? He's a doctor, that's all," she replies to Maddison's and Blake's shocked expressions. They don't seem so sure about it, and I'm not saying a word.

"I am a pretty good one too," I say, giving Tahlia a lopsided grin.

She rolls her eyes and smirks back. "I would hope so."

Maddison and Blake finish their drinks, and as soon as Tahlia notices, she says, "You guys ready to go? I've gotta work tomorrow."

And I wonder if she's speaking the truth, or if she's trying to run away from me.

"Yeah, good idea. I'm done," Blake confesses, running a hand through his sweaty hair.

"I guess I'll see you next time," I say, waving at Blake and Maddison.

I turn to Tahlia, and I can't help the way my hand reaches out to touch her waist. "Nice seeing you again."

Her gaze drops before looking up. I take in her flushed nose where her makeup has worn off. It's adorable. "Same. Bye, Alex."

"Night." I don't remove my hand, and she doesn't twist out of my grip until they all turn to walk away. And I can't help but watch her walk out the door, stopping myself from offering to make sure she gets home safe. Even though I know it's ridiculous, because she lives with Maddison.

What on earth is wrong with me?

Must've been the alcohol tonight...maybe it was stronger than usual.

Yeah, that's it.

∞

"Where did you go?" Ryan asks sliding his arm around a woman he was kissing passionately only moments ago. He's wearing a smug grin, probably thinking I've been hooking up with someone.

I wish I had another drink in hand. "Dancing."

I take my seat back on the sofa and, suddenly, I want to leave too. Being here is no longer appealing without Tahlia.

"I saw you talking to Alice's friend. What's her name?" He clicks his finger.

"Tahlia," I answer, but immediately wish I didn't.

"You going to tap that?"

I scoff. "No way. Mike and Alice would cut off my balls."

Ryan snorts. "That's true. But she's hot, even if she's a tad quiet—"

"But it's always the quiet ones," Jackson cuts him off and bumps his shoulder, winking.

I stay silent, looking down, knowing they might be right. However, it's not going to happen, no matter what I think or want.

Since I've been dancing with Tahlia, the guys have acquired a group of women hanging around us. Usually, I'd be chatting one up, with plans of taking one home for the night, but it's doing the opposite. My stomach rolls as I think about it, and bile rises when one sits down beside me, purring into my ear and asking if I want to dance with her.

No, I don't. As a matter of fact, I want the petite blonde to get her sweet ass back here so I can dance with her instead. The woman lays her hand on my thigh and squeezes, and I immediately rise to my feet, hating her touch on me.

Peering down at her, and then over to Ryan and Jackson, I clear my throat. "I'm out of here. You two comin'?"

"You want to leave already?" Jackson bellows with a frown, clearly upset I'm even asking.

"Yeah, a big week at work," I lie, not wanting to tell them I had a feel of Tahlia, and the idea of another woman touching me irks me. That isn't something I want to confess to my buddies right now, if ever.

"Can we stay a little longer?" Ryan asks.

I don't want them to leave because I'm being a grumpy dick. "You two stay. I'll call my driver."

"You sure?" Jackson asks.

"Yep. I'll talk to you tomorrow," I say, pulling out my phone and texting my driver to meet me out the front.

I stop by the bar, grab a shot, and walk through the crowd, and straight out to grab my ride. Sitting in the back of the car, I slump, staring at my phone with deliberation. I want to text her and see if she got home okay, but I don't. Instead, I stare out the window, replaying the night in my head. From how she looked in that sexy dress, to the way her warm skin felt, and her sweet scent causing my brain to misfire. It was a good thing she left, because if we were to hook up, I know how it works the next day. I know how I am, and she wouldn't be any different. Would she?

CHAPTER 6

TAHLIA

SURELY, THERE IS MORE to life than making coffee?

Yeah, that's the same question I keep asking myself as the manager's son, berates me for burning a customer's coffee.

When your head is thumping and your eyes feel like they are going to come out of their sockets from sleep deprivation, the last thing you care about is coffee. I want to go home and sit on my sofa with Maddison and eat cheesy pizza and chug soda while watching trashy movies until I fall asleep. But I'm here, getting my ass handed to me for making a mistake. Does he think he's perfect? Has he never used the wrong temperature water?

That's right, he doesn't know how to make one. The way he struts around, belittling everyone. Acting like we are nothing more than a piece of gum on his shoe. He's such a jerk.

"How long have you worked here Ta-le-a?" He tsks.

I bite down on the inside of my cheek. He says my name incorrectly, but I'm the sweet girl, not the one who loses their cool at the workplace. Instead, I stand here, looking glum and nodding, keeping my focus on him, flinching with every spit word that comes toward me through his teeth. His hands are on his hips and he's tapping a foot, waiting for my answer.

I want to say, "too long," but he's not worth it.

"Four years," I reply.

"Exactly. And you still can't make coffee," he says, screwing up his face and shaking his head.

I don't want to apologize, but I'm wondering how else to salvage this situation.

I stay silent, waiting for him to get everything off his chest before I can finish my shift.

"Do you think you can make another one without destroying it?"

"Yes."

He huffs. "Well, get back there and make a fresh cup, and I'll go calm the customers down and apologize for you."

"I can do it," I reply, not wanting him to do it for me. I'm capable of doing it myself.

He narrows his eyes at me, but I don't shrink inside myself. I stare back at him, taking his insult on the chin. "I think you've done enough today. Just get back there and make a fresh cup of coffee."

I don't want this job anymore. I'm so done with it. I officially can't take another second.

Removing my apron, I toss it on the counter with a deep breath. Then I straighten my spine. "You know what? I'm done!"

He crosses his arms over his chest. His bushy brows rise and pull further together. "Don't be ridiculous, Tahlia. Put your apron on and get to work."

I shake my head. "No. I quit."

"Who is going to make the customer his new coffee?"

I shrug, uninterested. "You."

"Fine. You were useless anyway!" he spits.

"Well then, it looks like I'm doing you a favor."

His jaw ticks, but I spin on my heel, feeling the lightest I have in a very long time.

The buzz in my bag frightens me as I exit work, jobless. I rummage through my bag, but I can't find my phone with the mountain of rubbish inside of it. I drop to the ground and follow the vibrations, my eyes widening as I see the name.

I accidentally hit the answer button. Bringing it up to my ear, I speak. "Mom. Hi."

"Tahlia, darling, where have you been?"

A soft sigh slips out because I know the words that will spill from her mouth next. I mime them as she says them.

"When are you coming to visit? It's been too long," she whines, and I can't help but smile to myself getting almost all the words correct.

"Soon, Mom."

I don't know how soon, but I figure it's an answer that I can get out of. After today, I need to go home and search through jobs until I find something fulfilling.

I stand up and reposition the bag on my shoulder as I walk to a vacant bench. She will want to talk for a while, so I take a seat, scanning to check no one can hear our conversation.

"Where are you?"

"Sitting outside. I quit Frank's." I turn around, looking back at the glass door leading into the coffeehouse, relieved I'm never going back.

"Finally. Well, remember, your father and I have told you that when you turn twenty-five, if you aren't married, you won't get your inheritance from your grandfather. Your stake stays with us to sell to another investor. That would be unfortunate. You know Emerald Designs is a good job. Well paying. You become the majority stake owner. Be your own boss..."

How could I forget? The Adam's family fashion business; Emerald Design's.

My parents took over the business from my Grandfather, who passed away recently.

"Mom, women don't need to be married off at twenty-five. They can run businesses and be happily single," I argue.

"Your grandfather made the clause. I have no power to change it."

Blowing out a breath, I run my hand through my hair and scratch the base of my neck. I'm not even dating, let alone engaged to be married.

His death was unexpected. So, to think about owning a majority of stake in a business I knew nothing about, in a short amount of time, was too much pressure. It's like there's a countdown hovering over my head.

But now, I know, I want to learn about the business. My inheritance. A fulfilling future. There's just one major problem. I don't want a husband.

I pause for a moment too long, because she adds, "You know we have a handsome young man who comes from a great family. You've met Ma—"

"I'm dating a guy named Alex," I blurt without thinking.

I'm lying to my mother.

I'm so going to hell for this.

Why do I need to be married, or settle down? Yes, I live with friends and go out clubbing to Luxe. I know they disapprove of it all, but I want to live like a normal twenty-four-year-old, not the old-fashioned way they want me to. I've never given them a reason not to trust me, but they continually want to control my future.

"And you won't marry him?"

Date him is one thing, but to marry him.

"I don't know what he's thinking," I lie again, because I don't know what else to say now that I've started this.

I stare out at the people walking around, couples holding hands, kissing, all the things a couple would do. Could I hold his hand, cuddle him, or worse, kiss him like we're dating?

Yes. It's not like I'll get attached.

I just need to do this until I get my part of the business transferred to me.

Could I get him to go along with it?

I hope so. I probably should have thought of that important bit before.

"So, how is it going between you? This is the first time you've mentioned him," she presses, pulling me from my wandering thoughts.

I close my eyes and squeeze my neck before throwing my hand in the air. Why did I think it was a good idea to lie?!

"We're good, Mom. I was going to tell you and Dad next time I saw you."

"When do we get to meet him?"

And by *we*, I know she means her and my father.

I chuckle, but it's not a light, funny one, it's an awkward, strained one.

"Soon."

She gasps excitedly, and I almost feel bad, but I need to take this chance at a career change and a way to make something of myself. Make myself proud. I'm desperate for this chance, and I'm willing to sacrifice a little to make this happen. I'm going to blame the movie Maddison and I watched the other night with this 'fake dating' premise.

I just hope Alex won't mind. I don't think he would. But then again, he's a player and will have to agree to not see anyone or sleep with anyone else while being with me. Could he do that? I won't be giving him sex in any form, that's for sure. A kiss, well, I could do that, but anything further is out of the question.

"Send me a picture."

Panic clutches at my throat. I don't have a picture of us. Think, Tahlia! Think!

"I'll show you in real life. Pictures don't do him justice."

"Okay, well, tomorrow night, you come here for dinner and bring your boyfriend, Alex. Your father and I can't wait to meet him." She sounds happy, and I can't believe she bought it. I just need to get Alex to agree and somehow act like a real couple in front of them.

This is so bad. I have dug myself the biggest hole and I don't know how I'll get out of it. If they were to figure out the truth, I can only imagine the disappointment I would be to them.

"I don't kn—"

"Tahlia, I'll see you and Alex at six p.m. sharp. Don't be late."

I slouch down on the hard wooden bench and give in to her request. "Okay, Mom."

We hang up, and I sit staring at the phone.

How am I going to ask Alex?

I picture it. Me nervously trying to explain that I need his help to be my fake boyfriend so I can get my inheritance. Then I say, "Oh, but we need to get married." I can imagine the horror on his face. Yep, I'm so screwed.

But if I at least get him to agree to fake date me, I might be able to figure out a way to convince him.

Do I turn up at his work, home, or call him?

I don't have his address, so that rules out the home option. He could be in surgery or on the ward or not even be at work...Calling is my only option at this point.

I suck in a big, deep breath and scroll through my contacts. Thankful we swapped numbers for Mike and Alice's wedding present.

It isn't long before my thumb hovers over his name.

I can do it...

Shit, I'm doing it.

It's ringing.

Butterflies hit my stomach, and I don't know if I'm going to be sick. But it's too late because he answers.

"Hello?" he says, clearly without recognizing my number. I'm a little bummed, if I'm honest.

"Ouch, you don't even have my number saved."

A deep chuckle sounds down the line, and it makes me smile. "Ahhh, T. I better get to saving, then. Can't have my favorite girl upset."

His flirty words cause my stomach to flip, but I laugh it off and mutter, "I bet you say that to all the ladies."

"Nope," he says, and then whispers, "Only you."

My heart picks up speed, and I'm trying not to overthink this and let it derail me.

"I don't know how much you're going to like me soon."

He clears his throat, and I tilt my head and close my eyes as I let the sun hit my face.

Just say it.

"Wha—" he asks curiously.

My nerves are bubbling, and I can't help but cut him off, trying to hurry the words out.

"Would you be my pretend boyfriend?"

"What? Why would you need a pretend boyfriend?" he chokes out. I've definitely surprised him.

"I need my parents to take me seriously."

He coughs and splutters before composing himself. "What the hell for? That's a big favor without giving me all the details."

I sigh loudly and drop my chin back down. My nerves hit my chest as I talk. "My grandfather left a will. He owned a fashion business called Emerald Designs. He left my parents with 40% stake, and me the rest. But there's a clause. I can't inherit my stake unless I'm married by my twenty-fifth birthday. Otherwise, my parents can sell my 60% stake to another investor. When I quit Frank's today, I realized I want my stake in the family business."

I figure I can't hold anything back if he is to play the part for real. He needs to know all the lies I spilled to my mom.

"Shit! You really want this, don't you? I wasn't expecting this call today."

I can't help but smile at his rambling. It eases my nerves a little.

"I know, and I'm sorry. I'm just sick and tired of my life. I'm going through the motions without enjoying it. Quitting Frank's is one way of taking back my happiness. And getting my stake in the family's business would be another."

"How did Frank. I'm guessing that's his name, take it?"

"He told me I was useless anyway."

"Do you want me to come down after surgery today and yell at the dumbass?"

I giggle, but it turns into a snort, loving this protective side to him. "Nah, I'm good. It's nothing I can't handle."

"You shouldn't have to handle that." His voice is serious.

"Well, hopefully, I'll have a business to run, and he won't matter anymore..." I trail off, hoping he agrees to my offer.

"Oh, yeah. That's where I come in, right? Boyfriend. But let me get this straight; I have to do this until your birthday, which is in December, right?"

Him saying he has to do this gets me excited. He may actually say yes.

"Yeah. Does this mean you'll agree?" I ask with the sweetest, pleasing tone.

"Are you going to beg me?"

I grumble, and he chuckles again.

"I'm kidding...sorta," he teases.

"Fine. If I have to beg, I will."

He sucks in an audible breath. "For anyone else, I'd say hell no, but for you, T, I'll do it."

My breathing shallows, and my heart thumps loudly in my chest. I'm lost in the thought of being special to him. I'm somehow different. But why?

I don't dare ask that. I need to stick to the point of the phone call.

"But there are conditions," I say to stop my racing mind.

"Like what?" he asks.

Do I say it now, or wait to see him face-to-face? Nope, that would be worse. Rip the Band-Aid off.

"It would mean you're exclusive to me. No one else," I say, much too quietly. I'm surprised he even heard it, but when he answers, I know he did.

"Right," he mumbles. I can imagine him thinking it over, but then he asks, "What will we do?"

My throat is dry, constricting. I'm suddenly feeling warm all over.

Gripping the phone, I try to act like this is a totally normal conversation. "Hold hands, cuddle, and um, kiss, probably, just for show."

It's silent for a beat, and I hold my breath, waiting for him to say something. All I can hear is him breathing heavily down the line.

"Okay," he finally answers, after what feels like ten minutes.

"Okay?" I clarify, my heart thundering in my chest.

"Okay. But I have my own condition."

"Anything," I reply immediately.

"I can tell getting the business is important to you. So, if it requires you to get married, let's be engaged and get married," he suggests, as if it's not a big deal.

I gasp. *Wow*. I wasn't expecting that.

My brain falters a little in shock. When I let his offer sink in, I clear my throat, not hating the idea. "You'd do that?"

"Yeah, why not? It'll be fun, and you get something that means a lot to you." He states it so easily. Yet I'm trembling with the trouble I'm getting myself into.

"What time tomorrow?" His voice pulls me from my distracting thoughts once again.

"Dinner is at six."

"All right. We need to meet before dinner to talk things over, and then we can leave together."

"I can drive to Bar 9 at five. It's on the way to my parents," I say, as I could do with the wine.

"Are you telling anyone?" he asks.

"Not yet."

"Why? Are you embarrassed?" he gruffs, sounding hurt.

"No, no, no," I rush out, sitting taller. "I hung up from my mother after blurting you're my new boyfriend and called you immediately. I haven't had time to get my thoughts together yet."

"Your mom believed you telling her that you have a random boyfriend?"

I sigh. "Seems so. She was trying to set me up with someone. And I'm not being fixed up with her choice."

"Should I be worried about you being able to lie that well?" He isn't serious; he's teasing me, and it makes me giggle.

"No, I detest lying. But the will my grandfather left, leaves me no option. I had to tell them a small white lie to get my stake."

"Whatever you need to tell yourself to sleep at night," he jokes.

We laugh together and I have to pinch myself with how easy it is to talk and laugh with him. Maybe a little too easy...

CHAPTER 7

TAHLIA

AT FIVE O'CLOCK, I walk into Bar 9 and scan the room. The dim lighting makes it hard to see faces clearly. As I make my way through the crowd hovering around the bar, then over by the tables, I see Alex waving me in. His face lights up as I walk closer, and I don't miss the way his gaze drops over my outfit.

I dip my head and run my hand over my black leather skirt, and then re-adjust my off-the-shoulder sweater. It's a mix of sexy and comfortable.

When I approach, I begin internally panicking. How do I greet him? Kiss on the cheek? Shake his hand?

He pulls out my chair, answering my overworking brain.

"Thanks," I say as I sit down.

I feel the heat tickle my cheeks, and I'm glad I put foundation and blush on. Hopefully, it's hiding the embarrassment written on my face.

"You look stunning," he says as he walks around to take his seat opposite me, but not before I run my own eyes over his outfit. My blush deepens. He's hot. His dark jeans cling to his thick thighs, and his brown sweater and denim jacket complement his five-o'clock shadow and blue eyes. His styled hair and smirk are the real killer, though. And before I know what's happening, I'm blurting out, "You look good, too."

His smile broadens, and his eyes crinkle, which adds to his appeal. Now my butterflies have turned into a full flutter.

A server comes over and we order drinks. I get a white wine and he gets a beer.

He leans to the side of his chair, rubbing his jaw roughly. The wheels are turning in his head. I'm about to ask what he's thinking about when he says, "You're not what I envisioned."

My eyes widen at his confession.

He straightens in his chair, shaking his head. "No. Better."

I let go of the air I was holding and giggle. "I was hoping it was a good thing."

"Oh, it is."

My interest is piqued. "Why?" I ask.

His brows pinch together in confusion.

I clear my throat. "Why am I better than what you envisioned?"

A chuckle rumbles from his chest. "Ah. Well. You're kind, obviously. But there's this adventurous spark with a hint of boldness about you. I can see it in your eyes."

His gaze holds mine a moment too long, and I find myself needing a sip of water. With Alex, I don't have to wonder how daring I could be. It would be a given. He knows how to pleasure a woman, and I'd have fun being on the receiving end. But here I am jumping right to steamy thoughts again...

I wiggle my brows to lighten the mood, which causes us both to laugh.

"Am I what you were expecting?" he asks, and I think of how he hasn't made me feel icky or dirty. Instead, comfortable and sexy.

"You actually want me to answer that?" I tease, lowering my glass.

He leans forward, wiggling his dark brows. "Yes. Hit me."

I shrink a little knowing I judged him harshly. "I expected you to be obnoxious and full of yourself."

"Ouch," he says, rubbing the back of his head, careful not to mess up his hair.

I shake my head. "But you're not."

A playful yet dazzling smile erupts on his face. He liked my answer.

"You're thoughtful, caring, and surprisingly sweet."

"Sounds like I need to grow a set of balls."

My mouth opens and closes.

"Don't. They're great qualities. More men should be that way," I add with a soft smile.

"Sounds like you're ready to marry me, T," he replies with a dark stare.

"I wouldn't say that..." I trail off.

My hands are on my lap, gripped together, as I eagerly wait on my wine. I need it to take the edge off.

"You're clearly shitting yourself about this engagement." He smirks, as if it's funny. There's not a trace of nerves coming off him. I didn't need to worry about him charming my parents. He has charm in spades. It's me who might give us away.

"What are the details of this deal?" I ask, opening my bag and hoping I can find a pen.

"Don't tell me you're going to write it down?"

I pause my search and close the bag, dropping it back down beside me. "Fine. Let's talk."

He smiles smugly. "Rule one. Have fun."

I roll my eyes and shake my head. "Of course, you'd say that."

"No, I mean it. Everything we do, it's got to be fun. The venue, the cake, suits and dress shopping, bachelor/bachelorette party. It all has to be fun."

I rub my finger over my lip, thinking. It sounds less stressful and like something I could get on board with. He'd make it easy, I know that. "Yeah. I like that rule."

He leans back, asking casually, "What's one of your rules?"

Dropping my finger away from my lip, an easy thought comes to me. "No lying or hurting the other person."

"Respecting each other."

I nod. "Exactly."

"Can we tell people about what we're doing?" I ask, knowing I'll need to confess to my best friends. There's no way I could hold something like this to myself. Blake, Maddison, and Alice are practically my family.

He shrugs. "Just not the parents. Friends, sure. Why not? Oh, I'll probably tell Mike, but not my sister. She can't keep a secret to save herself. And the fewer people who know, the less chance someone will slip."

I smile at the tidbit of information about his sister. "Yeah, I'd tell Alice, so it would be good if they both knew."

I know they'd all be supportive of us. Everyone would think this was crazy, but they'd understand and help in any way they could. "I'll only tell them on an as-needed basis. I'm not hosting a party to tell them or anything," I admit, huffing a laugh.

"How did you want to break up?" he asks.

"Just say we weren't the right fit. And apply for a divorce," I reply.

He dips his head. "We'd need to wait for you to get complete control of your stake first."

"Yeah, good idea."

We gaze at each other in silence. I consider other rules but he's distracting. I shrug it off. I'm sure more will pop up at another stage.

"I have one more," he adds, looking me seriously in the eyes. "No falling in love with me, Tahlia. I don't catch feelings, so it's better this is out in the open, and there are no expectations that I'm some Prince Charming."

I scoff, which turns to a giggle, thinking he's joking. When I recover, I lean in so the whole restaurant doesn't hear. "You wish. You know it's not like that." I wave my finger between us. "This is a business deal, and that's it. By the way, these rules aren't helping. I'm currently still freaking out about it," I whisper through my teeth.

His eyes light up at my confession. "Don't be nervous. We need to know more about each other, though, so give me some basic information about you before I get to your parents."

"Good idea." I shuffle through the basics. "I'm twenty-four and my birth date is December 8. My favorite color is blue, and I'm an only child."

"Favorite food and drink?"

"Oh, yes. Italian food, and my drink of choice is white wine," I say.

He nods.

Our drinks arrive, and when she leaves, I'm quick to pick up my wine, holding it up. "Thank you, Alex, for helping me with this. I hope you understand how much I appreciate it, and you."

We clink glasses. And as our eyes meet, his dilate. It's quiet for a moment as we both take a good, long sip of our drinks.

Lowering his beer to the table, where he cradles it in his palms, he gazes at me, asking, "Do you have allergies? Or things you dislike?"

I hold my wine in my hand, enjoying the cold glass on my sweaty palm. "No, and ah, I don't think so."

His brows lift high into his hair line.

I tap the glass with my nail, mulling over the question. I wasn't expecting it.

"Rude people, liars, cheaters, and onions," I say on a breath. Thank God my brain decided to work again.

He chuckles, picking his beer up, but before he drinks, there's a soft shake of his head.

"What?" I ask.

"Just after that list, I wasn't expecting onions."

I take a sip of my wine.

"Oh, and Mom's name is Sonya, and my dad's is Hector. But what about you? I need to know your birthday, favorite color, and family."

"My birthday is March 1st. I don't really have a favorite color, but I have Mike and a sister Steph. My parents are both doctors, and their names are Margaret and Paul. Steph is a Dermatologist. Oh, and I like to play golf and watch football."

"I could've guessed that," I tease with a smile.

"But did you know I'm a better golfer than Mike?"

I roll my eyes playfully. "I bet you and Mike have always been competitive."

"Yeah, definitely about golf. But my dad kicks both of our asses," he says with fondness before picking up his drink and gulping some down.

"I think my dad will like that piece of information."

He drains his beer. "He plays golf?"

"Sometimes." I smile.

"I'll have to get him to play so I can win him over." He winks.

"I think you'll do it without that," I mumble before I drain my glass, too.

He stares at me with amusement, and I expect him to call me out on it, but he doesn't.

"I know you go to Luxe, and you used to work at Frank's, and you went to college for a bit for business but quit. What hobbies do you have?"

"I work out and watch a lot of movies and TV."

He nods and leans back in his chair, digging in his pocket for something. I take the opportunity to get a better look around the cozy bar. It's beginning to fill with more people. Groups of friends and couples. Tonight has been relaxing and I'm surprisingly having a nice time with him.

"T." His voice pulls my gaze back to him.

He's holding a velvet box open with an engagement ring. The solitaire diamond sits on a classic gold band. It looks to be at least two carats. This snaps me back to the reality of what we're doing.

My mouth falls open, and I stare at it as if it's going to disappear.

"Alex, it's beautiful," I breathe.

He clears his throat. "I was scared it was too simple."

I blink over and over, trying to make sure it's real.

"Do you want this back?" I blurt out.

He frowns. "What are you talking about?"

I whisper. "When this is over, what am I meant to do with this?" I point at the ring.

"Keep it."

"You bought this beautiful ring for me to keep? You realize that we're not staying married," I say, feeling like I need to remind him.

"I know. After you get your inheritance, and we break up, you could take it back to the Jeweller. It's up to you."

I push the hair away from my face and gaze back at him. I'm still in shock at the ring's beauty.

"This wouldn't have been cheap," I mumble, flicking my gaze back down to the box. It's hard not to stare at it the whole time.

"Your parents will find out I'm a doctor. If they're to believe the engagement is real, I needed you to have a ring. And I don't want you getting something cheap and fake. You deserve a nice ring."

I wish I had more wine right now. "Alex. This is a lot," I whisper.

"At least you like it. I was at the shop stressing."

I giggle, trying to picture the scene. "You in a jewelry store. Now that would've been funny to see. I wish I could've been there."

"I surprisingly didn't hate it. They just had too many options." He inches forward with the box, a silent urge to get me to take the ring.

I pluck it from the box, moving the diamond around between my fingers. The sparkle is captivating. "What made you choose this one?"

"I wanted a classic but elegant ring. When I saw this one, I knew it was the one."

I peer up from the diamond to stare into his eyes. His blue eyes gleam under the bar's lights. I'm speechless. How did he know this would be my choice? I shake my head at the silly thought. He didn't. It was a fluke.

The server comes back, asking if we want more drinks, but as we look at the time, his eyes hold mine. "Are you ready to go?" he asks, handing over cash to the server and rising.

I take a deep breath, slip the ring on my finger, and stand. "I think so."

"I got you," he says, trying to reassure me.

I offer a weak smile. I can't shake the fear that this will all crumble, and my only hope of a future will fail. Then all this will be for nothing.

CHAPTER 8

ALEX

SHE'S BEEN QUIET SINCE we left the bar. The pinch between her brows sits embedded, and I hate to see the stress having an effect on her.

We're on our way to her parents' house in my car. I prefer to drive, and it will look better for me to be driving us anyway.

Tonight, was unexpectedly enjoyable. The banter, chit-chat, and overall mood was fun and easy between us. At no time did anything feel awkward or forced, just smooth and comfortable. It's nice to see the outgoing T, not the one who reverts back into her shell.

The music plays in the background, but still, it will be a long ass drive if we don't speak. Especially now, since her knee is bouncing up and down. I'm a tad nervous about slipping up, but I'll do everything I can to help her.

"So, is the business successful?" I ask, catching a brief look at her before focusing on the road.

Her frame taunted me when she entered the bar in that sexy-as-hell outfit. The way the skirt rests on her waist complements her hourglass frame. I had to hold myself back from walking to her and laying a kiss on her exposed shoulder and dragging my lips up her neck.

I don't know what it is about her, but she has a way of getting me to not think straight.

"Yeah, very," she says too quietly. I could barely hear her.

"That will help when you take majority of it over."

She grumbles, "I don't know about that. I could screw it up."

"Is that what you're worried about?"

She stares out her window. I wonder what's running through her head.

"I've never run a business before. I didn't finish the business course at college. I haven't learned how to run a successful business or studied fashion...I'm not prepared for this at all. I just know I want it."

"Most people I know who are successful will say you don't need to go to college or have experience. The work itself will give you all the experience you need. You'll figure it out."

"I beg to differ."

"Why are you so hard on yourself? You have time to learn the ropes from your parents and ask questions as you go. You're freaking out because you're looking too far ahead. One day at a time, T."

It's silent for a beat, and I think that's all she'll say, but then she surprises me. "I feel like a failure to my parents. My friends all have their shit together, and I don't. I have money and the smarts, yet I couldn't figure out what I wanted to do before now. I'm already in my mid-twenties with no achievements under my belt."

I'm stunned by her confession. I'm also sad for her.

"You shouldn't compare yourself to them, because there isn't anything wrong with you. I'm glad you've figured out what you really want. Even if I'm on this crazy fake journey with you."

"Yeah, it's going to be a ride."

I look over at her again and see her slumped body is more comfortable. My gaze doesn't miss the way her skirt has ridden up above her knee, showing more of her leg to me. I bite back a growl.

"You know, my friends and I have joked about how I should be a stylist."

"Really? Then why didn't you work in the family business after school?"

"I wasn't ready, and seeing how much they worked, it was a turnoff. No life other than work. I wanted a bit of freedom."

"Being an established business, it shouldn't require as much work, right?" I ask.

I take a quick peek over at her, and she's staring my way. Her eyes have a way of pulling me in. I refocus on driving, wanting us to get there in one piece.

"They have a lot of staff in all different areas, so no it shouldn't be. But I guess I'll find out soon enough."

"You sure will. And remember, you can always discuss with them about changing the direction of the business. It's majority yours to do what you want with, right?"

She makes a humming sound. I'm surprised by how nice it is to talk to a woman instead of chatting them up with a purpose to fuck them. I've never spoken to them about life problems, or in this case, work issues.

I like the mental connection it brings. Physical isn't an issue whenever Tahlia is around. She's hot, but her vulnerability is killing me more than my attraction to her, and I want to make her better.

My phone rings through the car, and Nancy's number pops up. I cringe.

I plan to just let it ring, but Tahlia asks, "Are you going to answer that?"

"No."

"You can, I don't mind." She shrugs nonchalantly.

I clear my throat, wondering how I explain that Nancy will only be asking when she can fuck me, because I don't share my personal life with anyone.

"No, I'm good." I press the hang-up button. But of course, Nancy calls back. I hit the decline button again, and the temperature in the car turns up. I feel suffocated with having to explain, but knowing it's not something she'll want to know about me. Fuck, I don't even like myself.

Once the ringing stops, I get a message pop through, but neither of us speaks.

Before I get the chance to apologize to Tahlia, she cuts in.

"Just here." I follow her pointed finger through the trees.

I sigh. Ready or not, here we go.

I pull up to the double brick brown home and park in the drive. I take it all in. There's a manicured garden surrounding steps that lead to a pair of dark brown double wooden doors. We sit in the car a moment. I'm staring at her family's porch when her voice pulls me away.

"You ready?" she asks, biting on her nails.

I touch her hand, and she stops, allowing me to drop her hand away from her mouth. Her gaze flicks to me and the beginning of a smile tips the corners of her lips. I can't promise her this will go smoothly, or that they will believe us, but the look on her face makes me want to try harder.

"Ready? Let's go, soon-to-be Mrs. Tahlia Taylor." After the words leave my mouth, I'm surprised by how good it sounds. No feelings of dread take over.

"Let's go, Mr. Taylor."

"Dr. Taylor, but I'll let it slide for you." I wink, and a big open grin forms on my face.

I know the playful side of us ends now, though. It's time to be serious.

She opens the car door, and it makes me dart out like my ass is on fire, running around to finish opening the door for her.

She smiles when I hold out my hand and close the door for her. Her grip loosens, as if she's about to disconnect our hands, but I interlock them and tug on it to bring her eyes to my face.

When she holds my gaze, I lean into her ear, inhaling her sweet perfume, and whisper, "We've got this."

She blows out her cheeks and nods, as if trying to convince herself.

We take the steps. But before we hit the doorbell, the doors open to reveal an older couple, both smiling warmly at us. Her dad doesn't look like he wants to kill me, but I'm sure he will when we're alone and he berates me for not asking for her hand in marriage. If I were him, I'd cut my son-in-law's balls off for not asking me.

"Hello and welcome," her mom, Sonya, says as she flicks her gaze between us.

"Thank you for having us," I reply.

Tahlia drops her fingers from mine, and I mourn the loss.

She hugs her dad and mother, giving them double cheek kisses, and I wonder if I have to follow suit.

"Alex," I say, and extend my hand to shake her dad's. His handshake is firm, and his face wears a curious expression as he introduces himself. But before he can read my face, I move to her mother and kiss her cheeks like I saw Tahlia do a moment ago. Then I take a step behind and slip my hand on Tahlia's lower back, feeling her shiver.

We step inside the house, then follow her mom and dad farther into the house, we're led to the living room.

"Can I grab you a drink?" Sonya asks.

"A soda would be great?" I reply.

"You don't want a beer or whiskey?" Hector asks me, frowning.

"No, I'm starting early tomorrow," I reply, not wanting to drink in front of them. I need to be on my best behavior for Tahlia.

Sonya walks toward the kitchen for the drinks.

"What is it that you do?" Hector asks.

"I'm a neurologist," I say proudly.

Hector's face softens, and he nods. "Good job."

"It's very rewarding," I reply, knowing there's more to being a doctor than the money.

Sonya hands us our drinks and I thank her. I watch her grab Tahlia and pull her over to the sofa on the other side of the room. I stay standing with Hector. Who starts firing questions at me.

"Will my daughter be left alone a lot? I know doctors' schedules are very busy."

I hope not.

His question is fair, and I think for a moment how to speak the truth but also keep up with our lie.

I glance over to where Tahlia sits talking with her mother. She must feel my eyes on her because she turns and the lift of those lips in a secret smile causes my breath to catch.

Turning back to face her father, I can only be honest. "I will do my best to always be there for her in all ways. I can't promise to give her a nine-to-five job, but I promise when I'm home, she will be all I focus on every minute of the day or night."

He dips his head and sips his amber liquid, and I sip the refreshing soda and wait for the next question. Because it's her dad, after all, so I'd be stupid to think he would only ask one.

"You're engaged?" her mom shrieks.

My head whips back around, and I watch her mom pull out of a hug and grab Tahlia's hand.

Tahlia's face has a dusting of pink as her mom moves her head this way and that to get a good look.

"Hector, come look at the size of this ring," her mom gushes, smiling brightly, pushing Tahlia's hand out in our direction.

"In a minute, Sonya."

I turn around again, knowing this means he hasn't finished drilling me.

"Why didn't you ask me?" he asks in a deep, yet quiet, voice.

Oh, fuck. Here we go.

When I don't respond right away he asks again. "Why didn't you ask me for my daughter's hand in marriage?"

I swallow hard. I need to be convincing.

"Well, I..." Clearing my throat, I take a breath. "I hadn't met you yet and didn't think telling you over the phone was appropriate." I'm rattling off bullshit, and I just hope it saves me.

He stays silent, his eyes trained on Tahlia. I decide to turn the conversation around. Get it off Tahlia and our fake engagement. "How long have you been married?"

He twists his face to me, bringing his tumbler to his mouth and taking a sip before answering. "Thirty wonderful years."

I want to ask him how he knew she was the one, but considering I'm marrying his daughter, I should know that already. Only he doesn't understand that I'm broken inside, and this engagement is fake.

I'm totally fucked. I run my hand through my hair.

A woman wearing an apron comes into the room and informs us that dinner is ready. Taking my soda, I go toward Tahlia and walk with her to the dining room where a large rectangle table is. I'm careful to keep close to her. As I remember all the things Mike and Alice do, so tonight goes seamlessly.

However, I just realized that we have to keep this up until her birthday, so how many times will I see her parents?

I hope not many.

A couple of times I can handle. More than that, I can't promise not to slip up.

The table is already set for dinner. There's silverware, dinner plates, water glasses, bread, and butter.

Tahlia takes a seat, her face pinched. I lean down to whisper in her ear, "Are you okay?"

Her chest heaves, and I swallow a groan. Her breasts move up and down in her sweater, and the way the skin is teasing me, I have to take a seat to hide the tent that's forming in my pants.

I haven't even fucking touched her. Or even tasted her. Yet I'm rock hard and desperate to sink myself inside her.

That part of the marriage I could be good at.

Sex is easy.

A relationship, I'm doomed.

Everyone calls me the playboy, and that's all I am.

At least, I think so...

The steak, vegetables, and potatoes look delicious, and even though my thighs are spread while I wait for the uncomfortable erection to calm down, I focus on the food, which helps the deflation.

Sonya speaks once we've all taken our first bite. "How many children will you have?"

"Mom," Tahlia shrieks, her mortified expression making me cough.

Was she expecting kids? Because I really didn't sign up for that.

"What it's a legitimate question. He's..."

And I know she's asking me how old I am.

I swallow my mouthful of food and answer. "Thirty-two."

"See, in the next few years, he'll be thinking of children, Tahlia."

I lower my fork and knife, suddenly not as hungry. "We want to travel a bit before we have children. Right, honey?" I turn to Tahlia, trying to act calm, even though my body temperature is rising. As I tuck a loose strand of hair behind her ear, she melts into my hand with a soft smile. Her eyes have a sheen of relief, as if she's glad I got us out of an awkward conversation.

I finally drop my hand, skimming her exposed shoulder so I can touch her teasingly warm skin. It's tempting to keep my fingers there and seek more, but we are at dinner with her parents. So I curl my fingers and return them to my lap.

My gaze catches her father's, and it flicks to Tahlia and then me, a frown pinched between his brows. Suddenly, a slight worry runs through me. I try to think if I've not acted attentive or like a fiancé, but I'm coming up empty.

Maybe he just doesn't like the idea of me touching his daughter. Unfortunately for him, I seem to like it, and so does she.

"How long have you two been dating?" Hector asks, his finger rubbing along his bottom lip.

I tug at the collar of my shirt. It's a little hot in here.

"About six months," Tahlia answers.

"How did you meet? Seems like a rushed engagement. You're not pregnant, are you?"

My eyes widen. *Immaculate conception*, I want to say, but I keep my mouth shut.

"I'm not pregnant. And Alice's husband is Alex's brother," Tahlia explains. She speaks so easily. She's a damn good actor.

I wash down my food with more soda, welcoming the cold beverage.

"That makes sense," Sonya mumbles.

"It doesn't to me," Hector grunts, lifting his glass to his mouth to take a drink. He watches me over the glass.

This is not fucking good.

Sonya's clearly convinced by our relationship. But Hector isn't.

The way he's staring at me, I could bet on my life that he's not buying our relationship or that I love Tahlia.

"Where do you live Alex?" Sonya asks, lowering her silverware.

I'm grateful for the question. It pulls me away from her husbands death stare.

"In the Park area," I answer.

Hector lowers his glass back to the table, then sits back in his chair, arms crossed, and keeps his eyes trained on me. I'm really feeling the heat of meeting the parents. No wonder everyone always dreads it.

"It's a nice brick home." Tahlia says, but her voice wavers.

We never discussed this question. But we need to up the stakes and get him to buy our love.

"Yeah. A tudor home. She actually just moved in," I blurt, like the dumbass I am. I seem to have foot-in-mouth disease.

I hear a small gasp leave Tahlia's mouth. But I try to stay calm. I need to play the part. As if it is true.

"Everything seems new," Hector mumbles, taking another a large sip of his drink.

Sonya widens her eyes at him. "Hector," she says through clenched teeth. "Be nice."

"I am. I'm just asking questions," he gruffs back.

"You're not. Stop being a grumpy old man and be happy for your daughter and future son-in-law."

"We'll have to drop in sometime," Hector adds, not responding to his wife's grumpy comment.

Tahlia and I remain quiet, giving them the time to squabble.

I reach over and grab her knee. I want her to look at me.

This wasn't part of the plan. Is she okay with me saying that? Her head flicks to me as soon as I squeeze.

I offer an *are you okay?* smile.

To my relief, she gives me an easy one back.

It still doesn't solve the huge shit I've put us in, but it can't be worse than what we were already doing.

I guess this playboy is getting a roommate...a hot one at that.

CHAPTER 9

TAHLIA

"THAT WASN'T AS BAD as I thought," Alex says as my parents' house disappears from view.

"Are you kidding?" I gape, turning the music down to talk.

"All right, your dad fucking hates me," he says, gripping the steering wheel.

I laugh at his words. "He doesn't hate you." I stare out the car window, watching all the stars light up the night sky.

"He strongly dislikes me?" he suggests in his teasing tone.

I recline into the soft leather seat and turn my head to face his profile. "Yeah, that's better."

"Not really. There's no chance you'll get your inheritance if he doesn't believe us."

I know my dad is a hard-ass, but I'm the only child he has. Therefore, it gives him a strong urge to protect me at all costs.

"Because I got Mom on board, Dad will automatically follow."

He tilts his head. "I'm not sold."

"Hey, you totally threw us under the bus in the end!"

"I did, didn't I?" He rubs at his five o'clock shadow. "I don't know what happened. It just slipped out."

My hands twitch, wanting to know what his stubble would feel like against my palm...or between my thighs.

"We need to talk out the details of the move."

"How about a drink at my house? I think I need one after tonight. Your dad drilled me hard."

I giggle. I've had a surprisingly good time tonight, and it would be a shame for it to end already.

"Yeah, I wouldn't say no to another glass. If we hash out some more details. I thought our meet-up was good and that we covered enough."

"Clearly it wasn't enough," he jokes.

I face the window watching houses pass by. I'm still unable to believe we made it through four hours with my family and now we're on our way to his place for a drink.

"T?"

Pulling my gaze from outside to him, I hadn't realized I'd zoned out. "Y-yeah."

"Are you okay?" His tone is soft, yet commanding, and I don't want to admit that guilt is hitting me. Lying isn't something I do. Yet I did it. And now we're adding another layer to it, so I'm still trying to process how that makes me feel.

"Yeah, I'm okay. Just a little stunned. That's all."

He reaches over and touches my hand, startling me. His large one covers mine and an unexpected warmth surges through me.

These tender moments he shares with me leave me astonished. I can't tear my hand away, even though my brain is yelling at me, telling me my parents aren't here, so we don't have to act anymore. He doesn't have to do this. For a brief moment, I wonder if he wants to, though. The throb in my temples from stress has me reclining the car seat, all the way back. "I'm going to close my eyes for the rest of the drive. I have a headache starting."

"Yeah, of course. Let me know if you need me to pull over or something. Are you comfortable?"

His soft leather seats and his warm hand in mine have me feeling just that. I smile softly. "Yes, very."

"Good."

My eyes are already closed, and the heaviness takes over.

It isn't until strong arms are lifting me that I feel like I'm floating. It's a nice dream. The cold night air gushes around me, and I snuggle into a neck.

A neck?

I take a sharp intake of breath and jerk. My body is currently flushed to a solid bit of muscle. Firm hands grip me harder as my eyes fly open.

"Shhh, I'll take you inside."

I blink rapidly. I fell asleep in his car?

I thought I would just close my eyes. I never thought in a million years, I'd fall asleep.

This thoughtful moment makes my brain turn to mush, and I just merely stare at him, blank yet amazed. With no fight in me, I simply nod, succumbing to his care.

At his front door, he struggles to open the door.

"I'm awake. Put me down, and I'll walk in," I suggest with a light tone.

"It's okay, I can do it, and hey, think of it as practice for our wedding day."

I shake my head, trying to ignore his heavenly scent. Being this close makes it stronger.

I wiggle out of his arms, giving him no choice but to lower me. Once my feet are safely cemented on the ground, I expect him to open the door. Yet, his hands stay touching my waist and mine on his shoulders. As if we are both enjoying the touch of each other too much for either of us to stop. It's as if this is natural.

He's staring down intently at me before he slowly and seductively gazes over my body. When he meets my eyes again, my blood is pounding in my ears. He leans in, and the emotions around us are melting my resolve.

"Are we going to practice kissing?" he asks in a hoarse voice, licking his lips.

"Do we need to?" My eyes bounce between his. I want him to kiss me. Badly.

"I think it would be good if we do it without an audience, just in case we suck." His breath dusts my lips, causing a shiver to run up my spine.

I laugh, but then I'm straight back into a lustful state. My brain tells me this is a bad idea and to take a step back and go home, but then the other side of me is saying I need to stop overthinking and just try to enjoy the moment.

It's just a simple kiss. After that, we can go back to playing pretend. I haven't kissed a man in a really long time. And I've never kissed a man this hot or oozing this much sexual energy.

I don't answer with words, because my stomach is in a wild swirl of anticipation. When our lips touch, my eyes flutter closed, and I sink deep into it. His strong hand is on the back of my head while the other roams over my back and rests on my crease of my lower back just above my ass. The trail of heat from where his hands are makes me inch closer, closing any distance between us. My hands move from his broad shoulders up his thick neck, and I run my fingers through his hair before curling my grip.

I'd like to think this kiss confirms there is nothing between us, but I feel everything. Our closeness is like a drug, only bringing me closer to euphoria. It's unhinged and feral and unexpected.

His tongue runs over my bottom lip, seeking entry. I groan from the feeling of his tongue inside my mouth. Sweet and warm and captivating. I want more.

I need more.

The erratic beating of my heart feels like it's about to come out of my chest. Everything around us drowns out and my earlier sleepy state is now the opposite. I'm wired with desire.

And it's safe to say he's feeling the same. The way his hand grips my ass and brings me flush against his hard erection, there is no mistaking the sparks. I grind myself against him, causing him to growl.

Our tongues move in fluid strokes. I lap up his taste, and a whimper leaves my chest. No time to be embarrassed or silent. I can't hold myself back even if I wanted to.

Every sweep of his tongue I match it with my own in perfect rhythm. He's a good kisser; it's borderline going to make me second-guess the fake part.

When we pull apart gasping for oxygen, I bring my eyes to his and hold them, seeing the same struggle and conflict I feel. And I wonder what he's thinking, but before I get a chance to ask, he pecks my lips with soft slow kisses. Not once, no, not twice, no, three times before he moves his lips to my hair, whispering, "Let's go inside and have a drink."

Once we get inside his house, it's too dark to take everything in other than his large sofa. I walk directly over to it. Sitting down, I sink into the fabric, feeling almost lightheaded from what we just shared.

"I'll use the bathroom and then fix you a wine or tea?"

Twisting my head, I look over the sofa to meet his gaze with a smile. I ignore how my body still hums with a strong need to kiss him again and focus on the gentleness that's written across his face. It reminds me why he's a doctor. How he likes to care for people. Even now with me, in his home. I've not had someone. Specifically, a man that I'm attracted to want to do that for me. And right now, I admit, after the hot kiss we shared, it feels nice.

Deciding I need the alcohol to calm me. "Wine sounds good." I reply, sounding breathless.

His lips twitch. "All right, won't be long."

The next morning, I open my eyes and realize I'm in a bed that's not my own. I last remember being on Alex's sofa, drinking wine. A lot of it. I must've passed out. Looking around, the other side isn't touched, so I must be in the guest room. It's light from the sun beaming through the curtains. I glance around at the wooden furniture, large TV, cream and beige bedding.

It's not the bachelor pad I expected. No, this is lovely.

Getting up, I leave the room and head down the light wooden stairs. I find myself near the living room which has the same white walls, beige, and leather furnishings. As I make my way to his kitchen and living area, his voice booms from behind me. "I got you breakfast and a coffee."

I jerk around to find him holding two coffees and two brown bags.

"Thanks," I say, taking in his soaked white training top, showing off his toned chest and every ripple of his abs. The dusting of dark hair between his pecs reminds me he's all man. I know I should stop staring, but I continue my inspection. His black training shorts cling to his thighs, and when I make my way back to his face, beads of sweat drip along his temples, causing some of his dark hair to stick to his forehead. My hand twitches to push it back off his face.

His lop-sided smirk has me thinking he knows exactly how much I appreciate his looks.

My throat runs dry, so I take a step and accept the coffee from his grip, ignoring the spark from grazing his hand with mine. I sit at the breakfast bar and sip the caffeine like it's water. It's definitely not going to calm my rapid pulse, but at least the warm, familiar latte comforts me.

"What's in there?" I ask, nudging my nose toward the brown paper bag.

He slides it across to me. "Croissants."

I open the bag and my stomach grumbles on cue.

"I didn't know if you wanted it plain or something else. So, I got one plain and one with ham and cheese."

Of course, he did, because he can't stop being nice. I peek up at him from the bags as he walks around the counter.

"You can choose, and I'll have whatever one you don't want." He takes a seat on the stool next to me.

"That doesn't seem fair."

He shrugs. "Why? I'm a guy. I eat anything."

"Always hungry."

"Always." His voice is gravelly, and we've fallen back into the flirty behavior of last night.

I tear open the bag to occupy my thoughts and eat the plain croissant, enjoying the buttery flavor on my tongue. I didn't realize I was hungry until I started eating.

As I chew, his phone chimes. He glances down with a frown at his phone before looking back at me.

"I just got paged for an emergency surgery. I don't know how long I'll be, but my guess is at least a couple of hours. You're welcome to stay longer. Your car is in the drive."

"How?" I ask, popping the last mouthful of my croissant in my mouth.

"I had it moved last night. When you fell asleep on the sofa," he says it like it's no big deal. But to me, it is.

"You didn't have to. But thanks," I say, grateful for his generosity.

"On the topic of moving. You're going to need to start moving your stuff here today," he announces. He doesn't bat an eyelid. He doesn't seem bothered I'm about to move in here. Unlike me, because I'm wondering how I'll be able to leave with the tension after last night. Will we kiss again?

"Is that right?" I ask in a light voice, challenging him.

He smirks back, knowing I'm playing with him. "Yes. I can help you after work, or I can swing by on my way home and grab everything from your old house and do it for you."

I shake my head. "No. I want to do it. I'm sure it won't take me long and I need to do something today."

I don't need him going into my room and bringing everything here. If I go, I'll know exactly what I need to bring and what I can leave there for when I move back.

"All right, but if you change your mind, call me." He dips his chin and takes my now empty bag, rolling it into a ball and tossing it into the bin. Then he grabs his keys. "I'll see you when I get home." He winks and walks out, leaving me alone in his house.

Soon to be *our house*.

Why does it feel comfortable between us already? It scares me a little. I could easily fall for him, and that's a huge problem when he's not the type of guy to settle down.

CHAPTER 10

TAHLIA

ALL MY CLOTHES ARE laid out in my room. It's daunting seeing the amount of clothes I've acquired over the years of living here. I need to cull some. But today isn't the day to do that. No, today is about moving. I'm still trying to wrap my head around how fast everything is happening and all the big changes going on in my life. One after another.

I never thought I'd be moving out of this house with a guy for a fake engagement. I always thought it would be for love. This isn't love, though. I run my hand through my hair, wondering how it feels for him to have me move into his space. If this is a lot for me, how does it feel for him? And after last night, there's a new dynamic. A playful shift between us. If it was flowing easily before, it's thickening with some heat now. Well, it is for me. Soon, we'll be under one roof, with a kiss between us and a whole heap of sexual tension.

I shake my head to clear it. I need to be a big girl and focus on packing. If my parents decide to visit, I need to be at Alex's.

I open my suitcase, but after a few hours, I need a break. Since getting back home, I haven't stopped. I make my way into the kitchen to make some tea.

The front door opens as I pour the boiling water into my cup, and Maddison enters the room, wearing an exhausted expression.

She gives me a half smile.

"Would you like me to make you some tea?" I ask her.

She lets out a loud sigh. "Please." She tosses her bag on the table.

"Bad day?" I grab a cup and make her one.

"Just long, and I'm tired."

Once it's finished brewing, I hand it over.

"Thanks," she mumbles, taking a large sip.

"I have to tell you something," I start.

She frowns. "Yeah, what is it?"

"I need to move out for a bit," I say, taking another sip of my warm tea.

Her forehead creases. "Why?"

"You know how I quit Frank's?"

"Mm-hmm," she mumbles, staring at me, perplexed.

"Mom called right after and reminded me I won't get Emerald Designs if I don't get married, and I realized I do want it. So I blurted out I was dating."

She folds over laughing. "To fucking who?"

It makes me laugh too. Because it's the only way to survive this whole ridiculous idea.

"Alex."

"Alex wh—" Her eyes grow wide as she figures out who it is.

"You told your parents your boyfriend is Alex Taylor?"

I nod. "Yep. And that we're engaged and living together."

I lift my left hand, showing her my engagement ring, letting the sparkle of the diamond catch the light.

"Get fucked," she scoffs. "Did he buy this?"

Her eyes meet mine. I can see the wheels turning at all this new information.

"Yeah. Crazy, isn't it?"

"You think?" She shakes her head.

"I'll still pay my half of the rent, and I'll be back before you know it."

"As long as this is what you want to do." I can hear the worry in her tone.

"It is. I have this new fire in my belly at the thought of getting a stake in the business. I really want it. So, yeah. I need to be at his house in case my parents call and want to drop in." I take a big sip to wet my parched throat.

She wears a knowing smirk. "You're screwed...literally. He'll try to get in your pants the first night you stay over."

"I accidentally passed out on his sofa last night."

"Jesus, this gets worse by the second. Did you sleep with him?"

I shake my head. "No. I must've been exhausted from the big day and the alcohol I drank." I'm not opposed to the idea of sleeping with him like I was before we started this arrangement.

"Sounds like you need wine, not tea. Do you want help packing?"

"Please," I say excitedly. I begin to walk to my room. She follows.

She looks around at my clutter. "Where do you want me to start?"

My mouth curves into the biggest, warmest smile. I'm so grateful for our friendship.

"Can you pack my bathroom stuff?"

"Into what? I don't see any spare cases."

I groan and scan the room. Finding a shopping bag, I shake it out and hand it out to her. "This will do."

She turns and walks off, calling over her shoulder, "You owe me, bitch."

I chuckle and refocus on packing more clothes into the case.

After an hour, I have a big case, and another smaller bag overflowing with my belongings. If I need anything else, I'll get it when I come by and visit Maddison.

"I'm kinda pissed you're leaving me alone, but then on the flip side, I get this place to myself. I can have a guy over and you wouldn't know."

My mouth parts in surprise. "You wouldn't," I say, clutching my chest.

"As if I could. I have the biggest mouth, and if I had gossip, you'd be the first to know."

I exhale. "Good."

"But that works both ways, T," she drawls out my name, and I know what she means.

I can be quiet compared to her and keep things to myself, but there isn't anything to share about Alex and me. We're friends with a mutual attraction to each other. Nothing more.

"Nothing will happen between Alex and me, I can assure you."

Her face brightens at the suggestion. "I didn't say anything about Alex."

The corner of my lip lifts into a small smile. "As if you didn't insinuate if something happens with Alex."

"Well, if something does..."

I don't bother replying, because I'm not going to win. And if something were to happen, I'd want to share it with my best friends.

I put my hands on my hips, looking at the two bags, and then back at Maddison.

"All right, that's it. I better get over to his house," I breathe out.

"Good luck." And as she happily waves me goodbye, she sends me a wink. Maybe I am screwed.

CHAPTER 11

ALEX

WORK ENDED UP TAKING longer than planned, but that's what happens when you're on call. You never know what you're walking into. Pulling into my driveway, I see her parked car and wonder what she did today. Did she leave my house at all, or did she stay in and relax?

The kiss we shared last night was more passionate than I would have ever expected. Our spark intensified as our mouths joined together. I never wanted it to end. I'd kiss her again, but I can't have more with her. I don't ever want to hurt her, and I know I will. I always end up hurting women.

I shake off any more longing thoughts and take a breath. I have food I picked up from the store.

Inside the house, noises clatter upstairs. I lower the food to the counter and dump my keys and phone before heading to find her. I've never come home to a woman, so this is something new. And surprisingly, I don't hate it.

I pause at the guest room door, but I can't see her. Moving closer, I find her sitting in the walk-in closet, finishing up unpacking her clothes. Her hair is in a messy bun, high up on her head, with tendrils falling down around her face. She looks like she's had a busy day.

"Hey. You went home and grabbed your stuff?"

Her head whips to me, and I get a good look at her flushed face.

"Yeah, it's a workout," she puffs out breathlessly. "This is a closet of dreams, though."

"I wanted my guests to have the same luxury as me." I step forward, pushing the strand of hair behind her ear. "You want a hand?"

"Alex," she murmurs, my name falling from her lips in a whisper.

I'm surrounded by her sexy body and those pink pouty lips, and as I stare at her, all I can think about is tasting her again.

She picks up a pile of pants, popping them into a drawer. Her case is now empty. I grab the case and zip it, standing it up for her.

I must stare too long, and with no words being spoken, she clears her throat and drops her gaze to my lips. "What are you doing, Alex?"

I'd like to know too. I'm confused by my reaction to her.

"Seeing if you want a hand," I repeat, leaning in.

Our faces are now so close that I can almost taste her strawberries and white chocolate scent. She doesn't pull away, instead her breath hitches from my advance. I look down to where her tongue runs along her bottom lip. It's a secret challenge. She wants me to kiss her.

"No, I'm done now. But I never got a chance to look around. I left not long after you to head home. I only got here, I don't know, maybe an hour ago."

My eyes meet hers again, and a smile pulls on her lips. She's so effortlessly seductive, and I'm feeling a pull toward her. "Do you want a tour before dinner, then?" I offer, needing to move and clear my head.

I offer her a hand, which she takes. My hand closes gently over hers, and I help her up. "Thanks."

Her soft, warm hand fits easily in mine. But she trips over the suitcases, causing her to land into my chest. I catch her. One hand settles on her lower back, the other on her shoulder. She gasps. Her hand lands on my heart, and I expect her to pull away, but she doesn't. Instead, she looks up at me with interest.

My eyes bore into hers. "Are you all right?" I ask.

My words seem to snap her out of her fixed stare. She gently swats my arm and takes a breath. "Don't think you're getting another practice kiss right now," she says, but it lacks conviction. I can read her easily. She wants to kiss me.

She steps back, and a deep chuckle leaves my chest. "Never."

"Good. Don't get any ideas now that I live here." She laughs warmly.

Looking into her green eyes, I can help but know there's something about Tahlia that's seeping deep inside of my chest. "Never. Now come on. I'll give you a proper tour of your new home."

I love this house. It's bright, with white walls and timber accents. Splashes of dark brown and leather to keep it manly. It was important that the designer make it suit me.

"Let's start downstairs. I need to pop some stuff in the fridge. I grabbed a few things, but until I know what you like, I didn't want to go overboard," I say, walking downstairs and into the kitchen. She follows behind me.

I open the shopping bag and pull items out.

"Thanks. I can pick up some food, though," she replies, nibbling on her bottom lip.

"I have a housekeeper who normally does it for me," I say as I put the milk, fruits, and veggies in the fridge.

"Does she cook for you too?" she asks jokingly.

My jaw twitches at being called out.

"She does."

She laughs. And my mouth forms a grin at hearing her laugh again.

"But in my defense, I don't have time. Work hours can be intense, and the call-in hours are rough. The last thing I want to do is cook most days."

"Yeah, I don't know how you can be a doctor. It's tough." Her tone drops, and I don't want her to feel bad.

"It is, but it's also rewarding. Enough work talk, let's continue the tour. I'm done packing food away." We walk through the lower section of the house. "There's a bathroom down here. And these doors open to the pool and barbecue area."

She stares out at the vibrant blue pool with lounge chairs around it. "It's okay. I won't need the barbecue I won't be hosting a party, but I might use the pool."

"Please. It deserves to be used more," I say, looking out to the pool and the garden before adding, "Let's head back upstairs."

I turn and wander upstairs, with her following behind.

"I'm surprised by how homey it feels, even though it's also very modern."

We stop at my large bedroom. I stand inside it, and her at the doorway.

"Here is the most important room."

Her eyes hold mine, and I wink.

She rolls her eyes, but they move lazily over my bed in approval, as if taking it in. "I'm not sleeping in your bed."

"Dammit." I shrug and enter my room. "It was worth a try."

She laughs. "It's okay. I don't need a tour of your space," she says, stopping me from walking farther inside.

I turn around, catching something intense flaring through her entrancement. "Well, I'm here if you need me, roomie. Or should I say, fiancée?"

"Are you going to make me regret getting married to you?" she says with a trace of laughter in her voice.

"Not at all. I'm just getting into the role."

She walks away, her hips swaying, calling over her shoulder, "Well, fiancé, I'm going downstairs to eat before I pass out."

I walk out of my room and follow her. Something I wouldn't normally do, but when it comes to her, I'll gladly follow her anywhere.

Chapter 12

Tahlia

My head is thumping from a full day at Emerald Designs. I shadowed the design department and finance. I'm trying to wrap my head around these numbers when footsteps pad down the stairs. I nibble on the end of a pen and keep reading.

Until Alex enters the kitchen in navy suit pants...and nothing else. My eyes widen at his muscular chest.

In the past few days, I've encountered him bare-chested numerous times. The other night, he came down after a shower with only a towel wrapped around his hips. His dark hair was damp and his chest still glistening with water. It was as if he didn't bother checking he was completely dry before padding downstairs for something to eat. He couldn't put clothes on for that? I know this is his house, and it's probably what he did before I moved in, but he's making me hot and bothered.

He pauses close to me, resting a hand on the counter, looking at my books and notes. The movement of his hand causes his chest muscles to twitch, and I remember when my hand landed on his chest on the dance floor at Luxe. How those same chest muscles contracted under my touch. My gaze drops to the dusting of dark hair between his pecs. My hands twitch to know what it would feel like to run my fingers through it and over every hard bit of muscle on him.

I drop my gaze lower, taking in the hard ridges of his abs. His half-naked body makes my face flush. The longer I live here, the more my attraction grows. Will it ever fade?

I should read my finance book instead of studying his body.

He's a tease.

Yet, he doesn't give a fuck that he's distracting me by only wearing pants.

I suspected he was solid muscle, but all the times I've seen him half-naked confirmed it. And it's the right amount of muscle, not too big to imply he lives at a gym, but the type that says he takes care of himself. The perfect shape.

Living with a man I want to kiss again is dangerous. What's even worse is moments like this. He tests my resilience.

He moves from the counter and saunters into the laundry, and I continue to chew on the end of my pen as I enjoy the image of his broad back disappearing into the room. His tapered waist and his tight ass in those pants make me twitch.

Once he is safely out of my sight, I return to the page I was on and get back to writing notes.

A crash sounds and I jump. My body is still worked up and on edge from seeing the hard lines trailing down into his pants. Is he doing this on purpose?

Unable to concentrate while he's near, I stare at the open door of the laundry room.

"Where are you going? I ask.

"Work," he calls out.

I shake my head for asking the obvious. Where else would he be going dressed in suit pants?

I'm going to blame his sexiness for making me dumb right now. Yeah, that's it.

Another bang sounds in the laundry. What the heck is he doing in there? I get up and take a deep, steadying breath. Then I cross to the laundry room, trying to prepare myself for the sight of him shirtless. If that's even possible.

"What are you doing in here? Murdering the washing machine?" I try to hold back a laugh from my own lame joke, but a small one slips past my lips.

He turns toward me with amusement on his face. His hand gestures to the dryer. "I think this is broken."

"Why?" I stare at the white shirt he's holding. It looks dry to me.

He peers down at the fabric and then back at me. "The creases are still there."

I roll my lips to stop the laugh that's bubbling inside my chest.

"What?" He gruffs with a frown.

"You need an iron to get creases out."

His brows pinch tighter together. "Right. Where is one?"

I pull on all the cabinet doors to look inside. So far, coming up empty.

I peer over my shoulder to find him staring at me with fascination. The heat returns to my face. "Who normally irons your shirts?" I ask, still trying to locate the iron.

"My housekeeper, but she was busy this week."

"And you thought you could do it yourself?" I tease.

I finally find the white iron in the cabinet to the far left and pull it out.

"This is an iron." I hold it up to show him.

"Okay, let's plug it in."

I shake my head. "You need to make sure it has water in it first."

He scratches his head, but watches me check the water-fill line. He's so close, it makes my pulse race, so I step away from his magnetism.

"It's good," I say, sounding a little breathy as I open the large cupboard and find the ironing board. I pull it out and bring it to the middle of the room. He doesn't move, and it causes my ass to brush against him. Memories of us dancing hit me, making it hard to breathe. The air feels thick, as if I'm in a sauna.

I force myself to keep my eyes off his chest and open the board, concentrating on the task at hand and not on him. His eyes don't stray from me and my body is so hot, I could probably use it to iron his shirt.

"Thanks for helping me," he says.

"No problem," I say, laying the shirt on the board.

"I can take it from here," he says, but I shake my head at him.

"Maybe you should watch me first."

He smirks. "That, I can do."

And he does. He moves closer, too close, and watches me with his hands settled on his hips.

Thankfully, I don't burn any holes in his shirt with my shaky hands. Once I'm done, I unplug the iron, and he shrugs his shirt on. As I watch him dress, my feet automatically step toward him. I help him with his buttons.

My knuckles brush the ripples of his abs underneath, confirming they are, in fact, hard as steel.

"I'll do the ironing for you," I offer, keeping my eyes on my shaky fingers.

"You would?" he asks. "Why?"

"I live here, and I enjoy ironing. It's relaxing." I finish the last button at the collar and he swallows hard. The same desire to lick his neck slams into me. I fight the urge, though. But his neck veins and Adam's apple are captivating me.

He points to where I was ironing, breaking my dirty fantasy. "That is what you find relaxing?"

I shrug. "Yeah, so?"

He shakes his head. "You're quite unusual." His lips twist in a slow, amused smile.

"Thanks. Now I can go back to studying." I say, tipping my head back to find his fixed glare. I turn before he can stop me and wander back out to where there can be more space between us. A whole kitchen counter, in fact.

"What are you reading?" he asks, following me.

"Finance," I answer.

We stare at each other a beat and then he says, "I won't distract you any longer." He gives me a crooked, knowing smile and leaves to head back upstairs.

He knows exactly what he did to me. But the prickles on my skin were hidden underneath my clothes and the ache between my thighs wasn't visible. So how did he know?

He didn't. I'm clearly becoming delusional living here.

A few minutes later, he leaves for work and I go back to reading and making notes. After a while, I take a break and call Alice to check in.

"Hello," she answers after a couple of rings.

"Hi. Is it a bad time to talk?" I ask. Not having kids myself means I don't know when the best time to call is. I'll call to check in when I can and she can always tell me to call back another time.

"No. Great, actually. I popped Ethan down for a nap."

"How are you feeling?"

"I'm tired and my nipples are sore from feeding, but other than that, I'm good."

"Alice, that sounds awful and not something to feel good about. Maybe check in with your doctor." I laugh as the words leave my lips and so does she.

"Oh, don't worry. Mike is loving being a doctor for me."

I want to say too much information, but I'm too busy laughing.

"Enough about me. How are you going? Living with Alex?"

I told Alice and Blake about the arrangement after I spoke to Maddison. They were very understanding and totally supportive. I did, however, have to beg Alice not to tell Mike, and let Alex tell his brother. She reluctantly agreed.

To answer Alice's question three words come to me.

Hard. Good. Hot.

I don't say that. Instead, I end up saying what's been on my mind for the last half an hour. "Alice, I don't think the guy knows how to wear a shirt."

A giggle sounds down the line. "Why?"

"He's constantly without one," I mumble.

"And? He's at home. Is it a nice body?"

I screw up my face. "Alice, he's your brother-in-law."

"I'm not asking for me..."

The image of him earlier plays in front of me. It's more than a nice body. It's one I want to get lost in.

I won't admit that. Instead, I swallow hard and say, "I'm not going there with Alex."

"I didn't ask that question. I asked if his body is nice. So, is it?"

I smile at her words, and I can't help but answer. "Yes. It's very nice."

"I say enjoy the show. But maybe you could tease him back."

"I'm not walking around shirtless, Alice," I say deadpan, ignoring the way my nipples stiffen at the thought of teasing him.

She chuckles, and it turns to a snort. "You idiot. I don't mean naked but tease him a little. Give him a little taste of his own medicine. It'll drive him wild."

It would be nice to have him on edge like I've been for him. "Not before he drives me crazy."

"You're in deep shit."

"I'm not," I say, trying to sound convincing. "I have control."

I think...

CHAPTER 13

TAHLIA

The next day we've just finished dinner in the dining room. I noticed he picked Italian takeout, knowing it's my favorite food. He even asked what specific items I normally order, so that next time, he can order that. He's being a lot more attentive than I thought he'd be. With my belly full, another big work day is finally catching up to me. I'm exhausted. And so ready to shower and fall asleep.

"I'm going to go shower and crawl into bed. Goodnight and thanks for dinner."

"Wait up," he says, walking over. A second later, he swoops me off my feet, and I squeal. I'm alert now.

"What the hell are you doing?"

"Practicing carrying you for our wedding night," he replies nonchalantly.

Like a husband carries his wife on their wedding night. Only, we aren't a real couple, and we are going to separate beds. Why does that sudden realization leave me on choke-hold?

I'm silent. I'm too tired to argue. He climbs the stairs, and I relax completely, enjoying being in his arms again. But smelling his woodsy aftershave is playing tricks on me, causing me to desire things with Alex.

He takes the steps to my room and pauses inside, slowly lowering me down. My feet find the plush carpet, and I wobble, but he holds my arms until I find my working feet. Tipping my head back, I stare into his blue eyes and his handsome face hits me full force. I need to move back, put some distance between us. Being close to him and having his arms hold me tenderly is messing with every thought I had of him. He's Mike's brother, for God's sake. He doesn't want me.

I force my feet to step back, and I offer him a genuine smile. "Thanks for helping me upstairs."

Once he is out of reach, I tuck my hands under my arms, suddenly cold without him holding me.

"Let me run you a bath; it will help you wind down before you slip into bed."

I'm too surprised to do more than nod. And the sound of a bath sounds exquisite.

He swiftly turns and enters my bathroom. The water tap sounds, and cupboard doors open, and I wonder what he's doing. Walking into my closet, I grab my sleepwear for tonight, then step into the bathroom. I find him whisking the soft pink water caused by a bath bomb.

"You didn't have to," I whisper, biting my lip.

His eyes flick to mine, and the way they look from the light in here makes the butterflies return.

"I want to," he breathes.

My mouth drops open, and I'm too stunned to speak, so I step closer to take a look at the flecks of gold floating in the bath water. I won't lie, it looks amazing, and when I'm chin deep in it, my muscles will appreciate him.

"Is it warm enough?" he asks.

I reach out and touch it. "Yes, it's perfect." I let my gaze trail over his strong body until I meet his blazing eyes, the twinge between my thighs returning.

I need him to go, but I want him to stay.

"Well, I think that's enough water. I better go." His deep voice causes my skin to prickle with goosebumps.

I hear the struggle he's having in his voice. I'm glad it's not just me feeling something between us. The way my body is reacting to him is unlike anything I've ever felt.

"Thanks for running the bath. I'm going to enjoy this."

"Good," is all he says back as he slips out of the room, leaving me alone.

I let out a sigh and undress, piling the clothes on the floor, and then step into the bath. A soft moan slips from the warmth hitting my skin, and as I sit lower and relax my head back, the water comes up to my neck. Minutes pass, and then...a knock sounds on the door.

"Come in," I call out

"You look relaxed," Alex murmurs, entering the bath-room again.

I inhale a sharp breath and stare at him. He's holding a glass of wine. This sexy man is taking care of me again. I wish it was in other ways.

He pops a brow at me, as if reading my thoughts. His eyes darken with a wash of hunger.

The air crackles around us. "Is that for me?"

My question has his face softening. He looks at the glass and then meets my gaze.

"Yes. I thought you might enjoy a glass of wine in here."

"Thank you," I say, needing to calm the butterflies in my stomach.

"How's the bath?"

I know this is my chance to be daring. Try to seduce him. I need to get him out of my system.

"Relaxing but I have these knots in my shoulders," I say, rolling my shoulders.

He steps forward, taking a seat on the edge of the bath. I reach my arm out, totally forgetting that I'm naked beneath the water, until his gaze dips down, and he swallows hard. Following his line of sight, my nipples perk into the tightest buds. I'm wearing my desire for him, pretty much saying I'm turned on for him and come fuck me.

He clears his throat and rolls his shirt sleeves up as I hold the wine and take a decent sip. Cradling the glass, I lower it to the ledge on the side of the bathtub, then sink back down.

When he speaks from behind me, my chest heaves.

"Close your eyes."

The way his gravelly tone coats my skin, I don't bother fighting. I ease back, and as soon as his fingers touch my shoulders, I moan.

"You have knots."

"All the stress," I mumble.

The way his fingers and thumbs work to rid my knots in perfect rhythm, it's like he's a masseuse.

"Let's eliminate them so you can enjoy your bath and sleep well."

I'm unable to speak at his touch. This is intimate yet respectful, and it's playing with my head.

His touch slides slowly to the sides of my arms, making their way across my decolletage. I stop breathing for a moment, but his soft touch runs slowly up to my neck, and then down to the tops of my breasts. I bite my lips together to stop myself from begging him to dip his hands under the water and touch my full, heavy breasts.

I don't know how long he's been sitting massaging as I've lost track of time, but when he stands, I groan from the loss of touch. I try to clamp my mouth shut, but he definitely heard it, because he chuckles.

My eyes blink open. I find him standing at the sink with his back is to me. He's drying his hands. I take the opportunity to admire his broad back, then trail my eyes slowly down to his tight ass. I'm practically panting when he turns his head to stare at me over his shoulder. Amusement is written on his face. I'm busted.

"You feel better?"

I nod sheepishly. "Much."

"Good."

I pick up my glass, and I watch him under hooded eyes as he steps closer to me. My breath hitches when he leans forward. He presses his lips to my cheek in a lingering kiss. His lips are soft, but his scruff feels good against my skin. I want him to kiss me on my lips again. Only this time, it wouldn't be for practice. I tilt my face, but he moves his mouth to my ear, and I hear his breaths before he whispers, "I should get to bed. You stay here and relax. Goodnight."

My skin scatters with goosebumps, and my eyes flutter, struggling to stay open. I manage to find my voice to say, "Goodnight." It's coated with confusion, hurt, and mostly desire. I know he wants me, and the way the corner of his mouth forms a sly smirk makes me want to cry from desperation.

I know he fucks every woman he wants, so he must not want me...this really is all for show.

CHAPTER 14

ALEX

WHEN I WALKED INTO my house, I never expected to find Tahlia skinny dipping in the pool at lunchtime. Her black bikini is scattered on the sun lounger. Two days in a row, I've found her wet and naked in my house. Taunting and teasing me.

She's fucking with me. Yet I can't help the way my legs move closer. I sit in another lounger and don't speak. I just watch her. She hasn't noticed me sitting here staring. Her plump breasts are hidden, and the memory of last night and the way they perched out of the water, showing me her rosy nipples comes to my mind. The tight pebbles straining, telling me just how aroused she was, had me leaving before my growing erection scared her.

I could get used to coming home to this...to her. Except the only difference is I'd be naked in the pool and fucking her.

I watch her gracefully swim, her head occasionally going underwater. The sun beams down on me, causing me to sweat, and I want to cool off too. Standing, I tug off my shirt, dropping it to the lounger.

"Hey," her soft voice calls out.

I give her a crooked smile.

"You're coming in knowing I'm naked? I thought you'd bolt again," she taunts, swimming closer to me. She isn't hiding her body and her face is relaxed. Not a pinch of fear in sight.

Fuck...

"I didn't bolt last night, and I'm very aware of your nakedness," I say hoarsely.

I unbutton my pants and push them down. I stay in my briefs as I move to the edge and slip under, welcoming the cool water on my skin.

"If that's what you wanna tell yourself," she murmurs.

"What?" My brows pinch together at her boldness.

"You heard me, honey," she mocks, sliding her hands up to her hair and gathering her long blond locks in her hands. I shouldn't look, knowing it's a bad idea, but my favorite part of her exposed neck is on full display right now. My fingers move under the water, remembering how her skin felt under the pads of my fingers. Soft, delicate, sexy. Tahlia is a deadly combination.

"Don't be a brat."

"Why am I frustrating you?" she asks with a devilish smirk, totally challenging me.

Yep, this woman is taunting me for leaving the bathroom last night. I float closer to her, forgetting this is a bad idea. I want this just as much as she seems to.

"Not at all," I lie. If she were any other woman, I'd have fucked her so many times by now. But she's not just anyone. She's someone I care deeply about and someone I really like. The more I've gotten to know her, the more I like her. And fuck, I don't want to hurt her. And that's how this always goes the moment I have sex.

"Liar," she argues with a knowing smile. Her cheeks are flushed from the heat of the sun. She looks incredibly sultry, and I'm struggling to hold back and not approach her.

"I have good control, unlike some," I taunt her.

"You wish." She bites back a grin and splashes me. Laughing hysterically, she swims away.

My dick twitches at how much I'd love to catch her and fuck her against the pool edge. Make her come so hard she'll beg me to do it again and again.

And then I dive for her. She squeals and peers over her shoulder to see how close I am before a screech leaves her as she realizes I'm going to catch her.

As soon as I'm within reach, I grab her arm and she spins to back herself into the side of the pool. She's breathing hard and fast. I remind myself she doesn't deserve a quick fuck by the pool with an emotionless bastard.

But I still want to be near her. So, I close the distance between us, leaving only a few inches.

"You wanted me to chase you, didn't you?" I ask, unable to tear my gaze away.

Her teeth catch her lip as she nods. "Of course. And you did," she admits.

Her eyes don't shift from mine. Holding strong.

"You thought I wouldn't catch you?" I whisper darkly.

A wicked laugh slips from her lips before she breathes, "I don't know what I was thinking, honestly."

"I do," I rasp, inching closer again, until my erection hits her stomach. She whimpers.

"No, you don't," she argues. "You wish."

My head dips to whisper into her ear through clenched teeth. "I don't need to wish. I know."

I tilt my hips up, and she gasps, her head rolling back. I move my lips to her neck, breathing heavily. She rocks her body, so she slips over my erection. Growling, my hands fly to her hips, and I hold her still. I grind my hard cock over her naked pussy, and she cries out in pleasure.

I'm about to reach out to grab her face and bring her lips to mine when my pager goes off. Emergency call-in again.

Seriously?

"Fuck," I grunt, dropping my hand back into the water. I get an idea as I pull away. With a playful smile on my lips, I splash her this time.

She squeals, "Alex."

I swim away fast.

Her undiluted laughter fills the air as I go.

CHAPTER 15

ALEX

THE NEXT MORNING, I'M standing under the hot water of my shower, welcoming the hard hot sprays on my back. Trying to wake up after the worst night's sleep.

Have you ever walked away from someone and felt tormented? Well, that's me, but I push away the heavy feeling in my gut.

Stepping out of the shower, I get dressed, then pad down the hall and stairs quietly, not wanting to wake Tahlia. But when I pass her bedroom, I notice her door is open. I hesitate, knowing this is a little creepy, but I can't help myself and think it'll just be a quick look. Once inside, I peer around, but she isn't lying in the bed. Other than getting hit by her scent like a bus, I see she made her bed, and there're no clothes on the floor. Her room looks like new, so I push on and walk down the stairs. I hope she hasn't left.

It's a strange feeling to not want a woman to leave, but I don't think anything of it. We've been friends for a bit now, so I'm sure it must be the company. We haven't even slept together; it's just a natural reaction to having a roommate.

And I'm sure if she left, I'd have heard her. In my restlessness, I was wide awake. I take the final step and round the corner and see her stirring cups. I can finally breathe.

Realization hits me. She has made me a cup of coffee, and fuck if it doesn't make me smile.

But what's even better is her wearing this tiny pale blue night dress thing. I see the outline of her nipples, confirming she's not wearing a bra. I know I shouldn't be looking, as it will only make things harder on me, but I can't help myself. My eyes rake down over her body to her hips, trying to look for an outline of panties. I'm hoping she sleeps with no panties either.

"Good morning," I say as I walk toward her.

Her face lifts at the sound of my voice, but I don't miss the cute bags under her eyes. Glad I'm not the only one who struggled with sleeping last night.

"Morning," she says cheerily.

The metal spoon hit the sides of the cup with a final mix.

"You're all happy this morning. Did you sleep well?" I ask. I'm stirring the pot because I can almost guarantee she thought of me all night. With that knowledge, I can't help but get off on it.

"Not really," she says, choking on the most adorable laugh. Picking up both cups, she ambles over to me. I carefully take one.

"You figured out the machine?" I'm happy she's making herself at home here, and when I peer over toward the expresso machine, I wince. It looks like a bomb went off.

Ignoring it, I take a sip of my coffee, but it's steaming and burns my tongue.

Fuck, that's hot.

She definitely needs to practice making coffee here.

"Not so much. I'll need more practice."

I pinch my lips together, because it's exactly what I was thinking. And with the way she peeks down when a blush creeps on her face, I'm totally unfazed by the mess.

"Didn't you make coffee using machines at Frank's?" I tease.

Her head whips up, her eyes glaring at me. "Hey!"

"Am I wrong?" I blow the steam off my coffee as I wait for her to reply.

"No. But every machine's different," she clarifies.

I nod, set my cup down, and move to make breakfast.

"Did you want some toast? Eggs? Cereal?" I ask, ready to whip us up a hearty meal before I head into work.

I don't miss the way her eyes flick over to the oven.

"I made us breakfast," she says between sips of her coffee.

"You made me breakfast?"

She shrugs. "Yeah. I was hungry, and I figured you'd be too."

"Well, yeah," I mumble. My mind is in overdrive as I watch her move to the oven and pull out a baking tray.

A fucking tray, not a plate of food.

"T, this is so not expected. But I can't lie. This looks downright delicious." My stomach is grumbling with the need to taste the food she's cooked. The other part of me is laughing with wonder.

Will it be as bad as the coffee?

This morning is so different from any other I've experienced with a woman. She made me coffee and breakfast. No one has ever attempted. They always expect to be waited on.

"You're not doing all this because you want me to sleep with you?" I wiggle my brows at her with an amused look.

Horrified, she blinks rapidly, her eyes wide and completely bewildered. "Of course not. I—"

I wave and put her out of her misery. "It's fine. Just checking you're not doing anything you don't want to."

"It's only breakfast. I need to eat too," she argues, pursuing her pouty bow lips. I love it when she bites back.

I pick up my coffee, needing to distract myself from her mouth, otherwise my morning wood will be back with full force. And I don't have time for a quick hand job before getting to work. The lack of sleep last night made me hit snooze a few times more than I usually would.

"I know. I'm just saying, you don't need to do this for me as some thank you for the fake fiancé shit."

Her lips thin into a straight line, and I expect her to argue again, but she turns and grabs plates and silverware and sets everything on the counter. Then she takes her seat on a stool.

"If you don't sit and eat, I'll eat it all," she says. "I need to get ready."

Her words snap me out of my daze. I move to the stool beside her and sit, taking in the toast, eggs, muffins, turkey bacon, and potatoes and filling my plate.

"What do you have planned today?" I ask curiously.

She's already eating, so she doesn't answer straight away. She covers her mouth with her hand and mumbles, "I want to head into work at 9:30, but it will take time with traffic. Plus, I want to go for a walk and shower."

Thinking of her all sweaty from a workout or even just watching her workout has my dick twitching. The damn traitor keeps ignoring my brain.

I widen my legs on the stool and ask, "Will you use the gym here?" I take a bite of toast.

I'm hoping she says yes, because I don't know how I would take knowing she would be in a commercial gym. I imagine all the guys perving on her. My body turns ridged, and I know my answer. Yet I perve on her too. Go figure.

"Yeah, if that's all right? I don't have a gym membership, but your setup here looks fun."

I chuckle at how adorable she is. "Definitely not fun if you do it correctly. If you need a hand..." I smirk at her, and she rolls her eyes playfully back.

"No. I'm good," she retorts.

I laugh loudly at how fast she turned me down. Being her personal trainer in my house spells disaster. I don't know if I'd be strong enough if I had to watch her cute nose scrunch up, or blow out breaths, or worse, sweat coating her delectable body. Suddenly, my mouth is bone dry, and I take a sip of the shit coffee, just to add enough moisture to speak.

"Offers always there," I say, before we eat in silence for a bit.

"So, you're going into work again after a long day and night on call? Have you always wanted to work as a doctor?"

"Hitting me with the deep questions before 8 a.m." I raise my brows and give her a smirk before answering. "Surprisingly, I found the brain and spinal cord fascinating, plus the surgery component sounded fun."

Satisfaction purses her mouth as she nods.

"Hey, how come I don't get to ask you the hard-hitting questions?" I ask.

She pauses, bringing her cup to her lips. "You know everything about me, Alex," she mutters before sipping.

The way her face sags, and she bows her head, has me drawing in closer to her. I reach out, and she intakes a quick breath as I lightly finger a loose strand of hair that's fallen on her cheek. Her eyes hold mine and I could easily lean in and devour her lips in a hot kiss.

"I don't know everything." I'm dying to know when the last time she truly enjoyed herself with a man was.

"Ask me. I'm an open book." She raises her brow in a challenge.

"What are you most scared of?"

Her gaze looks turbulent. "I don't know if I can run the business." It's only a breath, but I catch it.

I reach out and stroke her cheek softly. "Hey. You can. I'm not a guy who runs his own company, but I can try to help you."

Her mouth quirks, and I swear I see amusement, but I didn't say anything funny. "What? Why are you looking at me like that?"

I see an amazing opportunity to take over this company and do whatever the hell she wants with it. She just needs to see beyond her parents' company, because soon it will be majority hers. And the Tahlia I saw in the pool yesterday is powerful.

"You seem way too invested, considering you have to be in a fake engagement with me."

"With you, it's not that hard."

I didn't mean for that to slip, but now that it hangs in the air between us, I own it. If I was ever going to do something crazy, it's for Tahlia. The only woman I've fantasized about before. Being around her in any shape or form is better than not having her at all.

But I will hold myself back from hurting her by not crossing that line, even if it kills me.

CHAPTER 16

ALEX

I'm finally home from an afternoon shift, dumping my keys and case down in the kitchen. I rush upstairs, calling out Tahlia's name loudly, but I don't get a response back.

The pool was empty, and there is no evidence or noises she's here. I bet she's working.

Lately she's been working late into the night, trying to learn the new business. Which means I'll have time to jerk off before she tempts me with her presence all night.

Entering my room, I kick off my shoes. I need some alone time to deal with my erection that I've been fighting all day. Because of her and all the little things she does. She's literally driving me insane.

I don't even shower before lying on my bed, propped up by pillows. The sinking way my body relaxes into the mattress helps the tension ease.

I drag a hand over my face and new stubble. I can't believe I am about to jerk off when all I want is to sink my dick into Tahlia's mouth or deep inside of her pussy.

That's not an option, though, so I unfasten my pants and push my briefs and pants down past my hips.

My balls sit tight and heavy between my legs, and my cock is straining with excitement. I'm about to give it a release, finally.

I grip my hand around the base and pull in languid strokes. My breath catches in my lungs before I blow it out.

After a few hard pulls, I slide my hand over my balls and touch them. Giving them a squeeze as a groan leaves me. I glide my hand back up and return to stroking my cock. My body is feverish as my hand works me harder. I close my eyes and tip my head back, enjoying the images of Tahlia's face and how her kiss and body felt to touch and taste. Pre-cum leaks, I widen my legs and rub the head of my thick cock. Working it as if it was Tahlia's hand or mouth instead of mine. I pull harder and faster, chasing the release, unable to slow myself down now that I'm this close to the edge.

Suddenly, the heat in this room has turned up by a thousand degrees. I stop to tear my shirt off. As I lower back down, I glance over to the doorway. Tahlia stands there, her dazzling green eyes staring back at me with so much longing.

There's no shy smile on her face. No, she's fearless. It's like she can't tear herself away and I don't want her to walk away either.

I welcome her eyes on me. I can't believe I didn't hear her come in. No footsteps, no words, but this is a nice surprise.

A real fucking nice surprise.

And there's no need to keep my memories when all I have to do is turn my head and stare back into those big doe eyes in all their glory.

I wrap my fist tighter around me and return to pulling with rapid strokes. I watch her mouth part wider, and she inhales a quick breath. The rise and fall of her chest urges me on. I grunt as I feel my orgasm building. Her eyes flick from my dick to my eyes, and then back to my hand. This is hot, her watching me. If only she knew it was because of her. Maybe she does know. And that's why she is shuffling her feet and gripping the door. She's probably achy and throbbing, and I wonder if she will want to self-pleasure after this show. Would she let me watch?

Fuck, if I heard it, you wouldn't be able to stop me. I'd be like a beast wanting to ravage. I'd offer my hand, my mouth, anything. That thought alone has my balls tightening up to my body. I grunt louder as I stroke myself.

Her teeth sink into her full bottom lip as her eyes hold mine. Her eyes are heavy with lust and desire. I get lost in the forest color until I can't hold back anymore.

Her eyes drop to my hand again, and I want to beg her to hold my gaze while I come. But I also know if I were in her position, I would find it difficult. And it's as if she can mind read, because as soon as her gaze hits mine, I come with her name on my lips. My hot slick cum spills all over my stomach as I groan, not even sounding like myself. I swear I hear her moan, and if I didn't just come as hard as I did, I may have been able to back it up for another round.

But she takes the choice away from me. Pushing off the door, she smirks, but I don't miss the twinkle in her eye or the way her cheeks are flushed a cute shade of pink.

"T." Her name leaves my lips in a silent plea.

But she shakes her head and walks away.

Chapter 17

Tahlia

The next morning, I make my way down to the kitchen ready to tease Alex about last night, about how he called out my name as he came. But a disappointing sigh leaves me when my feet hit the bottom wooden step, and I realize Alex isn't here. He must be at work already. Approaching the kitchen counter, I see a note propped up.

Picking it up, I read.

To my darling fiancée.

I stupidly smile at his words.

He's being cute and funny in the only way Alex knows. But I'm enjoying the snippets of the genuine Alex seeping through. The playboy one only creeps back in here and there.

I open the note.

T,

I'm taking you out for dinner tonight. Be
ready by 5.

Alex

I set the note down and carry on with my morning, only now I'm excited at what tonight brings. At least I have Emerald Designs to keep me busy today. Otherwise, I'm sure I'd be watching the clock until it was time to come home and get ready.

We need to hang out like a couple, because we need to play the part. We need to test the waters to see how we are out in public doing couple-y things.

The rest of the day flies, and I'm home at four. I jog up the stairs and begin date night prepping.

I lay out a knee-length, tight black dress with a slit on one side, showing off one of my legs. This dress is sexy, and with the matching black stilettos, I know I'm going to make it a challenge to keep his mind off the tension between us.

I head into the bathroom, and I go to pull out my make-up and cleansers, but when I open the cabinet under the sink, I suck in a sharp breath. My perfume stares back at me. You know the signature perfume you're known for? Yeah, well, a brand new one is staring back at me, along with a range of shampoos, conditioners, body washes, and luxurious body creams. Even some more pink bath bombs. After the last bath I had, when he brought me wine, I'm definitely making use of that again.

But the perfume still mocks me...Did he buy this?

He must have noticed the other bottle running low. I was going to buy more. I just haven't had time to run to the shops.

I'm reading way too far into this, and I don't have time. It's a kind gesture, so I leave it at that.

After a shower full of shaving, scrubbing, and conditioning, I'm primed for a date.

I spray myself with the perfume, before running my hands through my freshly curled hair, detangling them to give it more of a wavy look. And then I keep my makeup simple. I suck in a deep breath, knowing it's almost time. I'm about to see him. See what he's wearing. He'll be looking handsome, that I know for sure. I can't seem to keep the swarm of butterflies away at the thought of what Alex will think of me. I hope he likes what he sees.

With no more time to think, I pull my door open. Let's do this.

I take the stairs slowly, so I don't trip. When I near the bottom, I see the back of his head. He's leaned back on the sofa, but as I hit the floor, my heels click and grab his attention. His head turns, and those blue eyes drink me in. I internally shudder at how sexual he is. He's definitely playing his role really well, and I need to remember that this is all just temporary.

But when he looks at me like he's starving, I'm worried if I have the restraint in me to hold back.

He stands eagerly and rounds the cream sofa, fastening his cuff while whistling at me.

"You look incredible," he rasps. His hungry eyes drop slowly over my body.

I smile proudly at his words. But I can't stop the blush that's creeping up my neck and hitting my cheeks.

My gaze runs lazily over him, and I can't help the shiver of a thrill that runs through me. The black suit with no tie and a crisp white designer shirt. His beard is trimmed and his dark hair is in that finger-swept wave I love.

"Well, don't you look handsome," I breathe.

He rubs his hands together, and a grin forms on his face. He likes compliments. Scratch that. He loves compliments.

"Thanks, but not only do you look beautiful, you smell tantalizing."

"I probably sprayed a little too much."

"It's never enough. It's so perfectly you."

My heart catches in my throat.

"How did you know what my favorite perfume was?" I whisper.

"I went to the department store and described it to the assistant and smelt a bunch until I found it."

"You went to the store?"

"For the perfume. Yeah, so?"

How doesn't he see how sweet that is?

How non-playboy an act like that is?

My mind is spinning.

"Are you ready?" He moves to me and holds out his elbow.

I nod, taking his arm.

As he drives us to the restaurant, he tells me it's a local Greek place that is always booked, but he's friends with the owner. His excitement about how good the food is makes my mouth water. The butterflies in my stomach today made me too nervous to eat.

He opens my car door, and I again loop my arm through his elbow. Inside, we are ushered to our seats.

The city views are beautiful from here. It's the perfect backdrop for dinner.

He shrugs out of his jacket, and I try not to let my eyes linger too much over how good he looks. The waiter takes it, and we sit.

"Did you want to share a bottle of wine?" Alex asks. "Or would you prefer something else?"

"Sharing a bottle sounds nice."

He nods and orders the wine.

"Doc, I'm so glad you finally took my offer."

My eyes flick to the male voice. This must be the owner and Alex's friend.

"Hey, Gary." Alex stands and shakes his hand. "I wanted to take my fiancée Tahlia out."

I smile when he says it, and Gary's face lights up. It's weird hearing Alex refer to me as his fiancée. Not in a bad way. More of a surprise still. I don't have long to think about it, because Alex faces me, and I know I'm about to be formally introduced.

"Hi, I'm Gary. It's so nice to meet you. I've been telling your man to come here for months as repayment."

"Hi. It's lovely to meet you," I reply with a grin.

"You don't owe me anything," Alex says, shaking his head.

"Garbage. I owe you my life."

The way Gary says it stuns me silent. I want to know the story.

Gary clears his throat and hands the food menu over. "Here is the menu. The way I'd order is one from each section and share. I made them to share."

Sounds good. I like to have a little bit of everything.

Gary gazes at Alex and me. "I'll be back to take your order soon."

"Thank you," I say.

Gary walks off and we read the menu. I'm thinking it will be better if Alex takes charge here. Everything sounds delicious; I'm having a hard time choosing.

"How do you know him?" I ask curiously.

He lowers his menu to the table and leans in, clearly not wanting to shout it out. I mimic him, understanding he'll be whispering. "I operated on him."

My brows rise to my forehead, and I lean back with an O-shaped mouth. "Ah. Right. That makes sense. So, you dine here often?"

"To be honest, I don't dine in at restaurants," he replies.

"Anywhere?"

"Anywhere," he deadpans.

"But why?" I ask, totally confused.

"I work a lot."

"That's a shame, and that's part of the reason having majority of the business that scares me. No life."

He shakes his head. "You can do whatever you want soon. You'll be one of the bosses. That's why you need to figure out where the business is right now and work out how you want to run it. You can hire people to work. You don't have to work twenty-four-seven."

"Yeah. I need to think more about the way I want to run it. At the moment, I'm listening to the way my parents run everything, just to understand things first."

I relax, realizing I'm taking this business as my own. And I'm really loving the work so far, even if I'm just standing back and watching for the moment.

"Definitely take this time to sit back and observe. Then after some time, if you see an area needing improvement, step in and change it," he says, offering advice.

"Good idea. Not just a handsome face, are you?" I wink playfully at him.

"If only I was handsome on the inside," he mutters.

My face drops at his words. "What makes you say that?"

"I'm ugly on the inside." Alex's words are ice cold. "But at least you find me hot," he adds in his familiar light tone and wiggling his brows.

I stare into his detached eyes with a gut feeling he's internally struggling with something.

If I'm right, I need to tread carefully. I don't want to push him and have him shut down. Instead, I want him to know if he's ready to share I'll be here.

"No one is perfect. We all have blemishes. Including me."

He puts his hand over mine on the table. His thumb swipes back and forth over my skin. It's hypnotizing.

"You're beautiful Tahlia," he whispers. "So, fucking beautiful."

CHAPTER 18

TAHLIA

AN INDISTINCT, SENSUOUS LIGHT passes between Alex and me.

Is it because he shows he cares about me, that he brings up this hidden, unnerving desire? He speaks directly to my heart in the most unique way.

I pick up my drink, taking a sip and swallowing, but keep my eyes trained on him. He unbuttons another button on his white shirt, showing more of his exposed chest, up to his thick neck. I know I shouldn't watch, but I can't help it. The sexual magnetism makes me self-confident and has me throwing my worries away. His hungry eyes leave no room for not knowing he wants me, and I can't hide my attraction for him either. I admire the way his massive shoulders fill the white shirt he wears. My fingers tingle with a desperate need to touch him.

The food comes out, and I wince.

He must read my face because he's quick to ask, "What's wrong?" His voice is full of worry.

"Ah, I forgot to mention to the waiter that I have an intolerance to onions. It'll be fine."

He shakes his head, then he waves down a waiter, and I want to hide right now. Why didn't I keep my big mouth shut?

He sits back down and says, "It won't be long, and they will have one Pastitsio with no onion in the sauce."

"You didn't have to," I say, still mortified he wants the food replaced.

"And you shouldn't have to eat food you're intolerant too."

Fair point.

"You could have kept yours."

"No, I'll eat when you do."

I dip my chin and wonder how he can be this considerate.

"I'm sorry about the dishes, guys. Here's some flatbread to tie you over." Gary lowers a plate between us, and it looks puffed.

Alex chuckles and nudges his nose to me encourage me. "Poke it with your knife."

I don't argue; I'm way too intrigued.

I poke the bread and it loses the air, and I smile with utter fascination, mumbling under my breath. "That's cool."

"I'll let you eat the bread, and the pastitsio will be out with no onion soon."

"No rush," Alex says as Gary wanders off.

The warm bread aroma hits my nose, and I suck in a deep breath, my mouth watering. I'm so hungry, so I tear off a piece and chew. Alex copies and we stay silent as we eat.

"This is so good," I say when I finish my share, dusting my hands on my napkin. Leaning back, I add, "We need to come back here."

I can't believe how easy that was to say. *We.*

"I agree. It might be a weekly thing until we get married."

And I don't know why a wash of disappointment and a twang of pain hits me but hearing him admit this will be over makes me feel anything but relief.

"I don't know about weekly, but at least monthly."

"Deal. Before I leave, I'll let Gary know. It might be on different nights because of work, but I'll try not to work too much."

"You don't have to. That wasn't part of the agreement."

"I know, but the thought of you alone in my house doesn't sit well with me."

I don't answer. I don't know what to say.

Is he meant to care about me this much?

No. Not at all, because this wasn't part of our agreement.

But do I like that he cares about me? It blurs a line that was disintegrating anyway, and I know it will be dangerous since more time with him is tempting...

"Aw, look at you two. The perfect pair."

I jerk, turning to my mother's voice. My heart races. Do we look like we're on a date?

Reading her face, I can tell she's delighted. Her pouty lips are coated in her favorite plum lipstick, and she's in a navy Chanel dress and matching navy heels. She steps back to stand beside my dad, who finishes shaking Alex's hand. My eyes move to Alex, and he doesn't seem fazed they interrupted.

Waving her polished, delicate hand in the air, it's her way of getting him to say hello to her. Not subtle at all. I smile and watch the exchange.

Alex's attention on my parents is comforting. Even if it's all going to end soon, and he'll be back to his playboy ways. I'll treasure moments like these.

"Hi, Mrs. Adams."

He rises to give her a kiss on the cheek, and I shake my head at how charming he is. I don't miss the way my mom's face lights up. He makes everyone fall for him. Meeting my eyes, he winks. I peer over at Dad, and I'm surprised to find a relaxed face.

Maybe finding us out on a date was a great thing. Cementing to them it's in fact real.

We're real.

However, breaking up this fake relationship will be hard if my parents grow attached.

This is becoming more of a mess.

I grab some water. And then I rise to Mom.

"He's better than any pick I had for you," she gushes.

My lips twitch at her confession. She's happy with a choice I've made. Finally.

"He's a good man." My eyes move to him talking to my dad.

I wonder what they're discussing since I've been talking to mom.

I'm going to guess, work, golf, or me. No matter what it is, I'm humbled that he's trying with my dad.

They end up joining us for a while. I step closer. My dad is discussing their business.

Error.

Soon-to-be majority my business.

"She'll make the best CEO. I have no doubt—"

Alex's compliment, and the earnest way he says it, makes me shy...yet also giddy.

"All right, you two, stop talking about me and let me get back to my date."

Alex puts his arm around me and pulls me close to him. He peers down with fire in his eyes. Yeah, the tension between us keeps building, making all these moments more intense.

Both men look at me with warm smiles, and my heart swells with pure happiness. My parents joining us surprised me because I didn't hate it.

Is it possible that Alex could help improve my relationship with them?

I never used to see them this much. Because I felt like the biggest letdown. Their child with no finished college degree or aspirations. Worse, no partner in sight. My family looks at me differently now.

It's all thanks to him.

My parents say goodbye and turn to their table, but not before Mom mentions she's organized a wedding planner for us at their house tomorrow. There's no rebutting. It was an order.

I turn and Alex slips his hand over my shoulders and massages my tightening knots. A moan slips from my lips at how good it feels.

He's standing behind me, and he whispers into my hair so only I can hear. "I'm going to have to finish this when we get home," he warns, and heat floods my body.

Him and me alone, with his skilled hands on me.

Yeah, not a good idea.

But I don't think I have any resolve left to fight.

"Here's the pastitsio," Gary interrupts, and we smile back, giving him our thanks as we take our seats again.

"This looks incredible," I say.

Alex agrees, and we dig in.

Afterward, I'm stuffed and ready to curl up on the sofa and watch my trash TV shows.

"Dessert?" he asks.

"I'm full..." But my voice is unconvincing.

"How about we share?" he suggests with a sparkle in his eye.

I shrug. "Sure."

Scanning the menu, we decide on a chocolate mousse.

I look over at where my parents sit, but a touch on my thigh has me jumping in my seat. I turn my face, and I'm met with his mesmerizing eyes.

"Are you okay?" he asks quietly.

I welcome his hands on me, but at the same time, it awakens the burning desire I keep trying to bury.

It's been bubbling underneath the surface, and at times like these, it hits in full force. All I want to do right now is move his hands up my thigh to my pussy. I've never done anything in public but with him? Right now? I would. I'm desperate to ease the ache, but our dessert arrives, interrupting my thoughts.

I eat in silence. When we finish, he walks behind my chair. I peer up to find his blue eyes full of longing, and I know mine mirror his.

He leans in, his thumb wiping across my lips. My heart is racing watching him bring it to his own lips and suck mousse remnants off. I know I should be embarrassed I had mousse on my mouth, but if it got him to do that, I'd do it again happily.

He gives me an all-consuming grin, then dips his head and kisses my open lips before whispering, "You ready?"

The air from his breath on my lips sends a small shudder down my spine.

I nod. "Yeah."

He kisses my temple, his warm lips on my skin teasing me again before he stands and holds out his hand for me. I take it, knowing it feels so right when I do.

CHAPTER 19

TAHLIA

I LOOK DOWN AT my hand and twirl the ring, admiring the way the light catches it. It really is something else. But I'm pulled quickly from my runaway thoughts by my mom's voice.

"I'd like you all to meet Yolanda. She's a wedding planner, and I asked her here today to run through a couple of things. Because we're having coffee, how great would it be to do the cake testing?"

I'm surprised she isn't clapping with the way she is grinning excitedly at us all. I'm speechless at her audacity. No discussion. No warning. Just here, we're doing cake today.

I know she's excited, but this adds to my ever-growing guilt. Maybe I should confess? That this isn't real. It's all a setup and I'm doing this for my part of the business. Admit to her that Alex and I don't actually love each other.

I suddenly need wine. I get up, grab a bottle of champagne from their wine fridge, and then some glasses for everyone, and return to the table.

I open it and pour everyone a glass. Mom beams back, and I know it's because she thinks by me grabbing champagne, I'm loving the fact she's organized this. However, my stomach is hard from the number of knots inside it. This is serious. I was hoping not to do any actual wedding planning before my birthday.

Today is the start. Meeting the wedding planner and cake tasting. Soon she'll be asking to take me venue and dress shopping.

There's a piece of cake pushed in front of me, and I wish it had the answers. I didn't think this fake husband thing through. Stabbing a big piece of the white chocolate and raspberry cake, I welcome the sweet taste when it hits my tongue. It's delicious, but it can't replace the mess I'm currently in. However, at least, I can eat my bodyweight in cake. I'm excited to leave here with a full belly and go home to lie on the sofa, watching my shows with Alex.

My brows pinch when the doorbell rings.

"I have a little surprise for you both," Mom says, and a wave of worry hits me.

What has she organized now?

She doesn't stop to explain, instead she takes off to the door, and I turn to my dad for an explanation.

He's already shaking his head. "Don't ask me. You know your mother."

That's exactly the problem.

Next up, I'm saying hello to the celebrant.

I arrive back to Alex's house and make a beeline for his cream plush sofa. I need to sit in this food coma a little longer.

The sofa feels divine as I sink deeply and turn on a home renovation show and snuggle up.

"You don't happen to have a blanket?" I ask as Alex fusses in the kitchen, doing God knows what.

"Yes. In the drawer under the TV."

I grab a cozy fluffy cream blanket and amble back to the sofa. Tucking my legs under me, I cover myself in the warm blanket and get comfortable.

"Did you want a cup of tea?" he asks.

"Mmm. Yes, please."

My mind is a little lost in what he's doing right now. Surely, this little play will end soon.

"Herbal?" he asks.

"Peppermint, if you have any," I call back.

"Sure."

"Tea bag left, please," I call out.

"Demanding, aren't you, honey?" he teases quietly.

I chuckle softly to myself.

But a couple of minutes later, he brings over snacks and my tea. I grab the cup from his outstretched hand, and I'm careful not to touch him, but, of course, it's impossible when the cup is a lot smaller than our two hands.

I ignore the sparks and say, "Thanks."

He offers me cookies, but there's no way I could eat another thing. I decline. But when he sits beside me and munches on one, my mouth hangs open, and I sneer. "Unfair."

He looks at me, waiting for an explanation.

"You can eat desserts and cookies and still—" I purse my lips and hold what I was going to say, because he will know I've noticed how fit he is.

"Still what?"

He pushes with humorous eyes. I can't help but roll my eyes and wave my hand over his body. "You still look great." I sound annoyed, even to my own ears.

"Noticing me, are you, fiancée?"

"No, I just need your metabolism."

He eases back into the sofa to get comfortable, and he taps my feet, so I go to move my legs off. "No. Leave them."

I pause and look at him, puzzled.

He has no tea, whereas I'm clutching my hot one so I can't fight off his hands that are grabbing my feet and laying them in his lap.

My pulse picks up, and when he begins to massage the arch of my feet, I can't help the moan that slips.

I'm appalled and embarrassed, which I never thought possible. But with Alex, everything is possible.

"Just lie back and sip your tea. Let me ease some tension."

I follow his command. I can't argue with him when the strokes on my feet feel incredibly good.

I sip my tea and watch my show.

"What shit are you watching?" he teases.

"I don't know, some renovation show," I mumble between sips.

"More like reality."

I can't argue there, but it's more like a mash-up, and I explain that to him. He just nods, and we fall into a comfortable silence. Him massaging both my feet, and me sipping my tea and watching TV. As soon as I finish my drink, I put the cup down and rest my head on the arm of the sofa.

Somewhere along the line, my eyes grew heavy, and I must have dosed off. I'm being lifted from the sofa, and when my eyes fling open, I'm back up next to his face as he walks.

"I'm awake. Put me down, and I'll walk."

"It's okay, I can do it, and hey, think of it as more practice."

I slump down, too exhausted to care.

His scent this close is so heavenly, I just soak it in. Up the stairs, I know we are in my room, and he lowers me down.

His hands stay touching my waist and mine on his shoulders. The erratic beating of my heart feels like it's about to come out of my chest. Everything around us drowns out, and my earlier sleepy state is now the opposite.

He's staring down at me intently, before he slowly and seductively gazes over my body. When he meets my eyes again, my blood is pounding in my ears. Then he leans in, and the emotions around us are melting my resolve.

I wonder what he's thinking, but before I get a chance to ask, he pecks my lips with soft, slow kisses. Not once, no, not twice, no, three times before he moves his lips to my hair, whispering, "Goodnight."

Chapter 20

Tahlia

I'm so frustrated, I could cry. Why didn't he kiss me passionately last night? I was practically begging him. I even leaned in, but he just...pecked me on the damn lips!

He spun around and strolled into his room as if nothing happened. Leaving me shocked and breathless. When I finally got my legs to work, they were shaky. I barely slept last night, because I couldn't stop dreaming about him. The way his strong hands massaged my shoulders. Or the way his breath touched my ear when he whispered into it.

I know I shouldn't want him, but I can't rein it back in now. And if he didn't already turn me down, I would have crawled into his bed and begged him to touch me. But I've had enough humiliation.

I open my bedroom door, ready to stomp down the stairs, a mix of exhaustion and anger overwhelming me. I didn't bother changing into the sweats to cover myself. I'm back in my slinky nightie, wearing it proudly to fuck with him. I'm not covering myself up; I want him to walk around with the same amount of ache that I have. A wicked smirk parts my lips as I imagine him hard as a rock, walking around at work in scrubs for me. Yeah...I can't deny the thrill that thought hits me with.

Of course, he stands outside my bedroom with his hand up like he was ready to knock on my door. "Morning," he says in his gravelly morning voice.

I catch his eyes roaming up over my naked legs. Instinctively, I cross one foot over the other to squeeze the throb between my thighs. His eyes widen at the movement. I love the way he looks at me. It makes me feel adored...wanted. Yet his actions do the other.

He's so damn confusing. It hurts my brain to think.

The only sign he gives me, or at least I think I'm seeing, is a deep hunger in his glare. Then there're his heavy breaths and his Adam's apple as he tries to swallow when he finishes his inspection.

"Did you sleep well?" he asks through a thick voice.

I want to tell him I'm achy, aroused, and borderline close to begging him to fuck me here in my room. Even taking in his sweats, it's hard for me to focus.

"Yeah, all right." It's the best I can come up with. I try not to show him how affected I am by his looks.

The way his lips twitch and brow lifts, I expect him to call me out. But instead, he watches me closely.

Needing to break the tension, I cross my arms over my chest. I'm trying to calm the noise in my head that's telling me to step forward and capture his mouth with mine. My body is on fire, and I know he's watching me.

His hand reaches out to run a finger along my temple and over my lips. They part, desperate for him, just like the rest of me.

His touch on my lips is so delicate, it's like he's deliberating.

Do it, my head screams. Kiss me...

"Yes..." I breathe, my voice cracking.

His fingers trail down my neck, over my rapid pulse, before he moves to my shoulder. I watch him, and his brows pull down as his tongue pokes out of his mouth. My breath catches. His hand has moved to the divot in my chest, and his finger trails delicately down the center between my heavy breasts, my nipples tight and ready for his touch. His fingers linger over my wildly beating heart.

"I shouldn't..." His voice is low and strangled, mirroring my own struggle. But he has some kind of internal fight that he isn't voicing. His dark eyes stay trained on his finger that's headed back to the base of my throat, setting my body to shivering.

"Why not?" I push, ignoring my own dark thoughts coming up about how much of a playboy he is, and that he will only break my heart. I'll be the one left disappointed.

"I don't do this."

I frown, not understanding. I try not to focus on his finger caressing up my arm again and how he could see my nipples tight through my nightie. Instead, I force myself to focus on his words.

"Don't do what?" I whisper softly, trying to get him to let his walls down and allow me in.

He stays silent as he skims his finger over the strap sitting on my shoulder, moving it effortlessly. I close my eyes; my body frozen, hoping he will slide the strap off.

"Alex..." I say, a gentle plea, willing him to take this further.

His finger moves across to the other arm, repeating the same torturous motion. A deep, heavy sigh slips through my lips.

His eyes momentarily flick to mine, blazing with so much heat. A breath catches in my lungs at the sight. And I have to focus on exhaling to calm my erratic body down.

"This. T. I don't. I can't do this to you." His finger stops on my wrist, over my pulse. It's spilling my secrets without me having to utter a word. I'm desperate for him.

I don't want him to stop. I feel like I could break from the overwhelming need to have him.

But, of course, he fucking stops. My eyes sting, so I squeeze them shut and then re-open them. Steadying myself, I try to get a read of his face. His lips are thin and his face tight. I see the pain, but I don't get why. I'm offering myself on a silver platter, and he's denying us...why?

"What. Why?" I ask. Attempting to get him to talk without the distraction of our skin touching. Knowing how it short-circuits my brain.

He shakes his head as he runs his hand through his gelled hair, messing it up. Like he can't quite believe he just did that. "I've gotta go." His voice is low and defeated.

He turns around and walks to his room. When I hear his door slam shut, I sigh. I sit lightheaded and dizzy in lust...And a lot confused.

"Tea or coffee?" Maddison calls out from the kitchen. I'm sunk into the sofa with a blanket. The comfort of being in my own home settles in, where I'm not confused or sexually frustrated. What is going on in Alex's brain; I'd love to know.

Maddison is an open book, not hiding how she feels or what she's thinking. I welcome the familiarity, just like all the times I've been on this sofa with her and Alice.

Talking boys, food, or the latest episode of a recent TV show we're bingeing.

"Wine?" I ask.

"Sure." she says.

"Wanna hand?"

"Nope, I'll be a second."

A couple of minutes later, she walks in carrying our glasses, handing me one. "Thanks."

As she settles into the sofa, she speaks. "Wine for lunch. This is new."

I turn my gaze away from her wiggling brows. I take a big sip, welcoming the sweet taste on my tongue.

"Come on. Clearly, something is going on. You haven't been here since you left."

"I h—" My voice dies when I realize I haven't been back. And now I'm expecting to come here and hang out? We've been friends for years. Maddison speaks her mind. Her no bullshit approach is probably what I need to hear. But then I'd have to hear my own desperate attempts of trying to come on to Alex when he clearly doesn't want me.

"See. So, spill it."

I sigh. "Fine."

She chuckles, and I side glance at her with a sneer that turns into a giggle.

"One guess."

She gives me a knowing look. "Hot doc."

My lips twist, and I try to pinch them together to stop the grin that's forming on my face.

I've never been one to hide my feelings.

"Yeah, him."

She claps. "No denying he's hot. That's a start."

"We haven't hooked up, so slow down."

No, he prefers to mess with me instead…

I twist to face her. And she mirrors me, clutching the glass. I tell her what's eating me up. Hopefully when I leave her, I'm less of a mess.

"There is something going on between us. I swear, we've come close." I sigh, staring into the yellow liquid.

"Like how close?" she asks, sipping her drink.

My stomach is too filled with nerves to drink any more right now.

"He was touching my neck, shoulders, arms, and chest." I rub my finger along the same lines he traced this morning. It doesn't feel as good as his touch, but it still shudders me with the memory as if it was him.

She nods. "And you didn't kiss?"

I shake my head. "He said he needed to go and practically ran to his room."

Her eyes widen at my answer. I giggle at her reaction.

"Yeah. I'm hoping I'm not that repulsive..."

"T. He's into you. Maybe..." She doesn't finish her sentence, making me antsy.

I sit up, waiting for her, but she just bites her lip.

"Maybe what?" I ask.

She lets out a deep, loud breath. Her face is scrunched up. "You don't think there's...someone else?"

The words I kept deep down, hidden with fear that's what he's hiding.

But I need to trust him, so I shake my head. "We had a deal that while we're in this fake marriage, neither of us would see anyone."

"He agreed?" she asks in shock, draining her glass and lowering it to the floor.

"Yeah, he was believable."

She flips her hair to one side and leans on her elbow on the back of the sofa. "Maybe he isn't seeing anyone else."

"Then why not go there?" My stomach is less bubbly, so I sip more of my drink. "Why not kiss me?"

My stomach grumbles loudly, letting me know it needs food, so I decide to order us some takeout. It's the least

I can do for coming here and talking her ear off with my problems.

"My other guess would be Mike and Alice."

My brows pull together and crease. "It is awkward, I guess...but I didn't think it would be a problem."

I didn't think they would mind. Alice and Mike seem so happy in love that they want everyone to find what they have. Why would they care about me and Alex?

She taps her lip and then holds the finger up. "Wait. What if Mike told him he'd kill him if he touches you?"

That's more of what could be happening, because Alice would talk to me, and she hasn't.

"Possibly," I mumble. Not knowing if it is that...what do I do? Talking to Mike isn't an option. And Alice is recovering from having Ethan. I don't need to burden her again with my little crush. But I can't keep living there with feelings bubbling to the surface every time I see him. It's becoming worse with every minute we spend time together. I'm a band ready to snap.

"What's it like living together?" she asks curiously.

That part is easy. I smile as I think of our usual mornings. Well, except for today.

"Surprisingly nice." I smile and continue. "He makes me breakfast and coffee. We hang out and he watches TV with me. I even got a massage."

She giggles hard.

"What?" I clip, a little salty at her laughing at me. I'm lost. Not understanding what I said that's funny.

"You got a *massage*, huh?" She looks at me with a smart-ass grin.

I roll my eyes and softly shake my head. I kinda wish it was that type of massage. But it definitely wasn't. No, this was a PG-rated massage. I'd have happily taken an R.

"It was strictly on my feet."

She scoffs. "Boring."

"I kind of have to agree." I smile into my glass, draining it.

"Have you spoken to him about why he's not wanting to go there with you?"

"No. Not yet."

Which is why I'm so confused by what we are. It feels more than friendship. Like we're towing the line of more. It's too easy to be with him. And the way I feel about him is not the same I feel about the other male friendships I have. With Alex, it's different. There's sexual chemistry, but more than that, there's a deeper connection. I could sit with him for hours in silence and not get sick of him. A touch here or a hold there. Some feelings are happening between us. I just don't know what exactly it is.

"I mean, you need to straight-up ask."

I laugh. "I will. Give me sometime."

"Okay. Okay. Just checking. Sometimes you're not as forthcoming."

"Not everyone is an open book, Maddy," I argue.

"I'm not that bad. Come on. I just like to talk."

I smile, reaching across to grab her hand in mine. "And I love you for it. Thanks for listening to me bitch and moan."

She reaches forward, squeezing my hand. "Anytime. I wish I had an exciting story."

"You don't wish this."

My head hurts from thinking too hard. Or is it the wine? I don't know, but either way, I'm grateful when the bell rings. Jumping up, I grab her glass from the ground and make my way to the door. Knowing the conversation about Alex and me is over, and I've got no new ideas. I am where I was when I walked in. I'll just have to go home and go back to the awkward dancing around our attraction again.

Chapter 21

Alex

"I'm engaged to Tahlia," I blurt out as my brother swings his driver.

He hits the worst shot, and I burst out laughing.

Perfect.

He's beating me, and I can't have that. I need to win today. Take back some control. I haven't been feeling like I'm in control when it comes to Tahlia. She's consuming me without even knowing. Yes, when we're together, we're fiery and the passion is there, but what's worse are the moments we aren't together.

The unhealthy amount of time my mind drifts to her...I wonder what she's learning from her parents at work today. If she's thinking of me. If she's going to be swimming naked in my pool when I get home.

Mike spins, leaning on his driver for support. "What the fuck did you just say?"

"Nice hit," I taunt.

"Fuck you." He smirks. "Now tell me you're joking?"

"Nope. But it's not real," I admit.

Mike waves his free hand in the air before scratching his temple, utterly confused.

"I think I need a drink."

"You want to stop playing and have a beer?" I ask, hopeful. It means I win if we stop now. Yes, it's by default, but a win's a win.

"Yeah, I'm not going to be able to concentrate until I know everything."

"Okay, sweet. Let's get rid of our clubs and get drinks. You're a loser."

"You're an asshole," Mike grumbles.

"A winning asshole," I reply, laughing.

We get back to the bar, where we hold beers. Mike already finished half of it.

Mike's focus is on me. He wants me to spill everything.

There's a worried expression, and I can take a stab that it'll be for Alice. Alice and Tahlia are best friends, so if his wife's upset, so is he.

I'm trying not to hurt Tahlia, but it seems I keep doing it. When really, I'm trying to protect her.

"When did you get engaged? I never knew you two were a thing."

"We weren't."

"What the fuck, Alex. Spit it out. Stop messing around."

"She asked me to be a fake boyfriend to her parents—"

Mike interrupts, "Why?"

"She quit Frank's and wanted her inheritance. But to do that, she needs to get married."

"Christ," Mike splutters before taking a decent pull of his beer.

"I told her, let's get engaged so she can get her part of the business. I'm glad I did. You should see her slowly changing. The way she wants to learn everything possible about the business is so fucking alluring."

"So, hang on. Let me get this straight. You're definitely getting married."

"Yeah, we've been doing all the wedding prep, so I need to ask you something."

"Yeah, what?" Mike asks.

"Will you be my best man?"

He stares for a second before laughing. "Yeah, why not? I'll happily play the fake best man."

"This means I get to organize a bachelor party." Mike smirks, rubbing his hands together.

"Nothing that can get me in trouble."

"You sound like you've caught the feels."

I roll my eyes. "Yeah, so what? That doesn't mean I've acted on it."

"Why?"

"She deserves better than me. I don't want to hurt her."

"You won't."

The next day after I've finished work, I pull into the driveway, and notice her car is missing. I don't recall her saying she had work today, but this morning I wasn't thinking clearly. I park and wander up the stairs, admitting her not being home right now is probably for the best. This morning was intense. I had a hard time concentrating today, because of my wandering thoughts about Tahlia. Every gasp, shiver, and moan fixed into my brain. I'm annoyed at myself that I can't switch off these feelings.

When I step inside, I walk around through the quiet house. I hate her not being home. I miss the TV being obnoxiously loud and her mess in the kitchen. Or her warm, sweet chocolate scent that hits me as I walk up the stairs and past her room to go into mine. Even making her breakfast and coffee in the morning is a highlight, and I never thought living with a woman could be so easy. But Tahlia's presence has grown on me.

And now I've probably upset her by turning down her advances. She's given me every indication she's interested.

The only thing she hasn't done is kiss me. I know I've been teasing her, but not completely giving in. Just dangling her along with a carrot.

I'm such an asshole.

The player I'm known for.

I wish I could hold back from going near her, but I can't control myself. My mind and cock are at war with themselves.

So, can I blame her for being mad? I practically ran out of the house this morning like a child. Instead of opening my mouth and telling her why I don't think it's a good idea, we cross the boundary.

But whenever she is near, I choke up on the words and say nothing.

After changing into activewear I leave my room to hit the home gym.

I begin lifting weights, but after a few heavy sets, I rip my shirt off. I must be engrossed, not even hearing the door, because when I turn, I freeze. She's standing there with flushed cheeks and her bottom lip between her teeth as her gaze hits me. I like her in my house. A lot more than I thought was possible.

Peering down, I mumble a curse under my breath. The way her eyes are eating me up, is not making this easy on me.

"Hey." My voice is a little shaky, but I manage to hide it well.

"Hi."

I need to stop looking at those green eyes. "You want to work out with me?"

"I'm going out tonight."

The pit of my stomach hardens. A wave of jealousy hits me. She wouldn't go on a date right? Shaking my ridiculous thoughts off, I clear my throat to make sure I don't sound rude.

"Yeah. Cool. Where you off too?"

I turn to finish my set, watching her in the mirror. Her gaze shoots down as soon as I turn, and the flush across her cheeks tells me she likes what she sees.

"Just Luxe with Maddy and Blake."

A sudden wave of worry hits me. "You don't need me to come?"

I take in her heart-shaped face and prominent cheekbones. She's really beautiful in this light. And I don't like the thought of other men looking at her. Even talking to her.

Her face softens with slight amusement. "No. We've gone there plenty of times without you."

But now it's different. Now you're my fiancée. Now you live with me...

It's not my place to say any of that, so I hold that back.

"True. And you'll behave, right?"

Her eyes narrow at me. "Yes, Dad."

"Don't call me that," I say as nausea rolls in my gut.

She chuckles at my hard expression, clearly reading my unimpressed face.

"Makes me feel gross. I don't look at you that way."

She snorts. "I hope not."

Blinking at her, a new thought occurs to me. "You'll wear your ring?" My back is still facing her, because I don't want her to see my worried expression.

I trust her. I'm just...falling.

The thought makes my heart race and my throat dry. I've been falling for her all this time. Every moment we've shared together had a part of me becoming infatuated.

"Yes. We have a deal, right? Neither of us is seeing anyone else while we are in this agreement."

My shoulders sag with relief. Blowing out a breath, I turn to face her.

"I'll wear your ring." She holds up her hand, where my ring sits, and she waves, so it catches the light.

Her cute smile on her face is totally calling me out on my protectiveness, but I like that she isn't fighting me. Instead, she's reassuring me. I just need to relax and let her be without me for a night.

∞

BANG! I must've fallen asleep on the sofa, because it isn't until I hear banging and crashing outside that I'm wide awake. Standing up in a rush, I go to the door, hearing Tahlia giggle.

I open the door and the air leaves my lungs. She's in her sexy black dress, on her hands and knees. Her green eyes lock onto mine, and a hand covers her mouth. "I'm sorry. Did I wake you?"

"Not really. But what are you doing down there?"

Her face scrunches up, her eyes glassy from alcohol. "What do you mean, not really?"

"As in, I just fell asleep on the sofa." I huff, slightly annoyed, but also struggling with the sight of her on her hands and knees.

I hold out my hand. "Come on, let's get you inside."

She drops her head and feels around on the ground. "I can't, I'm looking for my keys. I was trying to open the door when they dropped. Probably all those shots."

I chuckle, knowing how shots get you from zero to one hundred in a matter of hours.

I drop to my hands and knees and help her look.

"What are you doing?" she asks. Her words are slurry.

I peer around for her keys. I pad the area with my hands, trying to locate them.

"Helping you find the keys."

"Oh."

I smile, spotting them near her. "There they are. Just reach over to your left."

When she swipes them up, we stand, but she drops them again. Both of us squat down to pick them up. Our faces are inches apart and her eyes bore into mine. The alcohol brightens up her irises, which I didn't think was possible. Her gaze roams over me leisurely, and she doesn't look away embarrassed. Drunk Tahlia is bolder.

She inches closer, her breath tickling my lips. Her lips are already parted and her eyes heavy, gaze flicking between my eyes and mouth. I'm frozen. I should stand.

"Here are your keys." I look down and watch as she opens her hand and I lay them in her palm. She closes her fingers over them. I run my eyes over the skin on her shoulder and up over her shiny blonde curls, and then over her pouty parted lips and cute dainty nose.

"Kiss me," she breathes.

The beg in her voice kills my restraint, and I can't deny I want it. I run my hand along the side of her face, brushing the hair away. Bringing my lips close to hers, our breaths mingle. Her warm, short pants hit my lips, and when she licks them, I pull back before I cave.

"Ahhh. What are you doing?"

"Going inside, it's freezing out here," I say.

"No. Stay here and tell me what—"

"Come on. Let's get you a drink of water and then let you sleep."

She mumbles, "Sleep sounds good."

I help her stand by grabbing her around her waist, but she sags against me. She's drunk so I pick her up and carry her instead. She doesn't fight me. Instead, she lets out a loud sigh. When I hold her like this, I enjoy the feeling of her luscious curves under my hand. She grabs around my neck and lays her head against my shoulder. I stop to grab a bottle of water from the fridge. Then I walk her upstairs and into her bedroom. Moving beside her bed, I pull back the covers, and lay her down gently. She immediately settles her head into the pillow and curls up on her side. Her eyes close, but as I go to move a step back, I hear her mumble, "Stay."

I shake my head. Telling myself to not even think about it. I lean forward, hovering over her, then kiss her temple and watch her drift into a deep sleep. "I wish," I whisper. After I pull the covers up over her, I walk out, returning to the safety of my bedroom.

CHAPTER 22

TAHLIA

MOVING AROUND MY BEDROOM, I'm quick to realize what a mistake it was drinking so much at the club last night. I'll blame Maddison for buying the drinks, but I only have myself to blame for the consumption.

The room seems to move when I feel the hard walls against my fingertips as I enter the bathroom. My stomach twists and my mouth makes excess saliva, letting me know I'm going to be sick.

I can't even run to make it, but I'm grateful I needed to pee, so I'm already here, and in two steps, I've thrown up my night.

And I repeat the sickness a few more rounds. I didn't think I could feel any worse until a gentle touch to my shoulder makes me want to hide somewhere. But unfortunately for me, this is Alex's house and there's nowhere to hide when my stomach empties again.

"Can I get you anything?"

I wipe my mouth, but keep my head down to the bowl, embarrassed to face him. "No. I'm okay. I deserve this." I laugh, keeping my chin down. Sitting back on my heels, my hands hold on to the rim.

His hand continues to rub slow circles on my back. "I would say no, but you did say you had shots."

The flashbacks of the night hit me...there wasn't just one round of shots.

I groan. "Yeah, shots. I can't believe I drank them. I know they are lethal, yet I did it anyway."

"You're allowed to have fun. Relax, you'll feel better in a couple of hours."

I wish. I launch myself forward, expelling whatever is left in my stomach. It actually hurts my stomach now.

His hands hold my hair before draping it over my shoulder and down my back in one soft stroke. "I'll get you some Hydralyte and Tylenol."

I nod. His heavy steps leave my room and move down the stairs, and I drop my head on my arm to close my eyes.

A few minutes later, he's back and lifting me in his arms. His hard chest, warm body, and calming scent surround me.

"What are you doing?" I murmur, half asleep.

"Taking you to bed," he whispers.

He eases me down onto the bed, and I blink, trying to focus on his face.

His hand reaches out to shift a strand of hair away from my eyes. "Hey." He smiles, and it's a boyish one.

If I had the energy, I would grumble, but I just muster up a smile back.

"Sit up for a second and take these, then let yourself sleep."

I nod as he turns and grabs the pills, helping me take them, and then I shuffle back down as he hovers over me to tuck me in.

When I next wake, I blink and stretch. "You're awake."

His deep voice has me tilting my head back, and I see him sitting in a chair.

"What are you doing there?"

The way he's easing back, scrolling on his phone with a leg crossed over the other knee, he's totally relaxed. It's as if sitting in the corner of my room watching me sleep isn't weird or abnormal.

I stare at his profile. I'm mad at how perfect his jawline is and the dark beard that's forming as the day draws on. The lines around his eyes give him a sexy older vibe, and his dark brows frame those damn captivating blue eyes.

His hair has managed to stay perfectly styled on top of his head, and I curl my hands to prevent myself from walking over and running my fingers through it. Messing it up. I liked the messy hair I saw the night I caught him jerking off.

I like the relaxed version. The charming version is nice, but I want the Alex who's reserved for just me.

Yeah, I want more of that. Except I shouldn't after he's turned me down.

His velvety voice takes me away from my lost thoughts. "Just making sure you're okay." He shrugs and uncrosses his leg as he tucks his phone away.

"Oh," I mumble, not knowing what else to say.

My mouth feels dry, and there is an awful taste, so I sit up and I expect to feel dizzy and sick, but I'm grateful that I only feel hungry and off. Not something I can pinpoint.

"Woah. Where are you going?" He moves fast to stand in front of me. It's like since our near kiss he is more attentive, and I don't know if I can handle it. I'm more confused than ever.

"Um. To get some food."

"You feel well enough to leave the room, or did you want me to cook you something and bring it here?"

This is definitely too much caring for me.

"I'm okay. I need to get out of this room."

"Need a change of scenery?"

"Something like that," I mumble.

I stand and move toward the bathroom. And he's right beside me.

"Thanks for helping, but I need to pee, and it would be weird for you to watch."

"You want me to meet you out here?" he asks, raising a brow at me.

I shake my head. "Downstairs," I say, knowing I need a minute without him clouding my head. He's too tempting when he's being all attentive, and I'm a hot mess from being this hungover.

He nods, and I go into the bathroom and close the door. A deep breath expels, and I decide to take a quick shower, brush my teeth, put some fresh sweats on, and throw my hair up into a bun. I know that will make me feel brand new.

Half an hour later, I'm making my way downstairs. The back of his head rests on the sofa as he watches football. I move to the kitchen to make plain toast with butter. His heavy steps come over, and my lips quirk as I look for the butter in the fridge.

"I hope you're not over here offering to help, Doc."

I find it, then turn to face him.

"Wouldn't dare to." He treks back to the sofa.

I turn to grab the bread before a big smile erupts on my face.

I can't help the silly flutters that my stomach makes for knowing he continually wants to check on me.

I bring my food and more Hydralyte over to the sofa and eat. When I'm finished Alex puts a pillow in his lap.

"Here," Alex says, patting it for me to lay down. It'll be the only thing between me and his dick. Thankfully. But I don't move. Sensing my hesitation, he rolls his eyes and smirks. "Come on I'm only offering you a place to lie down and relax."

I lower down. I don't have any energy to resist.

As soon as I relax, he flicks it back over to my reality TV show.

"I'm training you well," I joke.

"Hey, you. None of that."

A giggle rumbles out of me.

And he digs his hand into my ribs, tickling me. I wriggle around, trying to remove his hand to stop him. I'm laughing so loud, and his face wears the happiest grin. "You're very ticklish."

He stops, and I take short, sharp breaths, trying to recover before I ease back down. "Yeah, and now you know my weak spots."

A deep chuckle leaves his chest. "That I do."

We fall into a comfortable silence and watch the TV show. I'm surprised when his hand tugs gently on my hair tie. When he frees my strands, I moan at his touch. He rubs his hand along my scalp with a massage, easing the stupid headache throbbing in my temples.

I struggle to keep my eyes open with how good it feels. The simple atmosphere of us being here feels natural, and it should scare me. The fact it could ruin my journey to find a stable career for myself.

But it's not.

I stand behind Alex as he opens the door to welcome Mike and Alice inside for coffee. Alex doesn't seem the least bit uneasy. I'm not uncomfortable, but this does feel a tad strange between us—almost domesticated.

"Hi, T," Alice greets me with a smug smile and a twinkle in her eye. What is that about?

I don't get any time to think about it, though, because Mike is coming over to say hi.

Once inside, I head back to the kitchen to prepare snacks and Alice is quick to add that she'll join me. Adding to my curiosity if she's doing okay.

The boys go to the living room with the baby, leaving me and Alice alone.

I'm elated to have a friend over and just not think about Alex and the whiplash I'm getting. The moments of him stroking my back or running his hands through my hair. I wonder what he would be like in the bedroom. Would he be gentle or rough? The latter causes my sex to tingle. I really don't need more sexual frustration, as I'm borderline close to crying, or worse, begging for him to touch me just once.

And that would be utterly mortifying. I have never begged for sex from a guy, but with Alex, I'm contemplating it.

Why?

What's so different about him?

All I know is he's a player, but other than his words, his actions around me have been anything but. I don't know if it's just him pushing me away, or if he really is a commitment-phobe.

I may not have my shit together, but it doesn't mean I haven't wanted the perfect husband and children. And playing fiancée in this house is all too sweet.

Maybe if we had sex, I'd get over the fantasy. And the flutters will disappear.

But what if they don't...

I shake my head. I can't think about any of this anymore. I need to remember he isn't interested in a relationship. I can just push the silly feelings aside, and they will go away as soon as this deal is done and we are back to our old lives.

I shudder.

Old life...

I don't miss that.

Maybe instead of coffee, I should have something stronger. But then bile leaves my stomach at the thought of my head in the toilet.

Yeah. No.

There will be no alcohol today.

"It's so good to see you. How's life with Ethan?" I ask Alice with a warm smile.

"Wonderful, for the most part. But I can't pretend it's always great, because when I'm awake every two hours, I wonder why I did this to myself."

She laughs, and I'm unable to hold back my own laugh at her honesty. "I guess it's better than my life. Faking a relationship to get my inheritance."

She reaches out to touch my shoulder, gently squeezing it. "Don't be like that. You've needed to find yourself."

"I know." I grimace. "Even in this gorgeous place, it doesn't change the fact I need to figure out my life. Changing the house doesn't change my situation."

It's quiet for a moment before she nods. "And how's everything going since we last spoke?" Alice asks in a low voice.

My gaze flicks to Alex and Mike, and then back to Alice. The twinkles back in her eye, and I swear I see hope. Does she hope we are more too?

A heavy sigh slips, and I lean forward on the counter, ceasing any further preparations on coffee and snacks. Alex has given me a few lessons on how to work the machine now.

"Honestly?" I whisper. A swirl of nerves rolls down my stomach at opening up about my struggles with Alex and me.

"Tell me, T," she begs. "I know you like to keep things to yourself, but it's not healthy. Is he being awful to you?"

I shake my head. "I wish." I laugh, but it's strained.

Straightening up, I return to the plate of cookies, fruit, and cakes, arranging them in a nice order.

"What is it then?"

My eyes flick over to see Mike hand baby Ethan to Alex, and I bite down on my lip. The way my ovaries are dancing at the sight has me blurting, "This strange attraction I have for him."

"Oh." Her face opens up with surprise.

I turn back to him, unable to turn away for too long. The way he's rocking and peering down at Ethan is too sweet. I can see mouth movements but can't hear them. I'm guessing it's cooing to calm Ethan. And God, this makes me want to fall into a puddle on his kitchen floor. Dammit. Why does a hot guy holding a baby make my knees go weak?

"Have you acted on it?"

Her question has me taking in his biceps, which are on show at this angle.

He's hot, and holding a baby, it's like Kryptonite.

"We've come close," I admit.

"But you don't want it?"

I bite my lip, willing my blush to stay away. But it fails, and I feel the heat hit my cheeks. I drag my gaze to the food, picking up a cookie and taking a bite. "Just the opposite."

"Oh, T, don't be embarrassed."

"Why not? I've made it obvious on more than one occasion, and both times, he has turned me away."

Her head turns, and I follow her gaze, looking at Alex and Mike sitting on the sofa. Ethan is quiet and content, not making a sound. He's like a baby whisperer on top of a doctor. Maybe he should have worked with children instead. He seems to be good at it. But he also seems to be good at everything.

"I see something in him. He's a really good guy. From the moment I met him, I thought he was special, and hey, he agreed to be your fake husband. Let's remember that he did that for you."

I let her words sink in. But they make me a little irritated. Not at him, but at me. Why does he have to be so kind to pretend when there's nothing in it for him? I was sure he did it for me, but avoiding any advances and turning me down doesn't ease the turmoil running through me. "Then why avoid kissing me or taking things further?" I ask the burning question. I know she doesn't have the answer—only he does. But I want to hear her answer. I need to hear other people's thoughts and opinions, other than my own conclusions.

"Maybe because he doesn't want to ruin what you two have."

I've thought that too.

"Maybe," I say, but not really believing her.

"You could ask him."

"That's a bit awkward. Can you imagine me saying, 'Hey, Alex, how come you turn me down?'" I wince at how bad that sounds.

No chance.

I can't ask him.

I'm hanging on to whatever dignity I can.

She smiles kindly at me. "It's not mortifying, just ask him. You might be surprised by the answer."

I doubt it.

"I think I'm not his type, because he likes casual hook-ups."

"I think you need to talk to him."

"Maybe..." I ponder as I watch Alex lay a soft kiss on Ethan's head.

I worry the crack in my chest knows the real answer. Will I be able to do casual?

CHAPTER 23

TAHLIA

MIKE AND ALICE HAVE gone home, leaving us alone again. When I decided to work out, it didn't occur to me that he would join.

Now I'm in my room, overthinking about what outfit I'm going to wear. Down to the color and fabric of my panties. I must be going insane to be caught up on which active crop top will show off my curves the best. Blowing out a breath, I sift through the items one by one. Making a pros and cons list.

I've officially lost it.

I try to tell myself to not think about the panties, because he won't see them anyway. Therefore, I choose my favorite baby blue activewear set and basic cotton panties.

Dressing for me, not for Alex.

That's what I tell myself anyway.

I can't help the way my heart thumps at how nervous I am. I'm not great at exercising to begin with, so this session will be interesting.

Entering the home gym, I look around. My shoulders drop with relief, as I've beaten him here. Intimidated by all the unfamiliar equipment, I move to the treadmill. I warm up and peer around at his equipment, wondering what exercises I can do.

When I catch his bright eyes in the mirror, my breath hitches, and I stumble on the treadmill. I wince. How do I stumble walking?

Why is this happening to me?

His mouth twists into a smug grin.

"Are you laughing at me?"

"No, honey, I'd never."

The endearment washes over me like a cozy blanket. Makes me feel warm and fuzzy. I hold on to the sides of the treadmill and watch as he steps forward in his gray Nike outfit. The shirt he wears shows off his toned arms and broad shoulders, while his shorts give me a glimpse of his muscled legs. He heads straight over to the weights and curiosity gets the better of me.

"Why don't you warm up?" I call out.

He shrugs as he picks up weights. "I don't like cardio."

I frown. "But why do you have all the cardio pieces here?"

"For guests."

Like me.

I swallow the lump sitting in my throat, not understanding my body's reaction to his statement. It's not like I didn't know what this was. So why does the thought unease me?

I guess when it's said out loud, it hits me harder. I need to sweat out some of my sexual frustration.

I continue to walk slowly on the treadmill and openly watch him. He begins grunting, and I catch my shoe on the walking pad again, luckily saving myself this time. I'm curiously following his movements as he picks up a heavier pair of dumbbells and sits on a bench. Sitting up, he pushes the weights above his shoulders. With every flex of his muscles, my heart hammers inside my chest.

Looking at myself in the mirror, my cheeks are flushed, and I think it has more to do with him than from me working out, but I don't want to faint right now, so I stop the walk. Getting off, I move to stand in front of the weight rack. Feeling like I'm being watched, I look up to find his eyes on me. He's raising the weights to the sides of his body.

I look back down at the neatly racked weights. Picking up a pair, I lift them, but then realize they are too heavy and put them back.

"Do you want a hand?" he asks in an amused tone.

I giggle. "I clearly need it. I'm that obvious, aren't I?"

His sharp eyes drop over my outfit. "Not at all."

"Can you show me some basic exercises?" I ask, figuring if he's going to watch me, he may as well help.

He drops his weights to the floor and grabs a small pair of dumbbells.

I raise a brow. "Are you joking? These seem too light."

"Correct form is better than lifting heavy for ego."

My words are lost when I follow a bead of sweat that trickles down from his dark hair over his temple onto his perspiring chest. Being this close means I can smell his masculine soap mixed with sweat, and the way he looks is just making my flushed cheeks warmer.

I blink rapidly and try to refocus on what he's saying instead of what he looks like.

"Okay. What's the first exercise?"

"You can do the same exercises as me."

"You mean train together?" I clarify.

He shrugs. "Something like that."

"That could be dangerous," I mumble under my breath. It will be hard enough to get through tonight. Now to work out closely with him, this could really test my restraint.

He moves to stand behind me, watching me as I mimic what he did earlier. I stare at myself in the mirror, studying my form. I'm not great, but I'm not exactly bad either. With more of his help, I think I can improve.

After I finish those exercises, I move to the side raises before he shows me two more exercises to finish.

"That's it for tonight," he says, packing away the weights.

I help him, putting away my own weights. "That wasn't so bad." Even though I'm still catching my breath, it was surprisingly fun, and I feel better.

"Want to have a protein shake with me?"

I scrunch up my nose, totally confused. "Share a shake?"

He chuckles and pokes my ribs. "I mean, we both make our own."

I fold forward, laughing at the tickle. "Yes. I'll try one."

"You've never had that either?"

"Nope." I smile shyly.

"I'm teaching you so many things."

Things he has no idea about.

Approaching the kitchen, he gestures for me to sit. I shake my head. "Can you teach me?"

His eyes meet mine. "Of course. Come."

We stand side by side, and we add the ingredients in before using the Bullet to mix it.

Tasting the chocolate drink, I can't help but moan. "Yum."

"Good, right?"

I lower the cup and face him, noticing his blue eyes are now a shade darker. "This is really good."

His hand reaches out and his thumb dusts beside my mouth, grazing my bottom lip. I freeze from the warm touch.

He clears his throat to explain. "You had some on your face." Removing his hand, he picks up his cup and drinks.

"Oh. Right. Okay. Thanks."

I roll my lips and pick up my own drink. Neither of us say another word.

Later that night, I'm lying in bed, wearing my nightie. My back is to the door. I hear my door open and the bed dips beside me. A tingle runs over my body at him coming into my room like this. I don't want to turn over because of the nerves freezing me.

One of his arms comes around my middle. He's holding me. I don't know what to think about this.

"What are you doing?" I whisper.

"Truthfully. I don't know. But I couldn't stop myself."

With his honesty, I can't help but blurt out, "I want you."

He exhales deeply, and I expect him to pull away. So I'm surprised when he pulls me closer and his hand moves to touch the outside of my leg. His hot fingers skim my thigh, causing goosebumps to pop along my flesh. My body is coming alive from a single touch. On the next stroke, he moves to the inner thigh, almost touching my core. His fingers run along the edge of my panties, and I shiver with need.

"Fuck. You feel so good," he growls into the back of my neck, where his hot breath tickles my ear. His hand still caresses my inner thigh in a tease that makes me wriggle with a crazy need. I expect him to glide his hand inside to find me hot, achy, and ready. But he only runs along the edge, slipping in the smallest amount and bringing me to the edge of desperation.

I suck in a sharp breath and reach around to touch him. I want to encourage him by making him join me on the edge of desperation. My hand meets his hot skin, and he lets out a feral hiss. I'm thinking he's giving me the green light.

He sighs and grabs my hand, bringing it in front of me as he squeezes my middle, then mutters against my neck. "I'm sorry. I want you. I really do. But we can't."

The nearness of his face annoys me. "We can. You're choosing to say no." I turn angrily to face him.

"Fuck." He wipes his face with his hand roughly. "It's not that. I just. Fuck, I can't."

"Why?" I ask.

"Because there's something wrong with me. Can we just drop it?"

He leaves me gasping for air and wondering why. I'm still clueless what's wrong with him. I should tell him to get the hell out of my room, but the words won't leave my throat.

He kisses the back of my head before reaching out to touch my hair as he whispers, "I want you. But you're too fucking good for me."

Of course, with him here caressing my hair in soft, soothing strokes, I reluctantly find myself relaxing into him. His hand then wraps around my waist and holds me tight. I squeeze my eyes shut. I want to argue. But the words won't come out. Knowing I can't change his mind, I soak in this moment of comfort he gives because, truthfully, I want this. I want whatever this growing thing between us is.

He nuzzles his nose into my hair, and our bodies press together so tightly we're almost fused together. And I know in this moment, I'll sleep better with him here.

CHAPTER 24

TAHLIA

"I CAN'T WAIT." MOM turns in her seat to give me a side glance and a full smile.

We have both finished work. Today I learned all about spec sheets. How to fill the technical document in and how to measure each product with its functions and specific features. It's been my favorite thing to learn so far.

Now I'm in the car with her and the wedding planner, on our way to the florist. When she told me this morning, it wasn't like I could turn her down. I'm getting married in two weeks, so things like this need to be chosen and booked. I'm grateful she didn't insist Alex come. Right now, I need some space. He's consuming my every thought. I've never been this worked up over hooking up with a guy.

"Me too," I muse, but my voice lacks conviction, because in the next couple of days, I'm due to try dresses on. The thought makes my stomach flip with nerves.

I've never tried a wedding dress on. Heck, I haven't even looked at one in person. But lately, I've scrolled online and envisioned the style of dress I'd like. Never in my wildest dreams would I have believed it would be happening so soon. But here we are, having a wedding, all for me to have a career.

"What colors do you like?"

Staring outside the car window, I look at the trees and flowers as we pass. I let myself answer freely. "Elegant and classic."

"White roses, peonies, and hydrangeas?" the wedding planner asks, her notepad opened waiting for my answer.

I smile, seeing them as my bouquet. "Yes."

She hums her approval. "For all the flowers, including the ones on the tables and along the roof?"

I jerk. My head turns to face the planner. "The roof?"

"When your mom and I went to the Greek restaurant you requested the reception to be at, we wanted to make it more elegant. Here, look at these photos." The planner hands over her phone. "Scroll them."

Holding her phone, I stare down at the most breathtaking arrangement of flowers dripping from the roof. My hand comes to touch my lips. It almost feels like such a waste for a fake marriage.

"What do you think?" Mom asks.

"It's beautiful," I breathe.

"Which one, in particular, do you like?" the planner asks.

I hand back her phone and say, "The white one, where the candles run along the table. It's so..."

"Romantic."

"Yes," I say quietly. Romantic for two people who aren't in a romantic relationship. It's comical, only it's not. But if I can get my dream wedding, even if it's fake, I'm going to do it right. Get what I like, because God knows when I'll actually get married for real.

I swallow the bile rising from the lies I've had to tell my parents to get here. It's so against anything I'd ever do, but it's a necessary evil. Working at the company I can soon run gives me a thrill I haven't felt before. I just need to keep that in the forefront of my mind.

Not Alex...

Ten minutes later, we're at the florist. Thankfully, we don't have to spend too much time in here, because I've already made a couple of decisions. We also asked for some flowers to be on the cake to tie it all together.

Afterward, Mom drops me off at my car that's still parked at work. Sitting in the car, I can't bring myself to drive to Alex's house. Alex is on a afternoon shift today, which means I'll be going home alone. Which gives me an idea. A sexy and out-of-character idea...

Grabbing my phone with a new determination. Maddison answers on the second ring.

"Hi, where are you?" I rush out.

"At home, why?" Maddison answers curiously.

"I'm picking you up. I'm doing something embarrassing, and I can't do it alone. I need moral support."

She laughs. "What is it?"

Laying my head back on the headrest, I swallow past the shame. "We're going to buy me a vibrator or dildo. I don't know which one, just something to take the edge off."

The line is dead silent for a moment before she breathes. "You're serious?"

I sit up with a half-smile, knowing this wouldn't be something she expected from me. "Very," I say. "See you soon. Be ready."

I hang up and drive to the house I lived in with Maddison before I asked Alex to help me. Walking up the stairs and into the house now feels odd, and I don't miss it as much as I should. Living with Alex has become easy. But in five months, my life will return to the way it was. And I'll have to forget about our morning coffees together, his crooked smiles, our chats on the sofa, and, recently, him lying next to me in bed. I think this fake marriage has shifted my feelings for Alex. And it's dangerous. Liking a known bachelor is only going to end in heartbreak, but for some silly reason, I can't tell my heart to stop.

Hopefully, releasing some of this pent-up frustration will help re-center my thoughts.

"How's living with Doctor dreamboat?" is the first thing Maddison says on our way to the store.

I giggle, which then turns into a snort. "What made you think of that name?"

"You don't hate it...hmmm...interesting."

I try to bite my lips to prevent a smile, but I can't help it and a small smile breaks through. "It's cute and funny." And totally suits him.

"Are you actually falling for your fake fiancé?"

"No!" I scoff.

But I sound unconvincing, even to my own ears.

Maddison gives me the biggest side-eye.

"I'm not! I just think he's hot, and I'm..." I sigh, not wanting to say the word out loud.

"Horny," she guesses.

"Yeah, that," I mumble, embarrassed.

She laughs. "You can't even say the word. And yet we're about to walk into a sex shop. This will be interesting."

"Maddy, this is embarrassing," I whisper-shout, palming my head.

"Well, we could go to Luxe and find a real guy," she suggests, as if it's just that easy.

I purse my lips. The thought of another guy's hands on me feels completely wrong. "It's not allowed. It's part of our contract," I say.

She snorts. "Fuck, that's such a shit deal. Well, here's to finding the best dildo the shop can offer."

I scrunch my face up, hating the idea. I hope I don't end up regretting this. "This feels strange. I don't know if I want a dildo."

"Why? I have a couple, and they're great. If you can't bring yourself to pleasure, how can you expect someone else to make you orgasm?"

My mind thinks of Alex. If Alex were to touch me, I'd melt into a puddle. He doesn't seem to me like he would have any problems knowing how to please a woman. He's good with his hands at work. And when he's allowed himself to touch me, they've been perfect. Yeah...there's no chance I'd be teaching him how to pleasure me.

He would own me.

With one single caress.

And I'd fucking let him.

Bruised ego be damned.

Hence why I'm here in a sex store, staring at a range of different shapes and sizes of dildos and vibrators. Never in my wildest dreams would I have thought this would be a hard choice. The wedding flowers were easier than this.

I touch a hot pink one Maddison suggested. The ridges on the dildo are so lifelike, but the size of some of these…surely, these aren't lifelike. Having enough of touching the silicone, I remove my hand. Next minute, it's like dominos and one dildo hits the one beside it and they all go tumbling down. To the floor. My heart drops along with them. Dildos scattering the floor like confetti.

I squat and try to pick them up quickly, putting them back upright on the shelf before the worker comes over and sees the mess.

Maddison bursts out laughing. "I thought you meant one. Not the whole shop," she says between laughing at me.

"Please, help me," I beg.

My face is hot, and I bet my cheeks are the color of beetroot. I've never been this mortified in my life.

She starts to pick them up as the store worker comes over. A woman around my mother's age, with brown hair highlighted by her grays, wearing the kindest smile. "Oh no. Are you two okay?"

"Yeah, my friend here just seems a bit touchy," Madison says, erupting in a new fit of laughter.

The worker helps me pick them up, and when she stands, she pushes her glasses back up on her nose.

"I'm really sorry. It was an accident. I'm nervous. This is my first time in a shop like this." My words hang in the air awkwardly. I'm ready to run right out of here, but this lady's face lights up.

"Oh, don't be embarrassed, love. I meet so many people who've never stepped foot in a sex shop before. So, were you looking for a dildo?" she says, casually waving her hand toward the stand.

I swallow the shame and confess to her with a new blush forming. "Looking at them all now, I think it's a little intimidating. Is there something lighter to start off with?" I can't believe those words left my mouth.

The shop assistant beams. "Personally, if you're just starting out, a clit stimulator is a good one. I could show you what's popular for first timers."

"May as well, we're here now," Maddison interrupts, a hint of humor still laced in her voice.

My eyes flick to Maddy in a *please shut up* look. I love her, but right now, I need her quiet until we're out of here. I might need a glass of wine after this.

The woman's eyes flicker to Maddison's, and then back to mine. She waits for my direction.

I nod. "Sure, why not."

The woman wanders off and returns with two boxes.

"These are the two popular ones. Did you want to hold it? See how it feels and how big they are?"

I think I've touched enough for one day. I need to get out of here now. "No, it's fine. I'll grab them both, thanks," I say with a plastered-on smile.

Maddison snorts behind me. My word choices in the store are terrible, but I'm not thinking clearly right now. My mind is a jumbled mess. I just need to drop her home and never venture to a store like that again. Online only from now on.

CHAPTER 25

ALEX

"ARE YOU ON-CALL TONIGHT?" I ask Doctor Damien Gray. We stand side by side, washing our hands at the sink after working on a surgery together. The twenty-five-year-old, with a tumor in the right frontal lobe of her brain we just worked on removing, is being transferred to recovery.

"No, that's all for today. I need to get home to Samuel," he grumbles.

"Is your mom looking after him?" I ask, drying my hands and facing him.

"Yeah. You on call?"

I shake my head, but my mouth quirks at the corner. "No."

His brows draw together. "What are you smiling about?"

We walk toward the locker room to get dressed out of our navy scrubs into our clothes to head home.

Inside the empty lockers, I feel the need to explain. "I have someone at home...it's odd, you know, going home to someone."

I know I'm a selfish prick for holding her all night, but I can't help it. One moment, I was in my room, and the next, I was slipping into her bed, pulling her body close to mine. The caressing of her thigh, and then her sweet spot between her legs, was just an error in judgment. And I should regret everything I did. *Should*, but of course, I don't. How could I regret something that felt so right? I've never felt anything better in my life. In my arms, her soft, smooth, and perfect body snuggled into me was heaven.

"Couldn't think of anything worse," he mumbles as he throws his scrub top into the wash bin, breaking me from my thoughts.

I nod, understanding his reservations with women. His wife left him and his son for no clear reason. Now he's raising Samuel on his own.

"Yeah, I know. After what you've been through, I'd be the same."

We finish dressing in silence, and then I say goodbye. I take the elevator down and pull out my phone to write a text to tell Tahlia to let her know I'm on my way home. But my phone rings in my hand. My mother's name flashes across the screen.

I smile and answer. "Mom?"

"Am I interrupting?"

I exit the elevator and walk to my car. "No. I'm leaving the hospital."

"Finishing a shift?" she asks.

"Yeah, I just finished surgery," I say, driving out of the car lot.

"Are you bringing Tahlia to dinner this weekend?"

Shit. I totally forgot it was Sunday night dinner. We catch up once a month on a Sunday as a family.

"Yeah, I might be a little rough. Mike's throwing me a bachelor party the night before."

"I heard. I can't believe you're getting married." She sounds a little hesitant. I knew she'd be hard to convince this is a real marriage. Can't blame her when I've never brought a woman home before. Unless you count high school relationships that lasted for five months.

Yet Tahlia is meeting my family. I don't even know how to feel about it. My family is the best. I can't complain; everyone will be warm and welcoming. They'll love Tahlia. Fuck, anyone that meets her melts for her sweet and humble nature. And I guess my fear underneath the excitement that I'm bringing her to dinner is that they'll be so happy and get attached. And when our marriage ends, and we separate, I'll disappoint my family. And not to sound cocky, but I've never disappointed them. That sends a heavy feeling in the pit of my stomach.

This was supposed to be an easy fake relationship, but coming to my family Sunday dinner is more serious than I thought. I don't regret it. I know I agreed to this. I suggested the engagement and living together. Seeing and helping Tahlia with Emerald Designs confirms this was the right thing to do. She deserves the direction in life she's craving. This is her fresh start, and it's not my story to share, so I won't be telling my mom the truth.

"Neither can I. Are you proud, Mom? Your bachelor son is finally settling down?" I smile as I say it.

"Love, I'm proud of you. You haven't settled for any woman. You were waiting for the right one."

Gripping the steering wheel tighter with white knuckle force, heavy guilt twists in my gut. She really thinks I've fallen in love. If only she knew her son doesn't have a heart. He can't fall in love. He's fucking broken.

"Yeah. No settling here," I say, pulling up into my driveway, knowing Tahlia's behind my door...waiting.

If only I wasn't so fucked up in the head, I could be with her. Give in to her not-so-subtle hints for sex. I don't know exactly what we're doing; it's not like we're sticking to the friend zone, and yet I can't love her, so where does that leave us? I know I care a lot about her. More than I have about a woman before. I want to protect her and make her happy, but then what does it make us if we're not a real couple and not friends either? I rub my face with my hands. Utterly at a loss.

I put my car in park and push my head back on the headrest, closing my eyes briefly.

"You're at home," Mom says.

"Yeah, I just pulled in," I say and sit up, unbuckling my seatbelt.

"Well, I was just calling to check if she was coming for dinner on Sunday. I'm sure you're tired and just want to get inside to your fiancée." Her voice is lighter now.

Fiancée...

Want to get inside to your fiancée...

I'm waiting for the word to make my stomach roll. But I don't feel that at all. If anything, I'm thrilled to get inside to talk to her about her day. What did she do? What did she learn? What can I help her research tonight?

I've never given a shit about any of that with anyone else.

But with her, I want to hear about the most mundane details.

Things are definitely becoming way more complicated and less simple.

"All right, Mom. Love you."

I hang up on the only woman I've loved. Pushing open the car door, I trail the steps up to my house. I'm grinning as I go inside, ready to see the stunning blonde with the most magnificent green eyes curled up on the sofa, watching trash TV. And I'm going to shower and join her. I don't care what I'm watching, I just want to sit and unwind by listening to her speak about her day.

Except when I walk through my house, she isn't doing that.

The house is quiet, and if it wasn't for her car parked outside, I'd think she was out. Unless a friend came to pick her up?

I pull out my phone, but there's no message from her. My shoulders drop, and I dump my keys on the counter and stroll to the stairs. It's not like she owes me an explanation if she goes out, but I just can't shake the disappointment. In the back of my mind, reality is trying to remind me that this fake marriage will be over before I know it, and I will be back to coming home to no one. And I can't help the way my stomach drops from the knowledge.

A noise comes from upstairs...or should I say, a moan?

I walk upstairs and stride straight to her door when another raspy moan leaves her room. My dick twitches.

She's pleasuring herself.

It's only fair I take a peek after what she did to me, and I know how hot it was when she watched me. Walking the steps to her doorway, I'm hit with her sweet chocolate and strawberry scent. It's so strong and sexy. My mouth waters from the sight in front of me. Her laid out on her bed, her white bed sheets bunched down to the bottom, propped up on pillows, where her blonde hair drapes messily. But the knee-weakening vision is her legs bent, wide open, allowing me to see her pussy. She has a pink toy in her hand and she's rubbing it in lazy circles. The room is dark except for the lamp on her bedside table.

"Alex," she says, her voice strangled.

I step closer. Her chest is heaving from her quick breaths. I curl my fingers as I lower my gaze down to the peaks of her nipples. It makes me thirsty to see how rosy they are and beg for a taste. My legs move on their own accord as I step farther into her room. Crossing the boundaries I put on myself.

She's staring at me with a longing that is making it hard to resist.

"Tahlia…" I say on a ragged breath.

She moans and tips her head back, her eyes rolling as pleasure overtakes her. I'm so hard right now. She's more turned on now that I'm watching. I swallow the lust that's rising and step closer again.

Her hand comes out and wraps around mine. My gaze peers down at it. "Please," she begs, tugging my hand to her. It's almost like she's desperate for me.

"What's wrong with me?" Her eyes flutter open, and they are so bright and beautiful, but the pain of rejection sits heavily in them.

I fucking did that.

I put that pain there.

And I don't want her to feel rejected, because I want her. Fuck, I've wanted her so much, but I'm trying to protect her.

I'm breathing hard and fast now, struggling to get oxygen to my brain to think. But I'm so tired of thinking. I've never felt this way about a woman or sex. I've never wanted it or thought about it as much as I have with her.

"Absolutely nothing. You're perfect."

Her bright green eyes bore into mine. Moving closer to the edge of the bed, I sit on the bed beside her. My hand skims her jaw to tilt her head back, exposing her delicate neck and her heart beating rapidly. I trace my finger along it, admiring her full lips parted, before gripping her head and crashing my lips to hers. She kisses me back ferociously and my tongue skims her lower lip before tangling with hers. Reveling in her taste.

Our lips and tongues move in hard movements. It's desperate without being frantic. The sound of the vibrator hums in the background, and the buzz can be felt on my lips. Moving my lips away from hers, she lets out a whine. I smirk and move my lips to her neck, laying a kiss there and breathing into her ear.

"Can I touch you?" I ask.

"Yes," she says with need.

I have to take a deep, centering breath to take this slow and enjoy every piece of her. Keeping my eyes on my hand, I lay my finger on her lips and bring it over her jaw, down her neck, over to her right nipple. Grazing my finger over the stiff buds, her breath catches, and I flick my gaze to hers to find her watching me. I pinch the nipple lightly, and she arches into my hand. I do it again, but harder, and she moans and arches again. Leaning down, I capture a nipple in my mouth and suck, flicking my tongue over it again and again. Popping off, I bring my mouth to her lips. Her eyes open slowly, revealing heavy lust. I lay a kiss on her lips.

"Do you know how many times I've thought about you?"

"No." Her voice wobbles.

"A fucking lot, Tahlia. But nothing can compare seeing it in real life. No fantasy in my head could prepare me for the way you look. Look at my hand. See how your flushed skin looks with me touching you. You're so beautiful."

My hand skims her stomach, admiring the touch of her silky soft skin, and when I reach the top of her mound, I pause at where her hand has the toy. Her heavy breaths sound in my ear, increasing with despair. She rocks her hips as if she wants my fingers on her clit, and straight into her pussy, so when I move them, her thighs try to close.

"Keep them open," I say, pushing her thigh open, and then taking the stimulator from her hand. Her hand grips the bedsheets as I lower the toy to her swollen clit. Peering briefly up at her face, I find her eyes are heavy lidded and trying to close.

"Watch me touch you," I say gruffly, putting the toy aside. The blood rushes to my cock as soon as my fingers touch her wet pussy. Rubbing her clit in lazy but hard circles, then down to the opening and back up. Her back arches with every stroke, legs shaking, and I love how wet she is. What a sight to come home to.

I slip two fingers in slowly, and the sound of my name erupting from her lips is extraordinary. I move my fingers in and out and she trembles with the need to come. She drops the vibrator from her clit.

"Does this feel good?" I ask, as her hips rock, trying to chase an orgasm.

"Yes," she chokes out. Her hands reach out to clutch my neck and shoulders.

She rides my hand faster, and I pump harder, matching her rides with a pump.

"Good. Because feeling how wet you are and how tight you are is making me fucking crazy."

A deep grumble leaves my chest when one of her hands trails down my neck, digging in, and I'm sure she's leaving marks. It's sexy, knowing I'll walk around with evidence my fiancée is pleasured by me. Thinking of pleasure, my eyes drop to the pink toy beside her, and I can't help but ask, "What other toys do you have?"

"A dildo," she says quietly. "But they are new. I, ugh, just brought them today."

I smirk, loving the fact she's shy about buying toys. It's adorable, but to me, the fact she's purchasing toys is hot. Even though she wouldn't need a dildo with me. I'll happily fuck her anytime she needs, now that I've crossed the line. It would be a fucking honor.

My hand drifts to her thigh as it quivers, and her mouth falls open on a silent pant. As if hating the loss of my fingers inside her and chasing them again.

"What were you thinking about before I walked in?"

"You," she whispers back.

My mouth tips up even more, and I slip my fingers back inside her pussy. Her walls clench down hard on them, and her breaths become whimpers. I return to the slow movements, and she lets out a long, guttural sound. My gaze locks onto the pleasure exploding across her face. I don't stop my fingers from moving along her walls, hitting her G-spot. Her hips ride my hand, and it isn't long before her orgasm slams into her.

It's fucking hot to watch.

She's incredible.

"That was amazing," I say, slipping my fingers gently out, and her whole body shudders.

Her face tilts to the side, and I love the flush on her face. Bringing my lips to hers, I can't help but swipe my tongue along the seam of her lips, and then kiss her passionately with everything I have left.

CHAPTER 26

TAHLIA

I GUESS WE'RE EVEN now. I found him pleasuring himself, and now he's come home to find me doing it too.

The way he's looking at me, it's like I flipped a switch in him. Turning his brain off and finally allowing himself to give in.

Maybe the purchases today were worth the disaster to get them.

His lips control the deep kiss we've found ourselves in. With a moan, my hands jerk him onto the bed, and his body moves to hover over mine. Closing me in and trapping me under him, he's consuming me, but I'm not scared. No, I'm elated. Soaking in every sight, taste, and smell.

"What are you thinking about?" he whispers over my lips, his warm breath tickling my open mouth.

"Is this real?" I ask.

His boyish grin comes out, and I melt back farther into the bed. "I can't believe it either. I wasn't meant to touch you."

"Ouch." I wince.

He drops his chin so I can't see his eyes and shakes his head. "Sorry, I didn't mean it to come out like that."

Butterflies hit my stomach at the sincerity of his words. He tips his head up, his eyes stare down at me. Taking me in. It's as if he can't believe this feels just as good for him as it does for me.

His face tightens and nerves hit me. Biting my lip between my teeth, I wonder what he's thinking, but I'm giving him the time he needs to speak. The crossing of his own boundaries is clearly weighing heavily on him. His fingers touch my face in soft, slow strokes before he cups the side of my face. "I'm just messed up, and I didn't want you tangled up in it."

A frown creases deep between my brows. "What do you mean?"

He rolls to the side and onto his back. Tucking one arm behind his head, the other pats his chest with a small half smile.

I rise and rest my head on his hard chest, facing him. Enjoying the beat of his heart under my ear, I stay silent, waiting for him to speak. His hand goes to my forehead and then runs through my hair. My eyes flutter from the gentle touch.

"Tell me," I plead softly, trying not to scare him away. I only want him to open up to me. So I can understand him.

His lip quirks, but then he sucks in a deep breath, pushing it out on a heavy exhale. "Whenever I've slept with a woman, I've never felt anything."

I don't understand, but instead of interrupting, I give him the chance to talk. He's watching his hand move through my hair with fascination.

"Afterward, when they leave, my body doesn't react. There're no feelings and no desire for them to stay or see them again."

The pain etched in his face makes it hard for me to watch without encouraging him to continue.

"What do you feel?" I whisper.

His eyes hit mine. There's so much turmoil sitting in them. "Nothing. Kinda numb, to be honest." He looks away for a moment before holding my gaze again. "I didn't want to touch you. Hurt you. But fuck, you made it impossible."

I can't help but giggle at that, knowing what he means, because when I saw him jerking off, I had the same reaction. But we'd only just started to get to know each other. I bet if he was to do it now, I would've been on his bed.

"I know this is an arrangement, so don't feel bad. I wanted this."

I practically forced myself on him so I can't blame him for any hurt feelings. I pushed him into a corner. And he had no option but to sink or swim.

"Yeah," he challenges, and his hand pauses in my hair.

"I want more," I say, my voice dropping seductively, unintentionally.

His brows rise. "Is that so?" he asks with amusement.

I slap his solid chest playfully. "Even though I know you're a broken man," I tease, and his eyes sparkle with humor. His fingers are back combing through my hair, easy smiles on our faces.

I lick my lips. "I still want you, Alex."

Scrunching his shirt in my fingers, I push it up, lifting my head and holding his gaze. His mouth parts, watching every movement, hand slipping from my hair to my body. I want his skin on mine. I want to feel his hot body touch mine.

"I want you too."

We both know where I'm going as I slide his shirt up, enjoying the feel of his powerful body under my palms. He lifts until the shirt is off and tossed to the floor. I lean down and take his lips in a quick kiss, unable to help taking another taste of him. Especially when he looks up at me in awe. Having him look at me like I'm the sexiest woman in the world makes me wet. Plus, he's a damn good kisser. Skillful. It's not like I have much to compare with, but still.

Dropping my gaze to his pants, his dick strains against the fabric. I reach out and trace his waistband, watching his skin prickle in goosebumps. Loving how he's affected by me, just as much as I am by him.

I want his hands on me, but I also love the act he's watching me and allowing me to explore him. And I already know I want to ride him. I haven't stopped thinking about what it would be like since I saw him on his back. Tonight, I want to own his pleasure.

"I know they call you a player, but I'm not sure you really are."

He narrows his eyes at me. "What do you mean?"

"For a player, I expected you to fuck me already."

His chest rumbles with a loud laugh.

"Why are you holding back?" I ask sheepishly.

"Do you know how badly I want to throw you on this bed, spread you wide, and fuck you until you're screaming my name?" he rasps.

I can hear the struggle in his voice.

I blink rapidly. Well, okay, that's not what I was expecting him to say. My body tingles with new anticipation, and a wolfish grin takes over his face.

"You liked what I said."

My teeth sink into my bottom lip. "Very much."

My fingers drop back to his firm stomach, and I unbutton and slowly unzip him.

"So, you don't want me to be in control?" he asks as his hand comes up to skim along the side of my boob. I suck in a sharp breath at the soft touch on my sensitive skin.

"You're making me want to control now..." he taunts.

"No," I snap. Shuffling my knees over the sheets, I grab his pants and boxer briefs and pull them both down. Then he kicks them off. Both of us are now naked. Flicking my gaze up, I see his breathing has grown labored, and it spurs me on.

"You're enjoying yourself, aren't you?" he asks.

I hold his gaze as my hand touches his thigh, feeling it twitch. "So much."

He growls, and I feel it vibrate through me. Moving my hand to his big hard dick, I enjoy the hot and throbbing length in my hand. I break our eye contact to look down to where my hand has moved to the base of him. But I need...

I quickly move between his thick thighs as the words, "Fucking hell," leave his lips in a strain. "Tahlia."

But my tongue is already out, and I'm taking his dick into my mouth. Wetting him. Enjoying the taste of his pre-cum on my lips. One hand on his thigh holds me up and the other moves along his thick length. My mouth sucks the tip, and he groans.

"I can't see you," he says. His hands rake through my hair to make a ponytail, and he tugs it out of his way.

Peeking up under my lashes, I revel in the way his face is struggling to hold it back. I've only ever gone down on one guy before, and I didn't enjoy it, but here with Alex, I feel sexy and powerful, and I want to do this all the time.

"I want to be able to see you take me deep into your mouth and swallow me."

My core aches from his words, and I squeeze my thighs together to help, but it doesn't work. I try to concentrate on the feel of his smooth skin along my tongue and the swell of his dick. I suck harder and faster on his dick, squeezing the base of him. He moans, and his hand in my hair tightens in response. Pinching my scalp, it causes me to moan around him, sending a vibration through him, and a loud groan leaves his chest.

"Eyes up, T. I need to see your eyes as I come down your throat."

I open my eyes and tilt my head slightly. Our eyes lock. Staring back at me are a pair of blue eyes heavily laced with desire. I can only imagine my lust-filled ones. His hips rock, and I gag. His eyes widen, and a breath rushes out. He liked that, so I try to take more of him, and he thickens. He's close. I suck a little bit harder and squeeze my hand as he rocks his hips, meeting me with each stroke. I groan at the way he's enjoying this as much as me. He's giving me what I want.

"I'm going to come," he warns.

I mumble my approval around him.

"Fuck," he calls out as he jerks inside my mouth and cum spills down my throat.

He moans as I swallow him down. My wrists are sore, my jaw is on fire, and my core is aching, but I wouldn't change it for the world. As I slide my lips off him, his hand drops away from my hair and onto his chest. I sit back on my heels, gasping for air, looking back at him. There's a sparkle in his eyes, and if I didn't know any better, I'd think he's wondering what the fuck just happened. I've never felt that high, but I want it again already. It's addictive.

His mouth twists into a smug grin, and he crooks his finger. "Come here."

A shiver runs up my spine at his demand. I follow. He grabs my head, and I think he's going to kiss me, but he brings his lips to my ear.

"Now it's my turn."

My eyes widen. But I don't get a chance to think. He sits up and grabs me effortlessly, as if I weigh nothing, and lies me propped up on my pillows.

Leaning down, he whispers in my ear, "I'm starving," then bites my lobe.

He drops his lips to my collarbone, nipping it with his teeth, and then soothing it with a kiss. My breath catches at the sight of him moving over to one of my breasts. He blows on my sensitive nipple, and I let out a ragged breath.

I'm desperate to squeeze my legs together, but his large frame sits between them. He lays kisses over my chest, and between the gentle caresses, he nips. The push and pull of sensations is an out-of-body experience. I've never felt anything like it. Moving to one of my nipples, he sucks it hard into his mouth while his hand squeezes my other full breast. I'm close to begging him to hurry up.

Popping off my nipple, he whispers against my torso, "You're desperate, aren't you?" His voice can't hide the satisfaction.

His warm breath sends my body up in flames and goosebumps erupt.

"Yes," I whisper.

"Good, because I've also thought of how sweet you will taste. And just by the smell of you, it's going to be sweeter than fucking nectar."

His words are too much. And I'm about to tell him to shut up, but his mouth lowers down to the top of my mound. It's feather-light and teasing, but he doesn't waste time as he kisses the top of my slit. And when he sneaks his tongue out, touching my clit, my back arches into him.

He chuckles darkly above me. "So fucking ready."

His hand skims my inner thigh as he pushes my legs wider and drops his head lower. His thick tongue swipes in one long motion, and my eyes roll back into my head as I tip my head back and melt into the bed.

I moan loudly as his tongue laps over my clit before dipping down to my core.

"Look how wet you are. Is this all because of me?"

It's not like I can say no. I've been getting hornier and wetter by the second.

Dipping his tongue inside, I arch my hips into his face again. Enjoying his five o'clock shadow brushing me.

"Yes. All you. Oh, God."

"It's Alex," he mumbles over my clit before nipping my sensitive bundles of nerves.

"Smartass," I mutter between sucking in deep breaths.

My lower back heats, letting me know I'm already close. I run my hand through his hair, gripping it tightly. Rocking my hips up and down on his face, I let him feast on me. As the tension builds in my body, I close my eyes and moan.

"Don't close your eyes. Watch me eat you. Like the best meal I've had in years."

I peel my eyes open and meet his stare.

His eyes have the same longing and desire that I feel. It's scary. Onetime thing? He won't have feelings for me after tonight. But will I have feelings for him?

I already do…

Ignoring the little voice in my head that is throwing caution, I focus on the here and now. Enjoy the moment. If this is all I get, it was one hell of a fucking night. The best oral sex of my life. And hopefully sex.

I watch him from under heavy-lidded eyes. But I need more.

"What do you need?" His fingers grip my thigh as he breathes over my pussy.

"More. I bought…" I trail off.

He growls loudly. "You don't need a toy with me. I'll give you all the pleasure you need. Fuck, I want to feel you squeeze my fingers as you come all over them."

I swallow the butterflies. He's adamant he'll give me pleasure, and I'm not going to say no. I'd rather him than a toy anyway, and when he slides his fingers in, my toes curl. Yeah, that's what I needed.

His mouth goes back to my clit, and his tongue rubs in hard circles. I can feel the tension building inside me more and more.

"Alex. I'm—"

"Come."

And the orgasm hits me. He doesn't stop the torturous pace of his fingers or the sweet circles with his tongue. He continues until the waves of pleasure stop wracking my body and I become still under him.

He lifts his mouth off and removes his fingers, and I shudder from the sensation.

"You're so fucking beautiful."

"I thought you don't have feelings. This sounds like the opposite of that," I tease.

"So did I." He crawls over me, pausing to kiss my lips in a soft and surprisingly tender kiss. Not allowing me to respond. But I've been the one who's been actively pursuing him, so this was him telling me he's catching feelings too.

My chest warms as I look at his clear blue eyes.

His panty-melting smirk returns as he bucks his hips into me, and I feel his hard length. "Are you ready for the finale?"

Am I?

CHAPTER 27

ALEX

I've never wanted to be buried deep inside of a woman as much as I do right now.

I want to be surrounded by her and totally consumed until we come and pass out.

Staring into her eyes, I see nerves, shock, and excitement. And I can't help but give her a kiss. My mouth moves with hers, and her tongue skims along the seam of my lips. I tangle my tongue with hers, both of us tasting like the other and now mixing as one. This feels so surreal, and I kiss her harder. My hand is dusting her hip, and I grip it. Pulling her leg up to wrap it over my hip, she understands and follows with ease.

I run my hand up her thigh and over her ass, squeezing her full cheek in my hand. Loving how soft her skin feels, I move my hand to her pussy then give it a slap. It's gentle, and when she whimpers, I do it again, but harder. She tips her head back and moans.

Her hands grab the sheets, her pebbled nipples pointing up at the ceiling, and her mouth parted. She looks heavenly.

"Your body is incredible. So fucking perfect. I can't get enough."

I slap her pussy again, and a louder whimper leaves her mouth this time.

"You love it when I do that, don't you?"

"Yes," she moans.

Totally lost in the euphoria of pre-sex.

She's so fucking responsive to me, but my body is the same. My dick is so fucking hard, it hurts. Her face, her body, her taste, it's all fucking perfect. I can't get enough.

I reach out and graze my thumb over her puckered nipple. Her eyelids open, and she stares back at me hungrily. She fucking wants me just as much as I want her. She's never been as bold as she has tonight.

I slap her pussy one last time before I bend forward and bring my lips to her ear. Her hands snake over my arms, caressing my muscles before gripping onto my shoulders and digging her nails into my back.

"Fuck, your nails."

"Oh, I'm sorry," she mumbles, releasing her fingers.

"Don't be. I want you to mark me. It would be an honor to wear scratches from you."

"Oh…" Her voice wobbles with uncertainty.

But her nails dig in again and run down my back.

"Yeah," I murmur.

"Is this your thing?" she breathes out curiously.

"No. It's a *you* thing."

She bites her lip like she does when she's shy, and her voice is barely above a whisper. "Oh."

"What are you thinking about?" I ask.

Her gaze looks around before meeting mine. "I wanted to ride you."

I smirk, loving that confession. "Is this your thing?"

Her hands come to link behind my head, bringing my lips to hers so she can kiss them. "I don't know what my thing is. I haven't been with a guy in a long time and there wasn't much besides the basics."

Shit.

How the fuck can I say no to that? I want her to use my body to explore kinks. I'd do it proudly. Any position, in any way, I'll pleasure her repeatedly until she's seeing stars. Figuring out what she likes will be fun.

"Fuck, who are you?" I say with a crooked smile.

"Tahlia." She gives me a playful smile.

"You are, and you were made for me," I say, kissing her lips before I try to slide off the bed to grab a condom from my room.

She grabs my arm. "No. I'm on the pill. Please. I want to feel you with nothing between us."

Fuck. How can I argue with that?

I want that too.

"Are you sure?"

She nods.

I sit back and lean against the headboard. She watches me. My dick twitches in appreciation. She comes to sit on top of me, full of confidence. It's sexy as hell.

I lift my hand and drag my thumb over her bottom lip, and her tongue peeks out to graze it. I lower my hands to her waist, marveling at how incredible her hourglass shape is.

I move my hand and spank her ass. She moans, her body gliding over my erection. I grunt from the sensation, repeating the spank.

"Lift your hips."

She follows my instructions, and I grab the base of my dick, but her hands cover mine. "Let me."

I can't argue when she says it in such a husky tone. It's impossible to say no.

My hands drop to her thighs, and she lines herself up at her entrance.

"Are you ready?" I ask, because I'm so fucking ready. I'm barely holding myself back from bucking my hips to enter her already.

She nods and sinks down. The heavens have opened, and fuck, she's so tight. I have to breathe through it.

"Alex," she moans, pausing at my base to adjust to my size. Her head tips back in lust, exposing her neck to me. Her hands on my stomach steady her.

"I know, baby. I know." My hands rest at her hips, and I lower my eyes to her perfect creamy tits that are rising and falling with every breath she takes. Her rosy nipples are in tight peaks.

Her head lifts, and when her eyes meet mine, the air leaves my lungs. Her eyes glow with so much pleasure, I'm not sure how long I'll last.

She rises and sinks down again, and my gaze drops to where we join. I revel in how perfect her pussy takes me and she's watching our union with fascination too. It's hot, and I don't want this to end. I've never felt sex like this. The longing, the anticipation, the holding back, it's all lead up to this.

Now that I've had her, I don't think I'll be able to let her go. I've been attracted to Tahlia since I met her, but nothing prepared me for the way she makes me feel. I thought I was broken beyond repair, but I'm coming to realize I was just with the wrong person.

She rocks her hips, and her nails dig into my stomach, taking away my thoughts for a second. My hands glide up to her waist, and I lift her to help take her harder. Her eyes roll back into her head, and she gasps.

I thrust my hips up as she slams down on my cock. Her pussy clenches tightly around me. I grunt loudly. "Tahlia, fuck!"

Her head tips back as my cock jerks. We continue thrusting, until her legs tremble, and my name leaves her mouth in a whisper. The fact she's shattering on my cock, for me, is the best thing I've experienced in a long time. A cry leaves her mouth, and her body convulses as I keep thrusting up, trying to ride out her orgasm.

No sex will compare.

She's sexy and sedated as she comes down from her high, her body flushed with a just-fucked look. Flipping her onto her back, she squeals in surprise, and I stare down at the most beautiful woman I've ever laid eyes on. She brings me a happiness I never in a million years thought was possible. But here we are...

A sheen of perspiration makes her body glow, and I bring my lips to hers, devouring her. My hips rock into her, finding a rhythm that has her writhing under me. I want her to come again, but this time with me. Her hands grip my shoulders, and I pump my hips harder.

"Told you, you wouldn't need toys with me."

She giggles in the sweetest, breathiest way. And I slam my hips more forcefully, moving her body with each pump. I can't get enough of her. She's like a drug to me. A new addiction. I loved her body, but her heart and soul have crept beneath my skin. I've never felt like this. I'm hers.

"Definitely not."

I can't help but grin. The words every guy wants to hear, but only coming from the right person does it matter. And hearing it from her is everything. I don't even know why the thought of a damn toy being inside her over me made me see red, but it did.

"Good, because you have me now. And I plan on pleasuring my fiancée," I grunt out between thrusts.

Her legs quiver, and she arches her back as she cries out. "I'm coming!"

My orgasm hits me at full force, causing my vision to spot and her name to leave my lips on a groan.

Both of us are gasping and spent as I drop down beside her.

Once I've caught my breath, I press a kiss to her cheek and pull her body flush against mine. And then I sink my face into the crook of her neck, inhaling her scent.

Leaning to kiss the back of her head, I whisper, "Thanks for making me feel something other than numb."

I hold her tightly. I don't want to let her go from this position.

"Who knew you just needed to find the right person," she breathes, laying her arm over mine.

"My person," I say as I tug her even closer.

She tenses briefly before letting her body go lax in my arms.

Her sweet scent drugs me and helps the heaviness in my body drag me under. Not before I realize I'm at fucking peace.

I wake up deliciously hot from holding her all night. I've never thought much about sharing a bed with a woman. But she's changed that. With her body perfectly in front of mine, with my arms wrapped around her middle, I lavish in it.

I see her twirl the ring around her finger, and I can't help but grin proudly. I'm fascinated by the sparkles bouncing off it from the morning light. Going to the venue today doesn't seem so sickening at the moment. I couldn't be fucking happier.

"What are you thinking about?" I ask, watching her drop her hand back to sit on top of mine.

She sinks farther back into me. "How happy I am."

I love how easily that spilt from her lips. No need to hold back how we feel. Last night, our words were raw and honest, and it opened a new door. I'm still grappling with the idea that we're in this new happy bubble.

I growl and bury my head in her neck. Her giggle fills the room. And I love it. Her laugh is everything to me. It lightens up my house. It lightens me. Before she lived here, the only noise came from the TV. It was dull and unfulfilling. I never would have known that if she never moved in. I'd still be living the same life...but now, with her here, my life is different. Better. There is a future with possibilities I never dreamed of. Thanks to her.

"You make me happy too," I say, tugging her so she rolls flat onto her back. My morning erection hits the side of her body. For a split second, I wonder if we have time for a quick round.

"We have to meet my parents today," she says, as if reading my mind, and I give her a crooked grin.

"Yeah, we should get ready." I lean in, kissing her with a hot, demanding caress. My hands trail over her warm bare skin, and my dick twitches with excitement.

She hums in delight and disconnects our lips. "If we shower together, we could help wash each other."

I chuckle gruffly. "Is that code for sex? Because if it is, I'm down for that."

A full smile opens on her face and a flush coats her neck and cheeks. I get out of bed, and scoop her up effortlessly, she gasps.

"Put me down," she says with a wiggle, but there's no fight.

She's secretly enjoying this. And so am I.

"No. I'm practicing for our wedding night," I say, looking at her with a newfound intensity, reminding me that our wedding night is right around the corner.

"Well, I'm not here to stop you," she says as I carry her into the bathroom.

Lowering her in front of the shower, I open the door and turn the water on. Then move to set up our towels for when we step out. Her eyes glow as she watches me.

The room fills with steam. Her body is begging to be touched by me.

She steps in behind me, and I waste no time yanking her to me and locking lips with her. Pushing her back against the tiles, we disappear into the steam of lust.

"If we seat your family at this table and us at this one, would that be okay?" Sonya's eyes flick between mine and Tahlia's.

We're at the restaurant we're getting married in next Friday, looking down at the tables set up as a mock-up, so we can get the seating arrangements and menu decided.

I have my fingers linked tightly with Tahlia's, and it feels natural. To hold her hand and be out as a couple after last night is surprisingly easy.

"Please, take a seat," Gary suggests. He has staff beside him, holding plates of food. We all take a seat, and as the staff lower the plates onto the table, I don't miss the way the young server eyes Tahlia. His eyes drop over her face and then down the low-cut top and to her ample cleavage. My teeth clench. I know what he's thinking, and I don't like it one fucking bit. I'm close to telling him to keep his eyes where they should be and not on Tahlia or her goddamn body. The possessiveness pumping through my veins is foreign, and I'm worried about how fucked I am when it comes to her.

I've never thought of anyone as mine. But with her, I do.

She's fucking mine.

I'm tense until he leaves the room. I'll have to talk with Gary about his staff and let him know that guy will not be here on my wedding day.

No fucking chance.

"Are we going to fight over what we eat, or are we going to compromise?" I smile down at Tahlia before kissing her cheek.

She giggles at my pepper of kisses up her neck. "Depends if you like what I like."

"Oh, I think I like what you do," I whisper into her skin before pulling back and giving her a wink.

"Well, then we won't fight."

I shake my head with a smile and take a bite of my Baklava.

"Honey, try this," I say, holding the spoon up to her mouth. She opens her mouth wide and wraps her luscious lips around the metal. It immediately reminds me of how well she took my dick last night.

Fuck. This isn't the time to be thinking of that. I don't want to be getting an erection around her parents.

"What are the plans for your bachelor party?" her mom asks.

Internally, I groan. I don't want to go, but I know if I don't, it'll be suspicious. I asked for something low-key, but I'm not the one who organized it. Mike, being loved up and married with baby Ethan, should give me something quiet. Like dinner and drinks.

"I don't know. Mike said it's a surprise." I look over to Tahlia's dad, who's nodding between bites of food.

"What are you girls doing?" I ask, peering over to Tahlia, and then her mom, for answers.

"Alice is still breastfeeding and sleep deprived, so I said we'll have it at my house."

My back stiffens. She registers what she said and quickly corrects herself.

"At Madison's, where I used to live." She laughs, but I don't.

She has a new home, and it's with me.

Her mom picks up her wineglass, taking a sip before lowering it to the table. "Yeah, just dinner, some games, drinking, and that's it. Tahlia isn't into clubs and drinking heavily."

This intrigues me, and if my memory serves me correctly, there's been numerous times I've seen her at Luxe with Blake and Maddison. Dancing, drinking, and having fun. I think the person who doesn't like drinking and dancing and going out is her mom. Because the woman she's describing isn't Tahlia.

Touching Tahlia's leg, I squeeze it. I told her to not wear panties under her dress today, and I'm barely keeping my thoughts in check as I touch her.

"No, she's such a respectable woman."

CHAPTER 28

TAHLIA

I FEEL NERVOUS WALKING into the wedding dress store. My wedding with Alex is feeling real. I should hate the fact I'm making Alex marry me—but I don't. In fact, I'm beginning to really fall for him. Every day, I'm going to work, a job that I don't hate, and then coming home to him, and it's changing my life. A life that was so unfulfilling is now filling with a newfound happiness. And I have him and Emerald Designs to thank.

The nervous energy I'm feeling in the shop is about me unable to find a dress he'll like. I want to see his face transform when I walk toward him.

"This brings back so many memories," Alice coos as she touches the fabrics of different wedding dresses.

My heart is in my throat, and I feel too scared to touch them. My mind is spinning in panic. I haven't seen or spoken to any of my friends since I slept with Alex.

I told them to meet me earlier than my mom. I need to get it off my chest. They already know the wedding isn't real, but are happy to participate, but now things aren't so fake. Well, my feelings definitely aren't.

The vulnerability of his confession last night and his soft touches make me admire the man who most people wouldn't know. And I see why Alice always wanted me and Alex together. But it wasn't the right time. Until now...

"Can I tell you guys something before my mom gets here?" I walk toward the center sofa and away from the dresses.

Maybe that's why I can't touch them. Too much turmoil running through me to enjoy the process.

"What's up?" Maddison asks, taking a seat beside me.

"Tell us what's going on," Alice says.

"You fucked him, didn't you?" Blake blurts.

My eyes go wide, but my mouth parts on a laugh. I have missed my friends.

"You so did," Maddison adds.

My eyes look at Alice, who has a funny expression taking over her face. "What?" I ask.

Even though I know it's the *I told you so* face.

"Nothing. I'm waiting to hear what you've got to say," she argues innocently.

"We all are!" Maddison says loudly.

"Shhh! Calm down. For fuck's sake, let her speak." Blake spits.

"So, Maddy, you know how we went to the shop the other day?" I whisper. "A sex shop."

"No," Blake gasps, his hand covering his shocked mouth.

"She did," Maddison says, with a look of pride.

"*We* did," I correct her. But they don't bat an eyelid at me telling them she came. They'd expect that from her.

"Anyway, I bought some stuff. I'm not explaining that in detail, so don't even ask. He came home, and yeah, let's say, we crossed the friendship line." Suddenly, I'm embarrassed about what they're imagining now. This conversation is a lot for me.

"Fucked his brains out, didn't you?" Blake rubs his hands together.

I roll my lips, refusing to spill my dirty secrets. Even as the vision of me riding him flashes in front of my eyes.

"This makes marrying him a little interesting," Alice says with a smug look.

"I don't know how to feel. I'm nauseous being in here." I touch my stomach, trying to ease the flutters.

"Aww, sweetie, that's nerves," Blake says, reaching out to rub my arm.

"I'd say we can cancel, but with the timeline for this, you can't," Alice says with a small shuffle forward to me.

I suck in a deep, cleansing breath and stand, shaking off the strange feeling. "Let's start looking and maybe that'll help?" I say to my friends, who all look at me like I've grown two heads. "Come on." I walk away and hear their steps behind me.

"So what do you like?" Maddison asks, browsing the dresses beside me.

"I don't know. Maybe elegant? Lace?" I move one dress at a time and look over it with care before moving on to the next one. "It would help me if you could each pick a dress for me to try on."

Mom joins us a few minutes later, and chooses one too. Now I have a dressing room full of wedding gowns to try on.

I suck in a breath. Here goes...

"Are you ready?" the associate asks me in the changing room.

Am I?

I don't know. Yes and no.

"Y-yesss," I stammer.

She holds out the dress and I slip my mom's long-sleeve choice on; it has a high neck and flows out at the bottom. As soon as the woman buttons me up, I turn from side to side to look at myself in my first wedding dress. How do I feel trying a wedding dress on, as a fiancée to a man I actually like?

It's crazy. This whole experience is crazy, but a large smile breaks on my face.

"You like this one?" the sales associate says.

I realize by my smile, she must think I do.

"Actually, no, it's seeing myself in a wedding dress. It's kinda surreal," I babble.

"Oh. Well, explain what you don't like about his dress," she prompts, standing behind me, staring at me in the mirror and waiting for my answer.

I run my hands over the dress as I explain. "The sleeves, the high neck, the shape is just too proper."

This dress is my mom's choice, and not me at all. I want to feel sexy. I imagine Alex's blue eyes hitting mine the moment I walk down the aisle, and I love how everything else in the room disappears and I'm all he sees. In this, I won't have that confidence.

Walking out, my mom's eyes immediately well up, and I can't help but smile. This is a moment that feels special for us, even if our relationship has been strained due to the way she believes I should live my life. But with me "growing up," as she calls it, I see the change in how she views me. And God, I've wanted this so much.

My friends grimace, but they all stay quiet. No one likes it—other than my mom.

I try on Blake's choice next. It's way too short and when I walk out, they all admit they don't like the blush color.

I get back to the dressing room, where I decide to try on Madison's choice. But as soon as I put it on. It's all wrong.

There's one more left. Alice's choice. I don't have high hopes, but as I step into it, I know it's the one.

The soft lace feels so soft and feminine, and then the slight dip in the back makes me feel sexy. I imagine his hand on my back during our first dance together. And the front cinches in my waist, which I know is something he loves. His hands found any excuse to touch my waist last night. As the zip is fixed, I gasp at myself in the mirror. My eyes fill with unshed tears. I feel beautiful, and my nerves turn to excitement as I envision his face when I walk toward him in this.

I walk out to my friends and mom. The room is dead silent, but not for long.

Alice is a blubbering mess, and I can't bring my eyes to her because I know the tears I'm holding back will fall down my cheek.

I was so lonely before I met him. And I didn't realize it until recently. Living with him and spending time with him showed me how nice it was to have someone to listen to and talk to. Maddison is great, and I'll love her forever, but it's not the same. I feel different with him. When I slept in his arms, I felt like I had it all. We just clicked. We fit together perfectly.

Blake claps. "This is the dress!"

"It is." I choke on my tears.

My mom's dabbing her eyes with tissues. Maddison's eyes are glassy, Blakes crying, and Alice's damn sobbing hits me.

And my dam of tears releases.

I had a great day out. I've chosen a dress that I love and fits me like a glove. The moment I open the front door to Alex's house, I feel giddy. Walking through the entry, I find him sprawled out on the sofa, one leg hooked over the back.

His head lifts from the armrest. "Hey." His panty-melting smile hits me at full force.

"That was quick." I say, as I come to stand behind him, kicking off my shoes and rounding the sofa. I enjoy the cold wooden floors on my bare feet. Now the awkward *do I sit straight down, or do I kiss him?* I want to kiss him...

He tugs my hand, and I stumble. Making the decision for me, his hands grab my hips and lower me down onto his lap.

As he kisses me, I melt into him, kissing him ferociously. I've missed him so much today. His hands skim over my waist to touch my lower back and hold me. My heart beats frantically because my body remembers him and wants his hands all over it. It would be so easy to swivel my hips and grind into him, turning this sweet moment into hot sex in a second. But even though I want that, I also just want to eat and rest. Today was mentally exhausting.

I pull away from his sweet kiss, opening my eyes to find his shimmering ones looking at me.

"Did you choose a dress?" he asks softly. His hand reaches out to tuck a piece of hair behind my ear. I lean into it, looking down at my body on top of his. His hand lifts my chin.

I bite the inside of my cheek and nod.

He gives me a lop-sided grin. "What does it look like?"

"I can't tell you." I giggle and then lay a sweet kiss on his lips.

"Why not?" He frowns. He's being such a guy at this moment, oblivious to how special the moment will be when he sees me.

"It's the rule."

His fingers dig into my hips. He shakes his head. "I don't always follow the rules."

The way he's looking at me makes it hard to not give in. But I don't know if I could tell him without crying. It was a dress that made me feel heavy emotion, and he makes me do the same, so it's only going to end up with me looking like a mess.

"Well, bad luck, this is a rule I'm sticking to," I reply and stick out my tongue.

His hand moves to the front of my thigh, as he wears a knowing expression.

"And there's no way I could change your mind?" His husky voice is out, and all the humor leaves me.

His fingers drift down, caressing my inner thigh. My skin prickles with goosebumps from his tempting offer.

"No chance." My voice wavers, totally giving away how affected I am.

"Are you sure?" His tone is deeper now.

"Very," I breathe.

"That's a shame." His fingers stop, and his lips twist with a satisfying smirk.

I sigh. "Unfair."

"I know, honey. I'm such an asshole." He grabs the back of my head and slams his lips to mine, taking the air from my lungs.

I squirm on his lap, trying to rub the ache from my core, using his growing erection, but he pulls back.

"Dinner's ready? Are you hungry?"

Fucking starving for him.

How can he just stop?

He's clearly as turned on as me.

"Yeah, a little."

"Same, I'm famished." He's being such a smartass.

I climb off his lap, and he stands, adjusting his pants. I raise my brow at him. He's actually going to just end it here.

He smacks my ass. "Don't even think about it. You need to eat. I need you to have energy for later."

Oh. Here I was thinking that was it, but he has plans for us, and tonight I want him to take control.

"Did you cook?" I ask, following him.

"Yeah, why's that?"

"No reason," I reply, watching him move around effortlessly in the kitchen.

I didn't think he could cook.

"You cooked that?" I say, dumbfounded, as I stare at a large pastry crust pie.

"Yeah." But the sly smile tells me something different.

Squinting at him, I read his too amused face. A smile escapes my lips, knowing he's not telling me the whole truth. "You did not. You liar."

His lip twitches. "I may have bought it and I put it in the oven."

We laugh. It's so easy being with him. I can't wipe the smile off my face.

CHAPTER 29

TAHLIA

TONIGHT, I'M GETTING READY for my bachelorette party. Alice is coming to pick me up soon. I told her nothing fancy, but she instructed me to wear white. I've chosen a white simple dress, and I'm finishing my hair, choosing a half-up, half-down look. And I kept my makeup simple.

The doorbell rings, and I open it. Alice stands there in a red midi dress, that compliments her bouncy brown hair and matching red lips.

"Alice, you look beautiful. I love the red," I say, standing back and letting her pass me to get inside.

"And look at you. Happy Bachelorette!" she says, hugging me. When we disconnect, she thrusts a bag toward me.

"What's this?" I ask, taking the bag with caution.

"Open it and find out," she encourages.

I smile. Pulling out the tiara and sash, I can't help but be happy she's putting in so much effort. I could argue and say I don't want it, but I'm not. I want this. Everything about this feels right. Just like my feelings toward him.

"Thanks, Alice, it's perfect," I say sheepishly. Taking the tiara out first, I walk to the mirror. Staring at my reflection, I place the tiara on top of my head.

"I just need to put my shoes on, and I'm ready," I say, turning around, where she smiles her approval.

I quickly head upstairs, and a couple of minutes later, I'm wearing my shoes and sash, and I'm in her car, heading to Maddison's.

Walking the path up to my old house, I realize I don't want to leave Alex's. This feels like my old life, and I don't want to go backward.

My new life is a fresh start.

Arriving inside, I walk into a party playing music. All my friends and family are dressed up, waiting for my arrival. The house is decorated with balloons, ribbons, and there's even a life-size picture of Alex.

I'm handed a drink by Maddison, and as soon as I taste it, I recognize the drink as vodka, soda, and lime. But the straw is in the shape of a dick, and I can't help but laugh. I seriously have the best friends ever.

Once we've all had a few drinks, we play one game where Alex had to answer a list of questions. If I got the answer right, they all had to take a sip of their drinks, but if I got it wrong, I did.

"All right, five-minute warning. Everyone pee, touch up, and get ready to party," Blake announces to the room.

"I thought this was supposed to be low key," I say to Alice.

She shrugs. "You know them; you can't rein them in."

True. And so far, my bachelorette party has been fun, so I just want to let go and enjoy the night. Whatever crazy ideas they came up with.

Heading outside, I take in the limousine and my mouth opens into a full smile.

Tonight couldn't get any better.

Sliding into the back, I ask Blake, "Where are we going?"

"Our old stomping ground." He winks.

"Luxe?" I ask.

He nods with a knowing smile.

I smile eagerly.

I do love that club. Private and elite. Fancy and perfect for tonight. It's also where I first met my now fiancé, and that knowledge alone makes me giddy. It'll be like he's with me without being physically there.

I didn't want to go out, but now with some drinks and everyone around me, I can't wait to dance.

Arriving there, we go inside and into a VIP area. This is new, as we've never rented out an exclusive spot before. We even have our own bartender, and we order a round of drinks.

My gaze drifts over the crowd until a familiar set of eyes stare at me from across the room.

Alex.

CHAPTER 30

ALEX

SIPPING MY SCOTCH, I welcome the warmth that spreads through me. Not from the alcohol, but from the woman I'm engaged to. Her eyes hit mine, and they widen before a smile curves her lips. My gaze runs over her, and I can't help but smile. She's wearing a crown and a white sash with gold writing that says *Bride*. Never in my life did I think I'd be here having a bachelor party. Me. Nope, I'm still in shock, but I'm fucking happy we are.

It still doesn't feel real.

Pushing that aside, I look at the vision in white. Pure heart, probably a little too good for me. But I'm selfish and won't give her up. The thought of anyone touching her has me clutching my tumbler a little more tightly than I should.

Her teeth sink down into her soft, pillowy lips. God, I want to march over there and kiss them. I'm about to cross the room when a hand slaps my shoulder.

"You're not meant to see her tonight, you know," Mike's voice says. He's teasing me, and I give him a smirk back.

"I know, but I don't like these rules."

Mike chuckles. "No one fucking does. But considering my wife is there, and if she hadn't just had Ethan, I'd impregnate her tonight."

"Jeez, that's a bit much."

He raises his brow in a challenge. "Let's see what happens when you get married and have—"

"We're not having kids. The agreement was to get married."

"And then what?"

I drain my glass and put it away before coming to stand beside him, my hands in my pockets, watching her swing her hips. I know it's all for me. The way her eyes flick over here to make sure I'm watching. Fuck me, I wouldn't want to watch anyone else. Only her. I'd choose her every single time.

Both of us are enjoying each other and living together has transformed our relationship from friends to lovers.

It was just a game to me, and I thought after we got married, she'd get her inheritance and move out. I don't want that now.

But what if she still wants to leave and move out? Doesn't want me or a relationship?

I shrug. "I don't know. We'll probably talk about that after the wedding."

"But you like her?" Mike asks, rubbing his brow, looking at the girls across the room. All dancing and having fun.

"I don't want her to move out," I confess.

"And are you in a relationship for real now?" he asks.

"I think so...At least, to me, we are. We're going to Mom's tomorrow for dinner as a couple. So, fuck, I hope so." I laugh, but it's without humor.

I need to find out tonight.

"This is why you're single," a familiar voice booms behind me.

I turn and do a double take. Not believing who it is.

It's Doctor Damien Gray.

"You came!" I light up. Happy to see my friend out...in the first time in years.

"I'm regretting listening to you two," he grumbles.

Mike throws back his drink and drains it. "Bullshit. Look at the place. It's a vibe. You don't even have to find a woman. Just come here and relax after work for a few drinks with friends and unwind."

"Kid, remember?" Damien grumbles.

"Oh, we remember," Mike says, being a smartass before grabbing another round for us all.

I don't have kids, so I don't want to get involved, but Mike is on the same level playing field.

"You have a wife and newborn. Let's see how long it lasts," he says as he takes the glass Mike offers.

"Not every woman is your ex-wife," Mike adds, a hint of annoyance in his voice.

"I guess not," Damien says through gritted teeth.

My eyes follow Tahlia and her group onto the dance floor. She's totally lost in the beats of the song and gaining male attention. The sash is adding more eyes to her instead of scaring them away. It's like a magnet to say *one last hurrah*.

Not a fucking chance. Before I watch any guy touch her, and allow for the potential for me to lose my shit, I start walking. "I'd love to stay here, but I have to go see my fiancée."

"You can't," Damien says, trying to stop me.

"When you have a fiancée—" The words die on my lips.

"I've had one," he says with venom, wiping his jaw.

"Well, I want Tahlia, and I'm not following any rules."

Mike's voice chuckles. "You can't leave your own party."

My feet stop moving. I rub the back of my neck, thinking of how I can be in two places at once.

"I'll go dance for one song," I say with a smug grin, knowing I figured out the best of both worlds.

"I'll do the same," Mike adds.

I shrug. "Whatever. I'll be back."

As I push through the crowd of moving bodies, I see her white dress, and the strappy heels make me swallow a growl. Those are staying on tonight. The rest of her will be naked, but those heels stay on.

Her friends' eyes bug out as I approach.

"Hey! You're not supposed to be here!" Blake cries out.

"One dance. Let me have one fucking dance with my fiancée." My tone is husky now, my throat filled with her heavy perfume.

Once again, her presence consumes me.

"Only one," Alice says.

I give her a nod before telling her, "Mike said he gets one next."

Alice's face brightens, and I would normally envy the love they share, but I have a woman looking at me like I'm the only person in her orbit right now. I no longer envy them, because I'm now living that life.

Grabbing Tahlia's hand, she steps over to me, and I move so we're flush against each other. She giggles, and it's a sound I love so much. Her hands skim up over my biceps and over my shoulders to link together behind my neck. I touch her waist and keep my hands just above her ass, gently pushing her body against mine. We move easily to the music together.

Leaning close to her ear, I whisper, "You look incredible. I simply couldn't resist."

"I'd tell you I'm mad, but I secretly wanted you to come over."

I chuckle at her confession.

"Not so secret now."

I lay a kiss just below her ear. With her hair half up, it exposes her neck, allowing me to get easy access. She winces from my breath tickling her neck, and I release a full smile. I'm so glad I ignored the boys and came over. Moving our hips to the music feels so natural.

I've never had a connection this deep, intimate, all-consuming. But with one touch from her, she takes over me. I welcome the warmth of contact. But the question from earlier enters my mind. I have to ask.

"What are we doing?" I ask, keeping my hands on her hips.

"Dancing," she teases.

"No. I mean, between us."

She hiccups. "We weren't supposed to end up together."

My body tenses before relaxing again. "But we are."

"Are you sure you're not normally into relationships?"

"I'm into you."

"You are?" She pulls back to stare into my eyes, bright and glossy from the alcohol.

"I am."

"I'm into you too. Alex, I really like you. Like, I'm falling hard."

I swallow a groan. There's something about her saying that about me that makes me feral.

"I told you not to fall in love with me," I breathe.

She brings her face closer to mine. "You made it impossible not to."

"Good. Tell me you're mine."

"I'm yours," she whispers.

"You're mine," I repeat in a mumble as we stare at each other, unblinking.

"And Alex...I love you," she whispers, as if scared I'll run. But the opposite emotions rush through me at hearing it. Because I know in this moment, I feel exactly the same.

"Tahlia, I love you too," I repeat back to her, not hesitating.

I dip my head and claim her lips in a sensual kiss. Hoping she can feel my love through my kiss, because I mean every single word.

She kisses me back with equal passion, trying to climb me, and a grumble leaves my chest. I'm overheating from our desire, and I wish I could rip her dress off her right now. A voice interrupts.

"It's been one song. My turn. Go get Mike."

I peel myself off Tahlia, and she's flushed and smiling sheepishly as I stare down at her.

"You better go," she mimes, wearing an amused look.

"I wish I didn't," I grumble, the erection making me edgy.

"Later," she whisper-shouts.

"Definitely. At our house."

She grins, and I think she liked me calling it *our house*.

Taking one last look over my shoulder, I feel settled, as I walk back to the guys.

I tell Mike it's his turn, and he's gone so fast, I barely get the words out.

After another round of drinks, I'm over it. I only want to dance with Tahlia, and because I can't, I tell the guys I'd like to leave.

Mike's happy with that, because he wants to go home and enjoy being with his wife alone while our mom has the baby for the night.

I can't imagine not having Tahlia all the time and having to have a baby around.

I say goodbye and walk to the exit, but a voice stops me. I suck in a frustrated breath. Fucking hell. I just want to get out of here.

"Where are you going?" she purrs. I stare back at the woman I slept with once after we met here. I can't even remember her fucking name.

Why does the sound of her voice now irritate me?

"Home," I reply. I don't want to lead her on, so I try to word it in a direct but kind tone.

"Why? I just got here. Why don't you come and have a drink with me? I'm sure you won't want to leave then."

You mean, buy you a drink? But I don't say that.

"No, I'm going home."

She bats her eyelashes and whines about joining me, but I'm distracted. In the corner of my eye, I see Damien talking to a woman. His face still wears the same thin lips and grumpy expression, but from the way he's giving her dopey eyes, I think he knows her. How? I don't know. Right now, though, I don't give a fuck.

I walk to the exit on a mission. I can't stop. I have a date with my fiancée, in my bed, and I'm not staying here for anyone. I only want to go home to her.

CHAPTER 31

ALEX

"You drove me crazy wearing this sexy little dress tonight."

My eyes travel slowly over every inch of Tahlia while my fingers twitch to touch her. Only, I don't know where to start.

"I'm sorry," she purrs.

"Don't be sorry. It's fucking perfect," I say. My gaze drops to her mouth, and then back to her eyes as I lick my lips.

"It is?" she asks.

I don't answer her with words, instead I do what I want. I kiss her.

My eyes shut, and I lean in, capturing her whimper with my lips. I try to take this slowly and enjoy every swipe of my tongue and every move against her lips, but that one caress of her lips on my own sent me into a frenzy. I've never been this desperate to kiss a woman. She feels amazing on my lips and between my hands.

We take a breath and I trail a finger down her chest. "This sash and bachelorette dress tells the world you're marrying me. That I get to have you in every way possible, including your body. All those guys wanted you."

"I don't want them," she rasps.

The knowledge makes my dick twitch. She wants me. I want her.

"Oh, I know. You belong with me. That ring on your finger is to tell them you're mine."

She moans. "Alex."

My mouth drops to hers again, and I swallow another one of her moans.

Her hands grab my shirt, clutching it and keeping me close. I swipe my tongue over her lips seeking entry, and she parts them easily. She tastes a mix of sweet and spicy, and I can taste the mix of drinks.

When we pull apart, I stare at her swollen pink lips, her hooded lids, and her rosy cheeks. This look is hot, but it gets me remembering what she looks like when I've just fucked her. Yeah, she's an angel with the just-fucked glow.

"That was nice." She hiccups.

I chuckle, but it turns dark. "Nice?"

She hiccups again. "Well, more than nice, but I don't need your head bigger than it already is."

"I'm going to do something un-nice and rip this dress off your body," I gruff. "That's what you want, isn't it?"

"Jesus, just do it already. You're killing me," she whimpers.

A sly smile spreads on my face. "You're desperate," I grunt. "That means you're achy, clenching, and so fucking wet."

"Yes," she moans, but I'm quick to swallow it with my mouth.

I do what I promised and bunch the soft white fabric in my hands and rip and it down the middle. Revealing her bra and panties, all white and fucking edible.

Tossing her dress on the floor, I don't move my eyes from devouring her body.

"I thought I liked the dress. But I prefer it on the floor."

"Please, Alex," she begs urgently.

I lay a kiss on her collarbone, and then on her plump breast. "These tits are begging to be freed."

Her head tips back and her hands find my hair as I pepper her chest with kisses. Then pushing the fabric of the lacey bra down, I tease her nipple with the slightest dusting of my tongue.

"God, Alex," she calls out.

Her desperation makes me want to draw this out. Make her release so much harder.

I unclasp her bra, and when my fingers skim her skin to remove it, her body shivers. Now those pink pebbles beg for attention.

I growl, "So fucking beautiful." I suck a nipple into my mouth hard, enjoying her cries of my name.

Twirling my tongue, I drag my teeth along the nipple as I pull off and kiss my way to the other, giving the same attention. When I pull back, I can see them glistening from my mouth.

I bring my hands to the sides of her panties and slide them down over her curves.

"Keep them around your ankles, but part your legs," I instruct.

"Why?" she breathes.

"You'll see," I murmur, and bring my fingers to her swollen clit, rubbing it in circles. She groans again, and her hands are on my shoulders.

I know I haven't gotten her to the edge yet, because I want her digging her claws in, begging for a release.

I press down harder on her clit, and she jerks.

Sliding my fingers to her opening, I suck in a sharp breath. "Already soaked for me. Good girl. Now, what will I do to you tonight?"

"Everything," she asks quietly.

Her eyes hold mine in a bold stare. "You are a dirty girl. That could be dangerous."

I move my fingers around the opening of her pussy, teasing her. Her breath hitches. I try to take it slow and not rush, but without warning, I enter two fingers into her snug pussy, welcoming the way her walls clamp down on the intrusion.

"I can't open my legs."

"That's the point. It's so tight. Can you feel how tight it is? I can rub your clit and have you coming in minutes."

Her nails dig into my skin, body shuddering.

"You liked the sound of that?"

"Yes," she breathes.

I move my fingers quicker to mimic a thrust.

"Ride my fingers. Ride them as if it's my cock and come all over my hand."

She's so close, I can feel the bruising pressure of her nails piercing my skin.

"Alex, I need to—"

"I know, and I'm not stopping you. Come for me," I rasp, struggling to speak.

A moment later, she's calling out my name as her body shakes and her walls clench down as she climaxes.

When her body slacks, and I know she's come down from her post orgasm high, I carry her to the bed and lay her down.

I pull her panties off and then grab both of her wrists in mine and pin them above her head. "You okay?"

"Alex, please fuck me," she begs.

I almost cave, but my mouth is watering to taste her. I want her to come on my tongue first.

"I know, honey, but I want you to come again, just as much as you do. Just not yet. I have one more orgasm coming out of you before I fuck you."

"Oh." Her voice hitches.

The pleasure staring back at me through her eyes matches my own.

"Spread those legs," I command and settle between her thighs.

"I can't," she tries to say.

I shake my head.

"You can and you will. It will feel amazing."

"Has sex always been like this for you?" she asks.

"Never. But with you, I want to pleasure you and make you come in every way possible before I fuck you."

I don't bother asking if sex has been like this for her, because the surprise on her face as I told her she's getting multiple orgasms before I fuck her answered it for me.

There's something thrilling about knowing I'm the only man to please her so much.

Lowering, I take one long swipe from the opening of her pussy, all the way up to her swollen clit. I grunt like a starved man. I continue to lick and swallow her flavor. My tongue is strong and slow, and the movements are controlled. Her body becomes a quivering mess under me.

Her hands touch my head, gripping my hair as she moans.

"Keep your hands above your head. No touching," I say hoarsely.

"I can't—"

"You can. Relax and breathe. Ride my face until you come. I'm right here waiting—"

I don't even finish talking, as she does exactly that. The smell and taste of her pussy riding my face makes me feral. I fuck her pussy with my tongue and my hands find her ass and give it a squeeze, lifting her hips to smother me.

As her thighs tighten around my head, I'm in heaven. Goosebumps prickle on her skin before she shudders uncontrollably.

I can't breathe as she tightens around me, but I could happily die like this. I murmur into her pussy, "How good," she is.

She's panting.

I climb over her, and my hands sit on either side of her head, caging her in. She stares back at me with heavy lids and so much desire it makes me feel complete. I've never felt like I do when I'm with her. She makes me get lost in all the little moments with her. She looks at me like I'm the only man for her, and she's the only one for me.

Her breathy voice tries to speak, but no words are needed right now. I understand this is different for her too.

I kiss her lips and ease my hips forward, my cock jerking at her wet entrance. When her eyes hold mine, I get lost in the dreamy look. Thrusting forward, I enter her in one swift motion, and as I move, she meets me thrust for thrust. As we always do. We meet each other in the middle, sometimes communicating without words.

I thrust again, and I'm all the way in, not a gap between us. Her back arches and pushes her pretty tits up high.

I reach out and squeeze one in my hand.

"God, Alex," she moans from my touch.

"You have the best tits."

"I'm glad you approve. But shut up and fuck me."

My eyes widen, and a smirk takes over my face. Her cursing is very rare, so I know she's desperate to be thoroughly fucked. It's so fucking hot.

"You better hold on. I'm about to fuck you so hard, you'll remember me between your thighs all day tomorrow."

Her eyes flare.

With no other warning, I slam my hips, and I expect her to regret her words.

Instead, she calls out, "Please. Harder."

Her words unhinge me, and I snap.

My name falls from her lips in a cry, and at the same time, I jerk as I grunt. My own climax slams into me. I come so hard, I lie down immediately after and hold her tightly. And to think I was scared of love. One affectionate hold, and she makes me feel worthy of it.

CHAPTER 32

TAHLIA

SUNLIGHT FILTERING THROUGH THE drapes wake me. My head is laying on top of Alex's warm chest. His soft chest hair reminds me just how much of a man he is. I can't help but smile.

"Morning, beautiful," he says gruffly. His morning voice is so thick, and if I wasn't sore from him fucking me hard last night, I'd be climbing up on top of him and using his morning wood to relieve me.

"Morning," I say, smiling before turning to him. God, he's even more beautiful in the morning.

He smiles softly at me, pushing the hair off my face. "What are your plans today?"

I lift my head. "I'm planning to finish studying the finance book I got from work...but I'd love some company."

"I have to work today."

"Boo," I say and push my bottom lip out in a pout.

Reading my sad face, he chuckles and brings my chin to him so he can kiss me briefly.

"Don't sulk. I'll make it up to you later. We've got dinner at my parents' house, remember?"

I nod and lay my head down for another minute before he heads for a shower. Meeting his family is exciting, but I won't lie. It's also a little nerve-wracking. I haven't met a boyfriend's parents in a long time, and I just hope I don't make a fool of myself.

I lie here, enjoying the scent left on his pillow, thinking about what I should wear that would not look like I'm trying too hard, but still pretty enough to impress them.

His phone goes off beside me, distracting me. I peer at the message and think it's work, so when I read part of the message, dread freezes me.

Unknown number: It was nice seeing you last night. Wish we repeated...

I can't read the full message, but last night meant at the club. Repeat what?

I can't pick up his phone and open the message to read it in full. It's not something I feel comfortable doing. Instead, I let the dread sit heavy in my stomach as I peel myself out of his bed and walk to my room and get changed. Purely for something to do.

I decide a workout will keep me busy until he leaves, and then I need to go to Maddison's to talk to her. The dull ache of the hangover has been replaced with the pain of confusion.

I thought we were in a relationship. I thought I could trust him. I thought he changed. But that message tells me he's still a playboy and I'm an idiot for believing him. I'm due for my period, so maybe I'm extra paranoid, but before I accuse him, I need Maddison's advice.

Is this all part of his charm? Am I a fool?

Downstairs, I move to the treadmill and begin walking slowly. His shape stands in the doorway, and I hate the way my traitorous body is enjoying the way he watches me.

My heart constricts as he walks toward me. I don't want to appear rattled by the text, so I hold on to the sides of the treadmill, so I don't trip or fall.

"You're back in here. I clearly didn't wear you out enough." He gives me one of his crooked smiles, and if I wasn't so numb, I'd feel hot from his suggestion, but every muscle is still tense.

I need to let this go for now. I can feel him staring at my profile beside me, so I turn to face him and look over him. Yeah, he's a delicious man. Bringing my gaze to his amused one, I answer honestly. "I'm definitely sore."

He frowns with deep concern. "I wasn't too rough, was I?"

I soften slightly and offer a small smile. "No, it was hot." And that's the truth.

"Good. My parents' house for dinner tonight?"

"Yeah, what time?" I ask, knowing I need to get my shit sorted before then and to make sure I'm ready on time.

"Six-thirty?"

"Sounds good," I say, and he kisses my cheek, lingering a little too long. My heart aches from the gesture.

When he leaves the room, I let out a heavy sigh and text Maddison to tell her I'll be around in a couple of hours.

I hit stop on the treadmill and walk into the kitchen to find he's made me a coffee. Damn him. Why does he have to mess with my head? I need to get out of here and think seriously about what we'll do after the wedding. I take the coffee and see the heart design on top, and I sigh. He's definitely trying to kill me.

I drink the delicious coffee he made me, and then hit the shower. My mind is still in a bad way when I get to Maddison's. I tried to eat breakfast, but the knots in my stomach wouldn't ease up. So, I skipped it and brought some snacks for us to have with tea.

"Is everything all right?" Maddison asks, opening the door and seeing the bag of food I'm carrying.

"Not really, but let me sit down and explain. I need to pick your brain," I mumble.

"Let's talk quietly. My head isn't 100 percent today." She gives me a knowing smile and closes the door behind me.

"Hungover? I didn't think you drank more than me," I question with a frown.

We take a seat on the sofa. She sinks low and throws a blanket over her legs.

"I brought snacks," I say, waving the bag between us.

"I wondered what you brought. Gimme." She curls her fingers into grabby hands.

I hand over the bag, and she pulls the bag of chips out and tears the packet open.

"Talk to me," she says before eating a chip.

I exhale deeply. "He got a text this morning."

"Mm," she encourages.

"From an unknown number, but it was clearly a woman. It said *it was nice seeing you last night, and wish we repeated*...but I didn't read the rest because I didn't want to open his phone—it felt wrong."

Her mouth twists in an unsure look. "Did you ask him about it?"

I grab some chips and munch on them.

My stomach welcomes the food.

"No, I was shocked, and he was in the shower for work. I wanted to think about it and then talk to you. I don't want to be a paranoid girlfriend, so if I come to him, I need to be controlling the situation, not emotionally driven."

She shuffles off the sofa to stand. "Soda?"

"Please." I smile back. I need the sugar to stay awake today.

"Be honest with him and say you saw part of a text on his phone, and you want to know if he's seeing other people. Just be casual, and I think it'll be fine." Her voice is soft as she walks farther away, but I catch the rest of what she's saying.

"Yeah, I was so shocked this morning, my heart couldn't have asked him about it."

"That's fair, but when he gets home, ask him." She arrives back in the living room and hands me a bottle.

"Tonight, I'm meeting his parents, so I'm also nervous about that," I say and gulp some of the drink, welcoming the bubbles.

"Meeting the parents is always nerve-wracking, but you'll be fine. Just be yourself."

"You're always so calm about everything. The text and now the parents," I say.

"Remember, it's easy to tell someone else how to be calm, but if it were me, I'd be losing my shit."

We laugh, and even though she didn't have much to say about the text, I just needed some time to digest it. Feeling much better now, I sit back on the sofa, and we watch a few old *Friends* episodes, eating chips and drinking soda until it's time for me to leave and get ready.

We arrive at the edge of a gated area, where we are buzzed in. Alex drives through the set of gates, following a long driveway up to his parents' house. It's a white, two-story building, surrounded by a beautiful garden full of flowers.

He opens the car door, and I step out on my shaky legs, grateful I decided on flats instead of heels. But butterflies hit my stomach, and I second guess my outfit. Is it too simple?

"Do I look too casual?" I ask, running my hands over my white blouse and light blue jeans. I look down, analyzing them before looking up.

He approaches with a genuine grin. "No. You look breathtaking," he replies.

"Please, be serious," I beg. How can such a basic causal outfit be breathtaking?

"I am," he answers. His blue eyes soften, and he grabs both of my hands in his. His thumbs circle the skin on the back of my hands in a caress. He's trying to pull my thoughts away by his touch. And of course, it's totally working. One single touch, and I'm weakening. Forgetting about any text or any other problem I have.

He leans into the side of my neck, and I wait for his next move, biting my lips together to prevent a sound, or worse, a moan. His mouth hits below my ear, and he kisses it. Breathing in my perfume, as if he needs to taste it. "Let's go inside."

I'm sure once I meet them, my nerves will settle. The longer I stand outside in this unfamiliar environment, the worse I'll feel. Holding hands, we walk up to the door. Alex opens the door, and I tug his arm.

"You didn't ring the doorbell?" I mutter.

His face transforms with humor. "I don't need to. It's my parents."

So different from my parents. They wouldn't accept me barging into their house.

I follow his lead, keeping my hand firmly in his.

"Mom. Dad. We're here," he calls out loudly as we step inside.

My eyes widen, unable to believe he just did that.

A gray-haired man a little shorter than Alex appears from around the corner. He wears the same smile as Alex too. If I hadn't already guessed it was his dad, this just confirmed it.

"Hi, welcome. You must be Tahlia?" he asks kindly.

"Yes." I smile nervously, offering my hand.

He shakes it. "Paul."

"It's lovely to meet you, Paul."

I hear shuffling as we wander farther into the house.

His mom walks toward me with a wide grin. Her bouncing gray hair that sits just above her shoulders is perfectly styled, and her emerald pants and white blouse make me feel settled about my outfit. "Hi, love. I'm Margaret. It's great to finally meet you. I'm grateful you could join family dinner, even though I'm sorry to say, Mike isn't able to come, and neither is Stephanie."

My eyebrows shoot up in surprise. Does that mean...

"It's just us. Sweet," Alex beams down at me. His hand disconnects from mine, sitting on the small of my back. I love how he always finds a way to touch me. As if he needs the constant connection as much as me.

I draw in a long breath and just try to enjoy the moment.

If he's happy, I should be too.

"Dinner is almost ready, but the starters are on the table. Come and help yourselves." Margaret walks us into the dining room, where a table is set up with lots of food, ranging from bread and dips, to fruit and meats.

"Would you like a glass of wine?" Alex asks.

"That sounds great," I reply quietly.

"Mom, Dad, would you both like wine as well?" Alex asks, turning his attention to them.

"Sure, let me help you," his dad offers.

Alex's hand drops away from my back, and he strolls into the kitchen with Paul to grab drinks.

"I'll have a small glass. They're in the fridge," Margaret calls out.

A moment later, Alex yells, "Mom, did you buy the whole store?"

I peer at her as I grab an olive to pop into my mouth. She smiles at me. "Maybe..."

I take a seat and nod, laughing lightly.

Alex and Paul arrive back with four glasses of wine. Alex lowers a glass in front of me, and Paul does the same with Margaret before they sit beside us.

We nibble on the food.

"Did you make the charcuterie board?"

"Yes, love. But wait until you eat dinner. It's going to melt into your mouth. It's Alex's favorite dish."

"Oh, is it?" I ask, getting my first piece of information out of her.

"What was Alex like as a kid?" I ask, just to be funny.

"Great, here we go. The next hour of mom spilling my secrets," Alex says.

I can't help but love it. I want all the details. I grab some bread and tear it apart as she speaks, her face lighting up with happiness.

"He was always so outgoing, but he's also the softest, most gentle soul. He'd always take care of Mike and Stephanie. When he loves you, he will protect you with everything he can." She meets my gaze before looking at Alex, who winks at her.

"We're incredibly proud of the man he's grown to be. We're glad to have met someone who means so much to him," Paul says.

"Yes, we've never met—"

Alex clears his throat beside me. "Mom, please. Now this is embarrassing."

"Oh, is it? Sorry, my love," his mom says, chuckling to herself.

"I don't think so; it's all the good stuff I came here for," I say, elbowing his side playfully.

His hand grabs my thigh, and I suck in a sharp breath at the sudden unexpected contact. Leaning into my ear, he whispers so only I can hear. "You know everything about me...more than they do, trust me."

His hidden meaning makes me close my thighs, but he slides his hand up farther. I excuse myself to the bathroom, needing a moment alone to take a cleansing breath as the dinner is brought out. Over dinner, we fall into more easy conversation. We talk about Mike, Alice, and baby Ethan, and I learn more about his sister Stephanie, her husband Chris, and their baby girl Ellie.

"Dinner was amazing. I wish I could cook this," I say as I eat the chicken potpie.

"I could teach you sometime. I learned it at cooking school."

Alex's chuckle pulls me. I look at him, confused.

"She finds any way to discuss cooking school," he answers me.

"What's wrong with that?" Margaret asks, offended.

He shakes his head, looking at her. "Nothing, Mom. I love how passionate you are about it," Alex replies, finishing his dinner.

I bring the wineglass to my mouth and enjoy the moment of being around his family. I think it was better just to meet the parents first. I don't know how I would've gone meeting the huge family at once. It would've been too much. Now I know more about them, and I feel more comfortable about the next Sunday dinner with everyone here.

My phone rings with my mom's name on it. "Sorry, I have to answer this. I won't be long," I say with a wince. I hope they don't think I'm rude.

"Go ahead. I'll get a start on dessert," Margaret replies as Alex's pager goes off.

I answer and quickly realize when Mom sneers "Tahlia Adams". That my world is going to be ripped apart.

Chapter 33

Tahlia

"How dare you lie to me to get your inheritance." Her icy tone freezes my veins through the line.

I swear I stop breathing.

"Mom. I'm sorry, I can explain. I'm coming over right now," I say in a hurry.

"You better have a good excuse. I'm extremely disappointed in you."

I swallow the sickness threatening to spill. Everything around me is falling apart.

When I hang up the phone, Alex is looking at me, confused.

Mom knows I lied about our engagement is sitting at the end of my tongue. But they don't come out, because I'm in a state of disbelief. And I need more details before I tell him. Especially now that work is paging him with an emergency. I don't want to take him away from that. From his patients. They need him.

"I need to go to my parents' house," I say in the most composed voice I can muster.

His eyes widen as he dusts his hands of crumbs. "Now?" he asks.

I stand up, shaking my head and collecting my stuff. "Yeah, sorry. They. Ah. Need me for something."

Margaret smiles and steps forward to hug me, and I didn't realize how much I needed it.

"Thanks for dinner, and I'm sorry to cut this short," I whisper as I take a step back. I was having such a good time. I could see how easy it would be to be a part of his life, his family. But now—

"It's fine. Family first," she says.

I swallow the guilt bubbling in my throat. "Thanks."

"Just be sure to join us for next Sunday dinner, and at least you'll meet the whole gang."

I give her a warm smile. "That sounds nice."

We say goodbye and on the drive, he gets another urgent call from the hospital.

He drops me off after some persuading not to come in. But he knows he has no choice when I remind him about work.

I walk up the steps to the house, and I don't even need to bang on the door.

"Tahlia," Mom's cold voice says as she opens the door. My dad's anger is radiating off him in waves.

I step inside, and we walk to the kitchen.

"Do you want a drink?" Mom asks. Even angry, she won't stop being polite.

"No. I just had one at Alex's parents' house."

"Do they know?" my dad asks with a bite.

I nervously moisten my dry lips with my tongue before answering. "No. Only Maddison, Blake—"

"Everyone knows but us?" Mom asks curtly.

"Let me clarify what part," I reply, holding on to hope they might be talking about something else.

A muscle flicks angrily in my dad's jaw before he scoffs. "You know exactly what I mean, young lady."

"I'm dating Alex, that's not a lie—"

"You two are not engaged?" Mom cuts me off.

"Not really. He asked me, but technically, no," I confess. I can't expect the truth from others if I don't speak the truth. No matter what it costs me.

I shouldn't have lied, but I wouldn't be with Alex if I hadn't, so I can't say I regret it.

"I'm glad your father is close friends with the jeweler Alex brought the ring from. Imagine if he didn't tell us that Alex had come in buying the ring but asked about returning it in a few months, or what happens if you divorce. It wasn't hard to figure out this was set up for your inheritance. But I have to know why you lied?"

That's how they found out...

"I wanted to get my stake in Emerald Designs," I admit. Unable to stand anymore, I pull out a dining chair and sit down.

They sit in front of me.

"You've wasted so much of your life. You should've finished college and listened to us and now you lie. Who are you?" my mom says with a loathing expression before looking away.

My dad's hands are clasped together as he leans forward and speaks in a cold tone. "We raised you better than this. We gave you the freedom you wanted, even if we didn't like it. We thought as you grew older, you'd settle down, but it went the other way. You went the other way."

"I'm sorry," I plead.

"I can't believe you would come up with a sick and twisted plan to deceive us." My dad's voice drips with disbelief.

"It wasn't a plan. The will said I need to settle down. So, I made it happen, but I should've been more honest about our relationship status. Again, I'm sorry. I really am," I beg, trying to get them both to understand it wasn't a disturbing plan, but more of a life raft for me.

"I don't know what to think." My mother dabs under her lashes with a tissue.

I hate how I hurt them.

"You will not inherit the business if you don't marry for love. No daughter of mine will get a business we've worked hard for after lying and cheating to get it."

"Please—" I cry, tears trailing down my cheeks. I feel my future slipping before he says it and my heart shatters.

"No. Tahlia. Your tears will not help. You cannot change the will. Emerald Designs will be sold to an investor, not to you, end of discussion." My dad rises from his chair and leaves to head upstairs, probably to his office.

I can't blame him. I just wish I was honest from the start. Now what do I do?

Leaving my parents' house feels like a blur. I can't even cry anymore because my body is in such a state of shock.

Alex's name flashes on my phone screen. For a moment, I just simply stare at it.

I can't answer it in this taxi. I'm too scared that between the mysterious text I saw and the deal being off, he won't want to be with me.

Alex: Where are you? Is everything okay?

The backs of my eyes prick with more incoming tears. Why can't everything stay the way it was? I was so happy, feeling like my life was finally having direction.

Now I have no inheritance.

No direction.

And maybe a relationship over.

What a damn mess.

The look of disappointment in my parents' eyes killed me. We haven't had the best relationship, and being with Alex gave it a new life. But now they think the worst of him and me.

I'm upset with myself. And at life.

Why can't it give me a break?

As I sit in the silence of the taxi, I think over how this is the first time in a while I've felt alone again, and I hate it. But I deserve it.

I deserve this soul-crushing feeling.

With only myself to blame.

I pick up my phone and try to write a message. The heaviness hits me and a tear leaks as I type.

Tahlia: My parents found out about the fake engagement, and they are selling my stake of the business. I'm going to my own place. I'm so sorry for dragging you through this mess. I bet you hate me.

He's reading it already, and the dots bounce.

Alex: Don't be sorry. I'm not sorry. It got me a girlfriend. I could never hate you. I love you. You've brought me so much joy. What time will you be home? I'm still at work but when I get home from the hospital we can talk then. I don't want to talk through texts.

More tears roll down my cheeks. What time will you be home? As if it's my house, too. One I don't deserve. God, I have fallen head over heels in love with Alex, and it's all going to be over.

I can't face him right now. I'm too fragile. I don't want to look into another pair of disappointed eyes. I also don't want to have a discussion about the text message either. I'm too exhausted from the emotional rollercoaster day.

Tahlia: I love you too. I'm here with Maddy so I'm going to crash at my old place tonight.

I don't see any dots bouncing, and I'm about to close my phone, when he finally replies. And my heart drops.

Alex: Ok.

But I asked for this. I just need to get my head right and figure out my next steps. I drop my phone into my bag and sob into my hands until the driver tells me we've arrived. Looking out the window, I sniffle and hand over the cash, then I drag myself up the path to my old place again. I open the door, and Maddison calls out.

"Hello? T, I hope that's you."

"It is." I close the door behind me and kick off my shoes, walking directly to the kitchen. I need wine and TV.

Neither is going to help me figure out any future steps, but I just want to relax and zone out and stop mulling over Alex and my parents.

"By looking at you and the fact you're getting wine and you're not at Alex's, shit has gone wrong."

I pour myself a glass. And then lift the bottle in her direction.

She nods. "Drinking alone is sad. And you look like someone already told you Santa isn't real."

I pour her a good helping before walking to the sofa and sitting down.

"Are you going to talk, or am I mind reading?" she says, taking her spot on the sofa.

Flicking my gaze to her, I take a gulp of the wine. "So, to keep this short, my parents are selling my stake of the business to an investor. I can't go through with the wedding if they won't support it. It doesn't feel right. I want my parents to be there."

"They're upset I get it. Sheesh. Like, I kinda get it, but it's your parents; they're supposed to be there for you."

"I know, but it's not like we've had a great relationship. They wanted to control my life. And everything had a hidden agenda. Well, until recently. Until I had a stake and interest in Emerald Designs, and I had a fiancé."

"It had to benefit them," Maddison adds.

"Exactly. This was the first time it worked in my favor...until it didn't."

"But you and Alex are dating now. Did you tell them?"

"Yep, but they didn't care. They said they can't believe I would come up with a twisted plan to deceive them," I say, the image of my dad's icy gaze flashing through my mind. He didn't believe a word I said. I broke their trust.

"Now what?" she asks.

I exhale. "We sit and watch TV and drink wine."

"Lots of wine," Maddison adds.

"And after that, I'll sleep in my own room...and tomorrow, I don't know," I admit easily.

"This isn't like you, T. I've known you forever, and you never avoid or dig your head in the sand about a problem. You're honest."

I sigh. "I know. I just need to do the opposite for once."

"I think you need to talk to Alex," she deadpans.

"I will," I say.

"When?" she asks.

"Soon," I lie.

"When is soon?" She smirks accusingly.

"Tomorrow?" I say, but it isn't convincing.

But instead of pushing me further, she drops it. Snuggling back into the sofa, I drink my wine and watch TV, but I can't escape it all, as he sends me a text.

> Alex: I miss you. The house feels lonely without you.

Tears fill my eyes as I type back a response.

> Tahlia: I miss you too.

Chapter 34

Alex

I barely slept last night. When I woke up after a couple of hours, I got up to make my morning coffee, figuring I may as well work out.

Instead of helping her learn or making us both one, I'm here alone like it used to be. Without her.

I run my hand through my hair as I look around me. This fucking house is filled with memories of her. Everywhere I look, I see her.

I can't have her walk away. That's what she's doing. I'm fucking crazy about her. I need to get her back. This is so unlike me to fight for a woman, but this feels right. For the first time in my life, I know what it feels like to be in love, and even with my stomach bottoming out with nerves, I want to be in love. I fucking miss it. I miss her.

The best way to do that is to talk to her parents. I need to figure out what was said. If I'm going to go to her and force her to talk to me, I need to know what happened between them.

I pick up the phone and call Sonya Adams.

"Doctor Alex Taylor, you lied to me." Her anger and hurt seep through her words.

"I'm sorry. I'd love to come and talk to you and your husband face to face," I say in a pleading tone I hope makes her give in.

It's quiet for a moment before she agrees.

"Fine. We're home. I don't want to be seen in public talking about this."

"Fair enough. I'll be around soon."

I hang up and suck in a breath.

I'm going to fix this.

With new determination, I grab my keys and get in my car.

Arriving at the house without Tahlia doesn't feel right. But I push it aside. Both of her parents wear thin lips and angry expressions, but they still act polite, asking if I need a drink or anything.

The nice act reminds me of her. She's always so kind and puts others first.

And here I am, putting her first. I like that I'm fighting for her. I've never done that for any woman. I've never been compelled to, but Tahlia is different.

Sitting down at a table opposite my girlfriend's parents should be good, but it's intense.

I clear my throat and start.

The quicker I do this, the quicker I can go to her.

"I want to know what happened. And why she can't get her stake in the family business?"

"Because your engagement and upcoming wedding was a sham," Hector spits angrily.

"But the business was on a hard-to-get clause. She was single and didn't have a boyfriend, so what did you expect her to do?" I ask.

"We had a husband she could have married," Sonya adds.

"She doesn't want him," I argue, my words cold, hating the idea of another man with her.

Fuck no, she's my girlfriend and my future wife.

"And what? She wants you?" Hector all but laughs.

I grind my teeth together, taking a moment to let the anger wash over me.

"Yes," I answer, my voice controlled.

"The relationship was fake," Hector scoffs.

I shake my head vigorously. "You're wrong. We've always been attracted to each other. This opportunity—"

Her dad snorts, and I crack my neck.

I remind myself this is her dad, and I need to be here for her today.

"Set-up, you mean," he argues.

Her mom stays silent. She's watching me. Listening.

"Yes, I told her to marry me. But the way she spoke about hating her current life, this fashion business was going to give her the direction she desperately craves."

Her mom moves. I bet she didn't know that.

I need to win them over. The next words that leave my mouth remind me of the little talks and moments we shared. I miss them already. I want her back.

"She was so excited to take the business on. We often spoke about the wedding. We were actually happy, and we started dating for real."

"It doesn't change the fact you two lied," Hector adds, as if my words don't affect him.

My body goes tense at the mention of lying.

"I admit that was wrong. My own parents would be disappointed, but Tahlia is worth it."

I am desperate to make this right. But so far, nothing is helping. No matter what I say or do, it isn't going to get her the business she deserves, or actually...I don't know how she'll take it, but I have no other choice. This is the moment I ask them.

"I want to buy the business as a wedding gift."

"You're going through with the wedding?" her mom asks.

My head shifts to her face. This is the first time she's spoken more than a few sentences since I entered the house.

Buying the business and marrying her is what feels right in my heart. I want to see Tahlia's full smile at home every day as she talks about what she's learned or implemented at work. I want her to tell me what new thing she's organized for our wedding. I want to be with her now regardless of how we got here. I can't apologize anymore. If Hector and Sonya don't accept it, I guess they'll witness it.

"Of course, and if you don't mind, can I do this the right way? Hector and Sonya, could I please have your daughter's hand in marriage?"

Sonya gasps and covers her mouth. A sheen covers her eyes, and she looks at her husband, laying a hand on his shoulder.

Her dad wipes his forehead with his palm. The look of shock hits him at full force. "Well, Alex...this is a lot to take in."

He looks to his wife with his brow raised, as if seeing what she thinks.

I need an answer now.

"I need your answer tonight, because she's upset, and I want to make her happy again. She's so beautiful when she smiles."

Sonya dips her head, and Hector sighs before turning to face me. "Yes, you have our blessing, and you can buy the business for her." His tone isn't warm, but at least it isn't as icy as before.

As I think about her and how to surprise her with this new information, a thought comes to me.

"Please don't tell her about the business. I want to gift it to her next weekend."

They both nod. Sonya cries as Hector speaks. "As you wish."

Checking the time on my watch, I stand. "I must go and talk to her. Thank you for hearing me out. And I'm deeply sorry."

"Please never lie to us again," Hector warns.

"Never, Mr. and Mrs. Adams. Never again," I say, walking to the door.

I kiss Sonya's cheek and shake Hector's hand. "Well, I'll see you both next Saturday for the wedding."

"You will," Hector says.

Sonya nods.

I leave and and pull out my phone to text Maddison.

Alex: Is she at work, or at your house?

Maddison: Actually, at yours. Please sort it out. I want my space back. She's miserable.

Alex: She won't be back at yours, mark my words.

Maddison: I knew you two were good for each other.

Alex: Thanks. See you next Saturday.

Maddison: Really?

Alex: The wedding...

Maddison: That's still going ahead?

Alex: Yes. She'll be my wife.

CHAPTER 35

TAHLIA

I'M EXHAUSTED FROM PACKING up my stuff and from the lack of sleep I had last night. My mind was too busy racing with replays of my conversation with my parents and the text message Alex received. It's strange how I feel more comfortable here than at my old place. I love Maddison's company, but my heart is here.

The front door opens, and my heart rate picks up, knowing I'm about to see him. It's been a day, yet it feels like a week.

"Honey, I'm home," he calls out, closing the front door as he walks in.

His shoes tap the wooden floors, and I peer up over the sofa to see him.

I struggle to find my voice as I sit up.

My nerves are back in full force, because I have to bring up the fact I saw a text on his phone, and I wonder how he'll take it. Will he lose his shit and think I was snooping?

We also need to talk about what happens now that the deal is off.

"Hi," I say back.

He leans over the sofa and kisses me unexpectedly on the lips in an all too brief kiss.

"I need to go shower quickly. I had to rush to work. Can we talk after that?" He sounds conflicted, but he always showers after work. It's his routine.

"Yeah, sure," I breathe.

"You won't run away on me, will you?" He winks.

His teasing. Another thing I missed yesterday.

"No, I'll be right here waiting," I reply.

"I'll be quick," he calls out as he jogs up the stairs.

I try to resettle on the sofa, but I can't concentrate on the show I'm watching. My mind is still overthinking, mostly about that text I saw yesterday. I need an answer about who she is. I can't wait. Being here, excited to be around him again, I'm desperate to know.

I walk up the stairs and find him unbuttoning his shirt. I rest my head on the door frame and watch his smooth hands slip the shirt off his shoulders.

It's sensual, and I can't help licking my lips.

"Are you going to stare at me? Or come join?" he asks darkly.

The corner of my lip rises, but it's a half smile. I can't shake the heaviness in my gut.

"I need to ask you something," I say nervously and walk into his room. I watch him pause and turn around, curiously staring at me.

"Yeaaah?" he draws out.

I peer down at my fingernails, picking at the skin beside the nail bed. "Yesterday morning, when you went in the shower, I saw a text from a woman, and it said something about seeing them."

I peer up from under my lashes to see his face soften. He sighs and stalks over to me, taking my hand and leading me to his bed. We both take a seat on the edge. He's looking at me with adoration, and I don't get it.

"It was one stupid hook-up before I met you," he says. "So that's why you were on the treadmill before I left for work? I thought it was strange."

My lips part and I try to act offended. "Are you saying I don't exercise?"

He arches one brow at me. "I've only seen you use it twice."

A loud giggle bubbles out of my chest. "Yeah, I'm not a fan of the gym."

"Well, I can give you more exercise," he grunts huskily, kissing my lips before he pushes me back on the bed and lays kisses over my neck and little nips up to my ear. He bites down on my earlobe, and a shiver runs through me at his promise.

I cry out from his affection, not hating it one bit after being in my head about us.

"I was leaving Luxe when she tried to get me to have a drink with her. Which I declined, because I had a sexy fiancée at home, who I wanted more than anything."

His fingers comb my hair and bring my face close to his. He whispers, "Were you really worried?"

I nod sheepishly, feeling the tears seeping onto my cheeks. I feel better now that it's off my chest. I've never been one to argue and fight. And the fact he was just as mature was surprising, but also a relief.

"Honey, there's no need. I only have eyes for you. In such a short time, I've fallen completely in love with you. Which is making it hard to fake this marriage. How can you fake something that feels so right?" His smile reaches his blue eyes, and up this close, the lines beside them are more evident. "I don't want our marriage to be over, do you?" he asks with so much trepidation, staring back at me. I want to put him out of his misery.

"No. The thought has been twisting me up and causing me so much anxiety," I say as a warm tear leaks and runs over my cheek at his words. I didn't realize how much I wanted to hear him say that until now.

The emotion is clogging my throat, and I can't speak. He takes the opportunity to talk more.

"You were able to love me even when I didn't love or believe that I was worthy of one person. I was always told I was a player and I let myself believe it. But that's not me. I hated myself every single damn time. And fuck, I tried not to let you in, but you barged through, and you took away my numb, hollow self. You have no idea what that means to me. I don't even know if I'm making sense—"

I nod through the stupid tears that fall, but I say through a sob, "You are."

"I thought I was broken. I can't go back to waking up alone without love. So, I'm sorry, but I can't let you go. I still want to go through with our wedding. I even asked your parents today for your hand in marriage."

"You what?" I gasp, trying to digest the fact he spoke to my parents, and on top of that he still wants to marry me. This is a lot to process.

"I asked if they'll let me marry you. But only if you still want to." He smiles down at me.

"You still want to get married?" I should be screaming out *yes, I still want to*, but I can't get my mouth to work.

"I do." He says it with these sincere eyes staring back at me.

This man. His heart. I can't even breathe. He loves me.

I sniff and bat all my tears away, drying my face.

"I love you, Tahlia. You're it for me. Please, say yes," he pleads.

I smile. Those words hit me in the center of my chest, and I feel every word. I believe him and I love how raw and open he is right now. It's time I'm honest with him, too.

"I'm scared," I whisper.

He leans his forehead on mine, our breaths loud. "Do you trust me?"

I don't have to think about it. "Yes, I do."

"Then let me love all of you. Give me your heart and I promise not to break it."

I nod, moving my head against his.

"I want you," he rasps in an authoritative tone.

He wins, because my resolve is melting. I can't say no to him. I'm officially addicted. Running his nose up my neck, he whispers in my ear. "I know you want this too."

"Yes," I breathe, fixing my gaze on his handsome big blues. I want us naked and making love. I know right now that I don't ever want him to let me go.

"Good, because I want to reassure you that you're my woman—my wife. You. No one else. You got it?"

CHAPTER 36

TAHLIA

I'M LYING HERE ON the sofa a few days later at my old house with Maddison. My mom organized for me to have a hair and makeup trial this morning. She's been surprisingly nice since our first argument. I haven't had a moment to dwell on it, because in a week, I'm getting married to a man I love.

"Here. You need to take this." Maddison thrusts out a pregnancy test.

My period is late.

It's never late.

Until now...

I missed my pill the morning after Luxe. I was vomiting and hungover. It slipped my mind. That's never happened to me before.

I grab the box with shaky fingers and sit up. My gaze flicks between the box and her.

"Don't be scared. Just go take it, then you'll know for certain," she says, as if reading my thoughts.

"I know. I'm just scared."

"I'll be here with you," she says softly.

I nod. "Thanks. I guess I'll do it."

She checks her watch. "Yeah, get it done. That way, you have the time to digest the news."

"Are you already predicting I'm pregnant?" I try to muster up a smile, but there's minimal movement on my lips. My nerves taking over, my stomach feels sick.

I stand and walk over to the bathroom, tearing open the box and following the instructions. I don't want to be alone, so as soon as it's done, I open the bathroom door. Maddison is standing right behind it.

I clutch my chest at the fright, but then I giggle. "You're more eager than me."

"Sorry. I didn't mean to scare you. I just want to know you're all right," she replies with a somber expression.

"I'm doing okay. I just can't wait three minutes and look at it by myself. I'm too chicken."

"I'll do it with you," she offers.

"Thanks, Maddy."

We're silent for a few seconds before she blinks and looks around. "Did you check the time?"

Eyes wide, I realize I hadn't. "No. I don't have my phone with me."

"Let's start the three minutes now, just to be sure," she says, tapping her watch face.

I bend my head and study my hands, desperately holding myself from picking my nail beds. "The longest three minutes of my life."

"Come on. Let's sit." She gestures to the sofa. Feeling a little lightheaded from the anticipation, I welcome the idea. We leave the test in the bathroom and sit back down. I try to concentrate on the *Friends* episode on the TV to take my mind off the test results.

"It's time," Maddison announces.

"Oh, God. I feel sick," I mumble, staring into her hopeful face.

She holds her hand out, and I accept her invitation to help me up. Standing tall, I stare directly in her eyes, and inhale deeply.

She gives me her friendly smile before spinning on her heel and tugging me along. "You've got this. Let's go see. You might be overreacting," she says as she walks us over to the bathroom.

"Jeez, thanks," I mutter.

"You know what I mean."

Inside the bathroom, she steps back from the counter, and it reveals the test stick. Immediately, I see the two pink lines.

I'm pregnant.

There're no tears. No nothing. I'm stunned. I'm waiting for it to hit me. I wander back to the sofa on trembling legs.

"I can't believe you're pregnant," Maddison says with a disbelieving voice from the other end of the sofa.

"Same. This was not in my plan." I rub my eyes, feeling the exhaustion hitting, but I can't lie here all day.

She twists on the sofa to grab the remote and play the next episode of *Friends*. "Nothing ever goes to plan. You should know that by now."

I sigh. "I know, but I feel like a burden to Alex."

I'm grateful for how he makes me feel and how he loves me, but I don't want him to think I'm taking advantage. He's had a lot of change already. Playboy to marriage and now baby. It's too much to ask. It's a lot for me, let alone him.

"He wouldn't. Have you seen him with baby Ethan? My ovaries flutter," she says, resting a hand on her heart.

I giggle at her dramatics. But she's right.

"Yeah, he loves him. How do I tell him?" I ask, trying to think of a special way.

Those pink lines on the stick are confirmation. Whether or not the timing is right, this is our baby, and I'll love it so much.

"Give him the stick," Maddison suggests.

"I don't know," I say, lost in thoughts. My brain already feels like it's not working. "I need to see him. He deserves to know." Standing up, I walk to grab my car keys.

"Are you sure? You could wait and gift it to him as his wedding gift?"

"I know, and that would've been a nice gesture, but my gut says to tell him now. I'll be back, but, Maddy, please, not a word to anyone," I plead.

"You got it. It's your news to share," she says with an understanding smile.

"I'll be back soon. Wish me luck," I say, spinning around and striding out the door.

"You don't need luck, silly," she calls out, and I leave, making the nervous drive over to his house.

At his door, I'm basically shaking like a leaf. The door opens before I can unlock it, and I see him wearing navy pants, no tie and an open white shirt. He was in the middle of getting undressed from work.

"Tahlia," he says, with his irresistibly devastating grin.

I drop my chin and swallow the lump in my throat as I look to the ground, trying to gain the strength to tell him the news. "I—"

He lifts my chin up with his hand, so I'm looking at him. He stares back longingly, and it cuts me up. "What's wrong?" he breathes.

My first attempt at talking just has my mouth opening and closing. I swallow the fear knotting inside me and speak the words in a whisper. "I'm pregnant."

His eyebrows draw up in surprise as his mouth slackens. I watch the wheels turning in his head as he tries to process the information. "What?" he replies coolly. He drops his hand from my chin and dives it into his hair, and he leans back, staring at the ceiling, mumbling under his breath, "Fuck."

Not the reaction I wanted. Any hope of happiness has been removed by him in one second. Why did I think he'd be happy? It was a lot for him to commit and love me, and now I'm pregnant. I've pushed him. But it wasn't on purpose.

Long silence looms between us, making me more uncomfortable.

"How...What...When?" Now he can't even form a sentence.

"What do you mean?" I ask shakily, looking up at him, disorientated. Hearing the fear in his voice is adding to my anxiety.

His eyes are wild. It's like the news has shaken him, and the next words cut deep. "I'm not ready to be a father."

My body tenses. I'm not ready to parent either. But it's happening.

It's silent again, and all I can hear is the blood rushing to my ears. So much turmoil pulsing through me. "I thought you loved me?" I ask in a broken whisper.

"I do..." he says in an odd, yet gentle, tone.

"This is a funny way of showing it," I mutter hastily.

His hurt eyes look around, as if he's seeking answers. I wish he'd hug me. Hold me. But I shouldn't have to ask for those things; he should want to comfort me. Fear is causing him to retreat. Withdraw in on himself.

"This wasn't planned," I say quietly, as tears fill my eyes, but I will not let them fall. Now is my time to be honest with him, even though my heart is splintering. I say the next words with as much conviction as possible. "I thought you'd be happy."

He drops his head and doesn't say anything, so anger seeps into my veins and replaces the sadness. I need to get out of here. But just as I'm about to move, he speaks, reaching out for me before pulling his hands back and tucking them deep inside his pockets. "I'm sorry. But I don't know what to think or feel right now."

I take slow, deep breaths, trying to calm my racing heart. "The first step would be to accept it," I choke out in a broken voice, wrapping my arms around myself. "If you knew me, you'd know I didn't want a kid right now. But look, it's here, so it's bad luck we both need to accept. No tricks, no nothing. It's what happens when you have sex. We need to talk about it."

His jaw ticks. "No. I can't talk right now," he says, before his mouth flattens into a thin line. He's holding himself back. Not saying anything else. We glare at each other. Both hurt, scared, upset, and confused.

I wait for him to change his mind. But it never comes. The quiet only inflicts more pain on me.

As my breath catches in my lungs, I mumble, "I need to leave." I turn and don't look back. He remains silent.

I jog up the stairs and grab my case and begin to pack.

"For how long?" he asks, entering my room.

I flick my gaze up, noticing his pained eyes stay on mine. My bottom lip quivers as I feel my eyes brimming with tears. It won't be long before I'm sobbing uncontrollably. I can't do that here.

"I don't know. What are you doing anyway? Get the fuck out and stop watching me."

I can't believe I swore at him. It's so not me. I'll blame the emotions of having my heart ripped out by the man I love.

He doesn't move, watching me continue packing my clothes into the case. Then suddenly, he sighs and spins around, leaving me alone. His heavy feet disappear down the stairs, and the front door opens. When the door slams behind him, I can finally breathe.

Sadness hits me deep inside the chest. The despair rips me apart, as deep sobs rack my insides. I'm sucking in breaths, trying to pull myself together, but they fall harder. Burying my face in my hands, I let myself cry, until I have no more tears left.

And then I suck up in one last calming breath and wipe my face with both hands. Standing, I walk over to my clothes and finish packing. As I drive back to Maddison's, I'm sad, angry and, of course, I stupidly miss him.

CHAPTER 37

ALEX

THOSE TWO WORDS "I'M pregnant" made something snap inside me. I can't be a father. I've just accepted I'm worthy of a relationship. A father is just too much.

Fuck. I need a second to think.

To breathe.

When I came back home from a long drive, she was gone.

I pour a good three fingers of whiskey. Bringing it to the television, I take a big sip and sit on the sofa. The stupid sofa reminds me of all the times we laid here. Watching TV, talking, and hanging out. My eyes drift to my pool. My stomach hardens as I remember the time I hadn't touched her yet, but the way her body looked submerged in the water naked...she made me hard.

Made me question things.

God, I wanted her so much.

Now I sit alone with my thoughts. I watched her pack her bags and said nothing to stop her. I let her go, even though it killed me.

I want to go one way, and my life pulls me in another.

How the hell did I get here?

I shake my head in disbelief. Where the hell did my life go? It seems to have spiraled. I pushed her away and shouldn't I be glad?

I should...

But fuck, I'm not.

Bringing the glass to my lips, I tip my head back and drain it.

I need to drink until I can't feel the fear thrumming through me anymore. I get up and grab the bottle and escape to one of the rooms that she's never been in, so I don't have to see her beautiful face when I close my eyes.

Visions of her blur the more I drink.

I wish I could be happy, but I'm fucking shit scared.

What if I suck at being a dad?

What if I revert back to my old ways?

I wake up delirious in one of my spare rooms the next day. It's the first time I've ever been in here.

It's for guests only.

To think now I'm a guest in my own house.

I peel myself up and stroll to my bathroom, ignoring the way my head is yelling at me for drinking last night. Nothing coffee and food can't fix.

I shower and dress and do the only thing that will allow me to run away from visions of her...work.

Before I think about hitting my office, I walk directly to the barista and order a coffee and a bagel.

But before I join the line, I hear my name.

"Alex," a familiar deep voice bellows.

"Damien, man, how are you?" I step forward and shake his hand.

He shakes mine back firmly. "Busy, but good," he says, stuffing his hands in his suit pockets after our exchange.

"Freshly shaven," I say, noticing his beard is gone.

"You could do with a shave," he says through a chuckle.

I rub my jaw, feeling the stubble under my palm, and with a smug grin, I say, "Nope, the wi—woman digs it."

I almost said *the wife*. Like the word just rolls off my damn tongue and we're not even married yet. If we even do get married now that I've made a mess of things.

My temple throbs. I can't think about it right now. The headache will form into a migraine if I don't stop with the running thoughts of Tahlia.

He laughs and shakes his head at me.

I ignore his tease and get away from my own shit to ask about him. "Talking ladies, how're the chicks loving the single dad tag?"

He pulls out a hand to scratch his brow before answering. "What women? I've been with none since—"

"Now you're really pulling my leg," I say, cutting him off, shocked.

He fires back quickly. "I'm a plastic surgeon with a young son. Not attractive to women at all."

My brows rise to my hairline. "You're kidding. You're a chick magnet. You just don't put yourself out there."

He snorts, as if I'm the one being ridiculous. "And how would you like me to do that?"

"Go out to Luxe with some friends."

He clicks his tongue on the roof of his mouth. "Son, remember?"

Think, Alex...

"Online," I say with a jackpot smile.

Damien scrunches up his face with disdain. "That's even worse. I suck at talking, especially small talk, and particularly about myself."

I can't argue with that, as he isn't as easy-going or as talkative as me. Hmmm.

"Well, I'm out of ideas. Let me grab us a coffee." I shrug and tilt my head to the barista.

He grins as if he's won. "Told you it's impossible."

I hate losing, so I shake my head and say, "Not impossible, but definitely not easy. Let me think about it and see if I can come up with any ideas. I'm running on a few hours of sleep."

"Were you on call?" He frowns.

"No. I was—" I stop speaking, not knowing what to say. I can't tell him Tahlia's pregnant and that I drank until I passed out.

"Was wha—" His pager goes off, cutting him off.

"Did you want a takeaway coffee, or is it urgent?" I ask, watching him.

He reads the message on the pager. I'm grateful that mine hasn't gone off, and I'm able to get in a much-needed caffeine kick.

Tucking his pager away, he looks back at me. "No, I gotta get back upstairs now. I'll have to catch you soon."

I nod, knowing I should start the mountain of paperwork I have let build up and get to visiting some patients. But I can't function properly right now without a hit of caffeine. "All right. Catch you later."

He wanders off toward the elevator, and I walk over to order my coffee. My phone rings, and I see Mike's name. I hit decline. I'm not ready to answer it. He will be angry. I don't blame him. I just don't have any answers.

Carrying my latte and bagel to the elevators, I become instantly awake without even taking a sip of my coffee.

Tahlia is walking with Blake toward the elevators. She's here. But why?

Is she okay?

Or has she come to confront me?

The glum look on her face tells me she's not here for me. I never got a text or call.

Suddenly a rush of panic hits my chest, and I press my lips together and stride closer.

Her eyes widen when she sees me.

"Tahlia."

Blake clears his throat.

I flick my eyes to his and nod. "Hi, Blake."

"Hi," he says curtly, but my eyes are already back on the captivating greens I've missed. Just now, she stares back at me with bold defiance. I know Blake probably wants to chop my balls off, but I don't care. I need to see why Tahlia's here. My hand grabs her waist instinctively, but she steps back, forcing my hand to slip.

She doesn't want me to touch her. And I can't stop the selfish way that hurts me.

I stuff my hand into my pocket to stop it from happening again.

"Why are you here?" I ask.

She winces, as if I wounded her by not wanting her to come here. But that's not it. If anything, seeing her now makes me miss her more. I've not felt myself without her.

"A doctor's appointment," she says matter-of-factly.

"Are you and the baby okay?" I ask.

"Routine one. Calm down, Daddy," Blake cuts in, the word making a wrinkle between my brows.

"Blake. Do you mind?" She turns to face her friend, whose eyes are still narrowed on me.

"You want me to leave you with him?" he asks.

Inside, I'm hoping she says yes.

"Please."

He blows out his cheeks in a frustrated breath, then turns to face her. "Okay but call me if you need me. I'll sit here and wait for you."

"Thanks." She gives him a small smile.

He snaps his gaze to me. Shaking his head in dismay, he strides to the tables and chairs in the cafeteria. He's not happy.

When her eyes return to mine, I patiently wait for her to tell me what's going on.

"Did you want to come with me? It won't be long. It will be a chat and blood test to confirm..."

"Confirm the pregnancy?"

"Yes," she replies sadly.

I nod. I'm still confused about how to feel, but the way I can't let her do this without me tells me to suck it up and go.

"Yeah, I'll come, if you'll have me."

Her mouth parts, as if she wants to speak, but she walks off, and I follow.

I stay silent the whole elevator ride, and even sitting in the obstetrician's office, listening to Doctor Paddock talk, I can't find my voice.

I'm confused, shocked, wondering when it'll wear off.

I can't believe we're doing this.

A baby.

CHAPTER 38

ALEX

After the appointment, I walked her down to Blake. She quickly said goodbye and left. My head has been spinning ever since. I couldn't concentrate on work, so I left and drove myself home. I've been lying on the sofa, wondering what to do. A part of me wants to go to her place and throw her over my shoulder and bring her home. This place doesn't feel right without her. But also, after the way I reacted, I don't feel worthy of her.

I rub my hand over my face just as the doorbell rings. I get up slowly, knowing deep down it's not her, so what's the rush?

The bell rings again, and it irritates me. No one is meant to be here. I need more time to be alone.

I stride to the door and open it.

Mike stands in my entry. I shouldn't be surprised. I ignored his call earlier.

I clench my jaw.

He knows.

"Mike," I answer, keeping my voice emotionless.

"Alex." He steps inside, and I walk to my kitchen to make some food. I need to eat.

I know why he's here, and I know I'm being a man child, but I don't want to talk about it. Because it'll mean I have to be vulnerable and that's not me. I'm the easy-going guy, not the talk-my-feelings-out guy.

Seeing Tahlia today has me feeling more restless.

I move to the kitchen and grab an apple. Mike stares at me. If he wants to talk to me standing up, then go for it. I don't have the energy.

"What happened? he asks.

I lower the apple with a sigh. "She told me she was pregnant."

He rubs his jaw in thought. "And what's so bad about that?"

"I'm not ready for a kid, Mike. Fuck."

He snorts. "No one is."

Staring at him, I ask, "How did you know you were ready for a kid?"

"I didn't," he says with a shrug, pulling out a stool and sitting down. "It wasn't planned either."

"So, you just accepted it happily?" I ask.

"It was either accept it, or lose her and the baby," he deadpans.

I nod. Understanding his difficult decision. I don't want to lose Tahlia, but a baby is a lot to take on. Listening to the doctor talk today cemented that.

"Do you want to cancel the wedding?" he asks, pulling me right out of my thoughts.

Cancel the wedding?

Looking down at my hand, where soon I'm supposed to be wearing a gold wedding ring, my answer is immediate. "No."

His firm grip grabs my shoulder, and he meets my eyes head on. "Do you want to lose her, dumbass?"

"Fuck no. I love her. I'm shit scared now that the things I imagined in a fantasy with her are coming true. Like having a kid and teaching him or her how to swim or playing with Ethan. I pictured it all, but now it's happening. I'm freaking out."

"I thought so. So, pull your head out of your ass, stop being scared, and go get her. Figure it all out together."

Mike leaves me sitting there without another word.

I love Tahlia. I need her. She's everything to me. I run my hand through my hair, pondering how to fix this.

I pull my phone out of my pocket and bring up her name to call her. But as I stare at the screen, I can't pull the trigger, as something inside me stops me. Even if it destroys me, I can't call her. I have to see her. I rush to grab my keys and run for the door to drive to her old house.

During the drive, my heart is pounding as I worry that I've fucked up the greatest thing in my life. Her.

CHAPTER 39

ALEX

WHEN I GO TO her house, Maddison opens the door. Her face is tight and her lips thin. I deserve the hatred. I hurt her best friend.

"I know I fucked up. Let me talk to her," I beg with a shaky voice.

She twists her head, looking inside the house, before bringing her icy gaze to meet mine. I'm slightly scared of this pocket-sized woman.

"If she wasn't so sad, I'd tell you to stick it where the sun doesn't shine, but because she needs you, loves you for some reason, I'm going to go out for a little bit. And when I get back, if you've hurt her more...watch out." She purses her lips, and I like how protective she is of her friends.

"I promise. I won't. I'm really sorry."

"Let's see if she'll accept it. I can't blame her if she kicks your ass out of the house."

I nod. She barges past me and straight toward her car.

I stand there for a second, a wave of guilt hitting me. I'm such an asshole.

Not wasting another second, I stride inside and close the door. Walking through the house, I follow the blaring noise of the TV, knowing it's an episode of *Friends*. I'm secretly happy she isn't watching our reality show without me.

Catching sight of her on the sofa, my heart lurches. I take in her appearance. Her blonde hair is messily tied up in a loose bun on top of her head. She's wearing a cream sweater and pants. Her knees are brought up to her chest...giving herself a hug.

And the sight of that makes me want to give her a hug and tell her I'm so fucking sorry. Even sad, she's fucking perfect.

"Hey," I say, staring down into her red-rimmed eyes.

The puffy bags under her eyes make me feel worse. She didn't look like this yesterday.

I keep hurting her. She deserves better than me.

But I remember what Mike said, and I don't want to lose her, or the baby, all because I'm scared.

"Hi," she says hesitantly. I can't blame her for being quiet. She probably thinks I'm going to storm off and have a tantrum, or stay silent, because that's how I've been acting.

Sitting down beside her, I inhale her scent deep into my lungs. I've missed the smell of her.

I just missed everything about her.

"What are you doing here?" she asks, keeping her voice low.

I shift closer to her, but she stiffens. My heart sinks. I did this. And I hate myself for it. I need to be completely honest with her.

"I'm so sorry for the way I reacted. I just needed time to process. Before you, I never wanted kids, but since being with you, falling in love, and wanting what my brother has...it's what I want too. To be honest, I don't know if I'm ready, and that's what's scaring me."

"I'm not ready either," she sniffles.

I nod. "I don't want to let you down. I'm scared. So, fucking scared. But Mike said something before we got together that's stuck with me."

Her head tilts up at me, curiosity etched in her face.

"He said you'll know she's the one because she feels like home. Keeping you safe, warm, and loved. And that's you. You feel like home."

Her eyes meet mine, and a flicker of deep emotion stares back. The cavernous pain from her makes my chest squeeze, and I have to look away for a moment before returning to her green eyes.

"I trusted you to be there for me..." she says, her voice husky with unshed tears. "And you broke my heart." She swallows and opens her mouth as she cries. "I don't..."

The blood pumps in my ears. Her hands covering her face make her ring unmissable. My own damn eyes sting.

Seeing my engagement ring still on her hand makes my heart pump harder. I reach out, unable to stop myself from touching it. She looks down at me touching the ring on her finger.

"I needed you," she adds, her voice broken and barely above a whisper.

Needing to touch her, I rest my hand over hers and speak the truth, no matter how painful. "I know, and I fucked up the best thing that has ever happened to me. I asked the world for one thing, and I got it. Yet I pushed it away from fear. Loving you scares me so much, but losing you would be worse. Fuck, no, even saying that out loud crushes me."

She stays silent. Tears still sprinkle down her cheeks as anguish looks back at me. With my other hand, I brush the tears away as I continue to beg. I'd rather give everything to at least know I tried, because I need her in my life, and I won't let her walk away from me. She's going to be my wife.

"Always getting accused of being promiscuous and a player, I guess I believed that to be true. That love wasn't in my future, let alone a family," I say in a panic. Pulling my hand away from her face, I hit my chest. I remember the numbness. It was so debilitating and so hollowing. "Tahlia, before you, I was so fucking numb inside."

"Alex," she sniffs, and there is a softness in her expression now.

"I swear to love you all my life," I say, grabbing her hand and turning it so I can lace my fingers with hers, admiring how perfectly we fit together. I squeeze her hand as my eyes hold hers. "You're my person. And without you, my life isn't worth living. I want a family. I want to fill my house with love, laughter, and happiness. I promise I'll make it up to you every day for the rest of our lives. Just give me a chance to prove how sorry I am."

Her green eyes fill with new tears, and my own finally trail down my cheeks.

CHAPTER 40

TAHLIA

THIS BEAUTIFUL, BROKEN MAN. As he swallows hard, clearly trying to hold back his struggle, I can't stop the tears that spill down my face from his words. I understand his freakout and that he needed a moment to digest. Staring at his solemn face, I know in this moment, my heart is his. The words he spoke were so vulnerable and honest, begging me for another chance. My heart aches as I look at the torment in his eyes. He's deeply sorry, and it's evident. I grab his hands in mine, calming from the heat of his skin. Entwining our fingers, I stare down at them. Everything is right when he's with me.

"I know you're sorry. I forgive you. But I'm sorry too, for not giving you a chance to digest things or talk it out when you were ready."

"Don't be sorry. I'm the fucking idiot. But do you really forgive me? Can we be a family? I so badly want to deserve this life with you." He speaks as if he can't quite believe it.

"Of course. I love you," I explain.

"I love you too. I want nothing more than to be your husband and a father to our baby. But I might need you to be patient as I ease into the fatherhood part."

"Why, Alex?"

He drops his gaze to our tangled fingers, as if looking for answers. I don't press him. I wait patiently.

"I'm not worthy," he whispers, like he's too scared to say them too loud. I catch it, and with those words, I feel his deep-rooted apprehension in all this.

It's my turn to be delicate and offer him comfort the same way he has given it to me. Grabbing the sides of his face, I welcome the rough texture of his scruff on my palms. The familiarity soothes me. His blue eyes are so bright and his pupils grow bolder with worry.

"You are, Alex. Look at the way you love and care for me. I can already tell you're going to be amazing. All a baby needs is love," I say tenderly, as if he may break if I speak too loudly.

He nods in my grip. "I can do that. I already do love our baby."

I smile, leaning up to kiss him. I lay my head on his chest, and he wraps his arms around me.

"I need to ask you something," he says, getting off the sofa. He drops to one knee and the dam of tears spill again.

"Tahlia Adams. I never would have believed we would be here today. What started as friends and then turned to a fake engagement to a real loving relationship is beyond my wildest dreams. It doesn't feel real that I get to come home to you. Me before you was so different that I would never have believed I could feel like this. This deep, earth-moving love everyone dreams about. But you make me feel every type of emotion, and I thank you."

"Oh, Alex." Clutching his hand that's holding mine, I inch forward.

"I was a shell of a man before I met you. I believed bad things about myself and couldn't see the good. You've been there every time I think I'm not worthy enough. I want to spend every day showing you and our baby how I'm worthy of both of you. That I am a better man. I promise to love you and our baby with everything that I am. I'll be there now and forever. Will you do me the honor and become my wife?"

"Yes, yes, yes!" I say, sealing my lips to his. He's mine, and I've never been surer of something in my life.

"Fuck yes! Let's get married then."

CHAPTER 41

ALEX

Alex: Did you take your pregnancy vitamins I had delivered to you?

Tahlia: Yes, Doctor Daddy.

Alex: Good girl. I can't wait to marry you today.

"LET'S GO, PEOPLE," BLAKE'S voice booms loudly over the music playing.

I quickly reply to Alex before getting in the car.

Tahlia: I can't wait to marry you.

Blake, Alice, and Maddison are in my bridal party. Mom and Dad are here too. Mom smiles kindly, and there's a twinkle in her eye. I think she's pleased I'm following through with the wedding to Alex, even though my stake of the business was sold to someone else.

Alex and I sat down with them and chatted about our relationship. We had the chance to explain what our honest plans were going forward with the relationship and the wedding. We haven't mentioned the pregnancy yet, but they were happy with our answers to all their questions. We aren't the warm and fuzzy family. But I'm fine with the relationship. I accept it for what it is, without expectations. It's better now than ever, and I'm excited to see how a baby will change the dynamic more. I do hope it brings us closer.

I'm still unsure about work and where I'll go from here. I'm disappointed. The business would've been great, but having Alex and the baby are more important.

Today is such a surreal moment. It finally feels real. I can't wait to marry him and start our new life as a family. I never thought this is where my life would've ended up in a short amount of time, but I'm extremely happy it's turned out this way.

"Come on, let's get you to him. Looking at your face makes me jealous," Blake murmurs.

I giggle and walk outside. There's no more time to day-dream. I'm about to live my fantasy in real life. I'm extra nauseas as I watch everyone climb inside the limo after me. I just want to see him already.

The drive isn't long, and once I get out of the car, I gaze at my dad. My dad's eyes are misty, and I can tell he's holding back emotion. He smiles at me before his elbow pushes out in encouragement, and I thread my hand through his arm.

"You've got this. You two love each other. The rest will come in time."

I give him as much of a smile as I can through my wobbly chin. "Thanks, Dad," I say, kissing his cheek.

The music sounds, and my heart thrums inside my chest.

When it's my time to walk, my breath catches. Alex is waiting for me at the end of the aisle.

His black suit and bowtie show off his broad frame and tapered waist. I try hard not to drool. Alex in a tuxe-do is scorching. But the most beautiful thing about my soon-to-be husband has to be his smile.

Today it's full and bright.

He's happy.

Which makes me happy.

We're both ready to take the next step toward making us permanent.

I walk on shaky feet, keeping my arm firmly holding on to my dad. Ignoring all the noise around me to just focus on those soft blue eyes drawing me closer.

My dad lifts my veil, and I hear Alex exhale.

When our hands touch, and we are standing face to face, he says, "You look beautiful."

His eyes drop over my dress appreciatively. When his gaze reaches mine again, they're full of silent approval. "I love the dress," he breathes.

My nerves fade away at the look in his eyes. I want to hurry up and officially be his wife.

I want to be Mrs. Alex Taylor.

We exchange vows and kiss at our ceremony full of our closest friends and families.

Later at the reception I'm sober and, of course, my husband doesn't drink because I can't. Instead, he takes my hand, and we move onto the dance floor for our first dance.

"This is nice, but I can't wait to get my wife home. And be alone with her."

"Is that a promise?" I challenge.

"Are you talking code, Mrs. Taylor? I was talking about running a bath and tucking you into bed."

I giggle. "It was code, but clearly you have much better ideas."

"Hey, now. I think you need all of it."

"It sounds like the best way to end a perfect day."

Our dance ends and we return to our seats.

A tapping sounds on a glass, drawing the crowd and us to a silence. It's Blake.

"Thank you, everyone, for being here for my good friends, Alex and Tahlia. I always knew these two had something going on. A spark that they grew to figure out. Can we all raise our glasses up and cheer for the new Mr. and Mrs. Taylor?"

The crowd erupts in clapping and whoops.

Alex stands, and I know what's coming, and that makes waves of butterflies swarm my stomach.

"Thank you, Blake. And thank you all for joining me and my beautiful wife, Tahlia, on this special day. We hope you enjoy the night. We thank you for your gifts. We have one to give back to you...I'd like to announce our pregnancy. Not only do I have a beautiful wife today, but also a beautiful mother-to-be."

The room applauds loudly.

I stare at Alex, lost in his adoring words. He peers down at me and kisses my lips.

"You guys surprised us." My mom's voice pulls me away from him.

Looking at my parents' faces makes me smile. Their proud and watery eyes have me getting up and giving them a hug. Alex's parents have also come over to congratulate us too. We spend the next couple of hours eating, cutting the cake and when we go around to the whole room and say our thanks and goodbyes, Alex leans into my ear.

"My beautiful wife, are you ready to go home?"

"Please," I exhale.

He nods. But before we leave, Alex pulls me aside for a moment. I can't help but kiss him.

He stops, smiling down at me, and I moan. "More."

"Soon. I need to give you your present," he says.

The nerves are kicking in, and my heart is in my throat. What is it now?

"Here you are," he says excitedly.

I take the envelope with deep concentration and open it. Reading its contents, I blurt, "No, you didn't."

He smirks at my reaction. "I did."

I drop my hand and hold the letter. My name is the majority stake owner of Emerald Designs.

"How?" I ask.

"Your parents like me. What can I say?" He laughs.

"You charmed them. And paid how much? How much do I have to pay you back?"

"Nothing. This was a gift to my wife. You gave me the most magical gift." He taps his chest before continuing. "To feel anything but numb, and you did that. No present will ever be enough of a thank you. I'll always be indebted to you."

I grab his hand and we exit, my heart warm and my body ready for him.

Back at our house, he carries me up the stairs to our bedroom and stares at me with a fire I've not seen before.

He carefully lowers me to the bed, and my stomach is in a wild swirl of anticipation. When our lips touch, my eyes flutter closed, and I sink deep into it. His strong hand is on the back of my head while the other roams over my back and rests above the curve of my ass. My hands move from his broad shoulders up his thick neck, and I rake my fingers through his hair before curling my grip.

I feel everything, and our closeness is like a drug that brings me closer to euphoria.

He parts our lips, and his tongue runs over my bottom lip, seeking entry. I groan from the feeling of his tongue inside my mouth. Sweet and warm and captivating. I want more.

I need more.

And it's safe to say, he's feeling the same. The way his hand grips my ass and brings me flush against his hard erection. There is no mistaking the sparks.

Our tongues move in fluid strokes. I lap up his taste, and when he teases my mouth with his tongue, a whimper leaves my chest. No time to be embarrassed or silent. I can't hold myself back, even if I wanted to.

Every sweep of his tongue, I match it with my own in perfect rhythm. He's such a good kisser. Kissing him has fast become an addiction.

When we pull apart, both of us are gasping for oxygen. I bring my eyes to his and hold them, seeing the same struggle and confliction I feel, but he has a little...excitement.

"Let me worship you."

CHAPTER 42

ALEX

"I don't think I've seen a better dress," I rasp, touching her hot skin that's exposed from the dip in her wedding dress.

The lace is a mix of soft and rough against my fingers.

"You like it?" she asks in a sexy purr.

"No, honey. I love it. Knowing you picked this to wear for me as we become one. My wife. My future. My love for now and forever," I murmur.

The green in her eyes glows brighter. I don't miss the misty look, though.

"Honey..." I start.

She shakes her head. "I'm okay. Just extra emotional."

I lay my hand on her cheek. She nuzzles into it.

"Are you sure? I can run you a bath and make you tea."

Her lips twitch. "No, Doctor, even though that sounds nice. I don't want nice right now."

My eyebrows draw together. "You don't?"

"No. I want my husband." She gives me a sexy smile, and I don't miss the hint of mischief in her eyes.

"My wife needs her husband to fuck her, worship her, and make love to her," I whisper, leaning in and bringing my lips to hers in a hot kiss.

Her lips part to breathe out, "Yes."

I drop my hand from her face. "Good. Because the look of you as my wife makes me want to come," I murmur darkly, before adding, "Turn around."

She spins slowly until her back is facing me. I take a steady breath and admire her curves, then my hand reaches out to unzip her in an unhurried movement.

My fingers grip the metal, and I pull down steadily, exposing her skin. No matter how hard my body screams at me to do it faster, I don't. The moment I make love to her as my wife will be worth it.

I finish unzipping her dress, and take it off. She turns to face me again.

"Something blue," I mutter as I look at her pretty panties.

"You know about that?" she asks, surprise dripping from her voice.

"Of course. The moment we were getting married, I wanted to know every single detail about weddings. And when the lines became blurry between fake and real, I knew the reason for my research was to please you. Because ultimately, I want to give you everything."

"I want to please you too." She drops to her knees and my eyes widen at her sweet offer.

I cup her face, staring adoringly at her. My dick is throbbing behind my black pants, begging for her hot mouth.

"How am I meant to worship you, if you're on your knees?" I grind out. I fight back with how much I want this, but also struggle to accept the pleasure she's offering.

"You letting me suck your cock will make me feel incredibly powerful. To watch you struggle and give me the power to bring you to your knees with just my mouth, that is better than anything you could do to me right now," she says, licking her lips.

She's fighting hard. My world is spinning. I'm so conflicted. She's on her knees, with her bright green eyes begging to suck me off.

"Fine but afterward, I'm going to make you come so much, you won't remember sucking my cock."

She smirks dryly at me. "I'll always remember. I don't want to forget the look on your face as you come down my throat."

Fucking hell.

"Suck my cock, my beautiful wife. Own me, as if you don't already," I murmur.

She swiftly works on my button and zipper. I'm so hard, transfixed, watching her pull me out of my briefs and trying to wrap her dainty hands around me. My dick jerks in her hands as she gets ready to take me into her mouth.

"You're already leak—"

I thrust my dick between her parted lips. I can't hear another word, otherwise I'm going to come all over her pretty face.

She takes me as far back as she can, humming around me. The vibration causes me to grow harder. The feel of her wet, warm mouth is incredible.

My hands fly to her hair, grateful her hair is pinned in a neat bun, so I don't have anything blocking my view. I force my eyes to stay open. I don't want to miss a second of her taking me deep. As if checking I'm still there, her eyes snap to mine, and a little pre-cum spills before breathing through it and holding myself back.

She pulls back, giving me a second, which allows me to collect myself. "You taste so good," she pants.

I shake my head. "You're too good at this," I grind out.

"What?" she asks, confused.

"Your mouth is wicked. Now the only sounds I want to hear soon are you moaning," I say, bending down to lift her to her feet. I need her wrapped around me.

"You like my dirty talk?" she asks, dazed.

I swallow the growl threatening to leave my throat. "Too much." I move my hands up the middle of her back, enjoying the softness of her skin and the heat of her. Slipping the dress from her shoulders, I watch the dress fall to the floor. Now standing in only the panties and heels, I soak in every part of her.

The sight of her pebbled nipples and her quickened breaths are the only giveaways she's holding back.

I bring my lips to her in a passionate kiss, only breaking it to lean my forehead on hers.

Needing more, I sink to my knees and look up.

"I'm yours, and you're mine."

She nods.

"Forever," I say.

"Forever," she repeats.

I grab the sides of her panties and slip them down. She steps out of them, and I lower a kiss to her stomach in a gentle caress. Just over our baby.

My world, right here.

I kiss the top of her apex. She gasps, and her hands immediately find my hair.

"Kneeling for you is my greatest pleasure," I say through a moan. Grabbing her leg, I lift it onto my shoulder.

"Ah. Alex," she gasps.

I lean in and suck her swollen clit, hard. Her hands tighten in my hair, urging me to go harder. When I lick her opening, her legs buckle. My hands fly up to her hips to hold her up. I'm not ready to let go of her yet. I need to devour her on my knees. So, I don't stop eating her pussy until she's coming in a quivering mess on my face.

Once she does, she lowers her leg, and I stand. I remove my tie, ripping it off and tossing it to the side before I remove my shirt as fast as I can.

Walking to the bed, I take a seat and pat my leg. "Tonight is all about you. So, sit on my cock in your favorite position and ride me. Ride me as hard and as fast as you want."

She doesn't hesitate. She hovers, just as urgent and as eager as me. Sinking down, her pussy takes my cock deep inside of her. She's right, warm, and perfect.

My hands grab her waist, and I admire the way she lifts and lowers on me. Watching myself be swallowed up by her pussy sends me wild. I tilt my hips up every time she slams down. I know she's climbing, so I help her. Reaching around, I touch her swollen clit.

"Alex. Yes," she cries, a breathless tone that I love.

I rub her clit harder and faster, and when I feel her pussy tighten around my dick, I grunt. "Good girl, use my cock to get off."

She moans louder as she continues to fuck me. Chasing her orgasm. "You feel amazing."

Her hips rock when she's fully seated again. She tightens and pulses from the intrusion. "Alex, I want to come."

"I know, honey, and you can." I slide my hands up her stomach to grab both her tits. Squeezing them both at the same time, I find her peaked nipples and pinch them. Feeling her around me as husband and wife makes my chest swell.

The loud feral moan she lets out is erotic.

"Alex," she cries out through her orgasm.

As she rides me through her aftereffects, I come the hardest I have in my life.

I lift her up and spin her around to face me, and I hold her against me. Our perspiring bodies moving together, our breaths are fast and hot.

Fuck. I love her so much.

"Are you okay?" I ask when I can catch my breath.

She nods. "Yeah."

I kiss her temple. "Let me run a bath for my wife."

CHAPTER 43

ALEX

"COME BACK TO BED," Tahlia begs with a purr.

From the side of the bed, I look over my shoulder at her. She's giving me her best *come fuck me* eyes, seducing me again.

And I can't resist.

I grin, rolling back under the blankets. "Ten more minutes, but after that, we've gotta get up. We need to go to your appointment on time."

My hand slides over her waist and I scoot so her ass is flush with my groin. My hand strokes her belly. I love holding her, sleeping next to her, and waking up with her.

"Someone's eager..."

"You have no idea," I say, laying a kiss to her bare shoulder. "I want to meet our baby already."

"We're way too early."

"I know. I know. I'm just excited to find out who he or she will look like. I hope it's you. You're so beautiful."

Her hand settles over mine, holding it still. "You have to say that. I'm your wife."

"I'm saying it because it's true." I pepper kisses over her shoulder.

I continue to hold her in my arms. I wish she could feel what I feel inside. Everything is hot, electric, and beating. I'm no longer the same person I once was.

No, I feel so much for this woman. Love, happiness, laughter. The list is endless, just like my love for her. I don't feel deserving of everything, but Tahlia reminds me every day she loves me and that's she's here for me. Heck, she even irons my shirts topless. I don't know why that happened, but I don't ask questions. I simply enjoy the fucking view of my wife ironing nude. That's my fucking life. A life I love.

"I love you," I whisper into her skin.

"I love you too."

I caress her bump. "We have to get up now." She turns in my arms to face me, and I kiss her lips. "Let's go see our baby."

She nods with a smile. "Let's."

We walk into the hospital holding hands. It's strange for me to come to work for a non-work activity, but today's all about our baby. The last time I was here, I didn't take anything in. It was all a blur. But now, I'm ready.

Ready to be a father.

We take a seat in the waiting area of our obstetrician's office. Doctor Paddock is one of the oldest and wisest ob-gyns working here. Tahlia chose well. She has great instincts, and I can't wait to see her as a mother.

While we wait, Tahlia pulls out her phone to reply to a work email. I'd tell her to stop working, just relax, but she'll be on maternity leave soon, and it's nice to see how much she's loving her job. I know the rewarding feeling of being passionate about your job, so I want to support her in any way I can.

"Welcome guys," Doctor Paddock says, standing at the entrance to the waiting room. "Come with me."

Tahlia tucks away her phone, and I put my hand on her lower back as we follow the doctor into the exam room.

"How is everything going with your pregnancy?" Dr. Paddock asks Tahlia as we take a seat.

I sit back and let them talk, taking it all in. I feel lost, like I'm waiting for direction. It's strange being on the other side of the table.

"I'm a little tired at night, but otherwise, it's easy," Tahlia says.

"Make sure you don't overdo it," Doctor Paddock replies.

Tahlia throws a thumb in my direction. "As if he would let that happen."

"I'm glad your husband is looking out for you. I wish more were like him."

I shift in my seat, suddenly feeling awkward and unsure why that was unusual. Not only has Tahlia got my heart, but she has another piece of me growing inside of her. Both are equally important to me. They are my reason.

"I will check your blood pressure before I do a small scan for you. You can book your twenty-week scan with my receptionist when you leave. I need you to get more bloodwork done then, too."

He stands, and Tahlia does too, walking to the exam table. Once she's situated, he takes her vitals.

"Did you guys find out the sex?" he asks as he finishes removing the blood pressure cuff.

"Not yet. I thought they were going to call, but they didn't," Tahlia replies, her brows furrowed.

"That's unusual. Well, I have the results here. Did you want to know?"

My stomach bottoms out, and I stand in a rush to move beside Tahlia. I want to be near her when we find this out. We've been waiting for this moment. I've guessed girl, and she has guessed boy.

I want another *her*.

A mini-Tahlia. Bringing me joy.

I hold her hand, caressing the soft skin in circles.

Her gaze stays fixed on the doctor, but mine is on her.

Her glassy eyes are already emotional as we wait for the results.

"Congratulations, Mr. and Mrs. Taylor, you're having a girl."

My smile nearly splits my face, and emotion hits me hard and fierce. I'll admit, my eyes sting.

Tahlia's lip quivers, and a tear slips down her cheek. "You were right," she says to me through sniffs.

"Are you happy? I ask worried she's disappointed she didn't get a boy.

She nods rapidly. "Yes. I'm so happy. Are you?"

"Over the fucking moon. I have two queens to take care of now. My heart has never beat so fucking fast in its whole life."

She smiles as more tears spill onto her cheeks. I remove my hand from hers and swipe away the tears with my thumbs before kissing her lips. "Are you ready to see our princess?"

A choke of a sob sounds out of her mouth as she says, "Yes."

She lies back on the table, and the doctor preps her stomach with gel and scans Tahlia's belly. The little baby girl comes onto the screen and a tear leaks from my eye. My world. These two beautiful women are mine. I'll do whatever it takes to make sure they know how much I love them.

"Do we have a name?"

"Not yet," I say in a shaky voice.

When he's finished the scan, while he wipes the gel from Tahlia's belly, I grab my phone and order something for her.

We move back to the chairs and discuss the next few weeks in detail. Dr. Paddock answers all Tahlia's questions and once we're done, he hands over forms for the upcoming scans and tests. Tahlia takes a detour to the bathroom, and I head to the reception desk to check out.

The receptionist hands me the box I had delivered for Tahlia. "This came for you."

"Thank you," I say, just as Tahlia enters the room.

Her eyes widen, and a grin transforms her face when she sees what I'm holding. "You didn't."

I smile. "I did."

She walks closer and lifts the lid to peek inside the box. The same bakery box I brought the time she dropped Mike and Alice's downstairs.

Cupcakes with pink icing. At least if she chooses to wear it, I'll happily help clean it up. Right now, seeing her carrying my child makes me want to fill her with another baby. Why? I don't know. But the thought and now seeing her pregnant is sending me feral.

"Get me home so we can enjoy these." Her eyes are no longer glassy with tears. No. They are full of wickedness. My wife's going to wear icing on her body, and I'm going to enjoy licking it off her. She's mine, and I am hers. I never thought I could have feelings for a woman, but every day I spend with her, I'm certain I couldn't switch them off. Tahlia fulfills me. My person.

Epilogue 1

Tahlia

Months later

I look out my new office window. The pool and city views as my backdrop are something out of a magazine. Alex wanted to move us into a bigger house, but there were too many good memories here that I wasn't ready to part ways with.

I like his house. It's loving, and everywhere I turn, I think of us. I want our baby to be welcomed and brought to this home.

Alex argues it's too small. Which is ridiculous. She will have her own room, and the house is modern, with more than enough accessories. Kids don't need all this. They simply need us. I know we're already going to shower the baby with love. The way Alex pampers me, you'd think I was the queen. The cooked food, medication, massages, and the coffee. I had to make the switch to decaf because I couldn't deal with his doctor's comments anymore. I just want the taste anyway.

I get it, he loves the baby and me, but damn, sometimes him being a doctor is a lot. I have to remind him I'm his wife, not a patient. On the positive, it always ends up in hot sex.

Since the wedding, life has been busy. The complete move here, with not a single item left at my rental with Maddison. The home office has only just been finished being built. It needed an upgrade to accommodate what I'll need to work from home.

Speaking of...my phone rings.

"Mom. Hi," I answer.

"I'm just popping over. Alex said you were working from home today," she says, and I can tell she's driving.

"I am. I have a new sample of the fall line. Did you want to come to help me approve it?" I ask with a smile, peering around the room to look for the box of samples. It just arrived.

I have accepted their help as a way of continuing our new relationship. Plus, I don't have time to train anyone new right now. I'm twenty-eight weeks pregnant, so to hire and train a new person to add to the business all while I'm still adjusting, is silly. This way, they help me, and I can still learn all from my house. The office and warehouse are not too far away if I need to go there for any reason.

The door rings, so I wander down and open the door.

"Hi, Mom," I say with a pinched brow when I notice she's holding something. "What's that?"

"Oh, it's for you." She hands me a white gift bag, and I take it as I close the door behind her.

"What is it?" I ask, unable to help myself.

She chuckles. "Open it and find out."

I walk to the table and lower the bag and open it. I pull out a long, white, flowy dress. The little flowers are beautiful.

I'm so confused.

"It's beautiful, and thanks…" I trail off, still not understanding. There's nothing else inside the bag.

"Your father and I designed it, and had it made," she replies softly.

Now I'm even more confused. "Why?"

"Your friends, me, and Alex decided if you weren't going to organize a baby shower, we would."

My hand flies to smother my gasp.

It dawns on me, my parents made this special dress for me to wear to my very own surprise baby shower.

"No," I mumble into my hand.

"Yes. It starts in one hour, and any minute, a team will arrive to do your hair and makeup. Also, to set the house up for guests."

I drop my hand and look down at myself in my Lululemon leggings and shirt. "Do I have time for a shower?"

I hope so.

"Of course," she replies.

"Oh," I say, as a wave of disappointment washes over me. I know it's not traditional, but I wish Alex could come and celebrate with me today.

"Alex needed to pick up a couple of things, but he'll come near the end," she says, smiling.

"The end?" I ask.

"Your friends didn't want him to hover and not let you have fun."

I giggle. "He's a little protective of us," I say, touching my bump.

"Who can blame him? I'm grateful you have him."

"I know he's taking extra caution, but...it's early for a baby shower. I'm only twenty-eight weeks."

We had our big scan recently. I received the all-clear and, finally, I feel like I can breathe. But realistically, I don't know if I will fully relax until I hold her in my arms.

"Again, he wanted you to rest in the final stretch not party."

I snort. "Mom, it's a baby shower. I'm not clubbing."

Her lips lift, and I know she agrees.

"You know Alex," she adds.

"I do. And I love him. My helicopter husband."

"Helicopter husband?" she asks, perplexed.

"Just a phrase, Mom."

"Okay—" she's cut off when the door sounds.

My eyes widen.

"Go shower. Take your time. I'll let them in and set up," she says, shooing me away.

I exhale and smile. "Thanks, Mom."

I grab my dress and head to the bathroom, but not before sending Alex a thank you text. I love him so much it hurts to be without him, even for a moment.

EPILOGUE 2

ALEX

One Year Later

I wake to a cold bed. Rubbing my eyes, I stretch and get up. It's just before seven in the morning. I stroll down to the kitchen, following the delicious smell.

A wide smile takes over my face as I see Tahlia making coffee. I come up behind her and wrap my arms around her middle. Touching her growing bump is my favorite thing to do. Resting my hands there, I murmur into her neck, "Smells good."

"Yeah, I've finished making your coffee. Sit down, and I'll serve breakfast."

"I'll help."

"I'm fine. You always cook me breakfast and coffee. It's my turn," she says with an odd twinkle in her eye. The curve in her lips makes me think something up.

Looking around the kitchen, I take a seat. I can't help but notice there are no dishes.

"Where're the dishes?"

"Ah. I cleaned up."

My mouth purses, trying to contain a laugh.

But she bursts out laughing first.

"Fine, you got me. I ordered delivery."

"That's still thoughtful, thank you." As I look at the array of food, my mouth salivates. "Looks like we have a bit of everything."

"Yeah, I couldn't decide on what to get, so figured I'll get everything."

"Maybe he's growing."

"It might be a she..."

"It might. I wish we could find out."

She shakes her head. "Nope. I want a surprise."

"We didn't have a surprise with Elsie," I mumble.

The sound of the monitor goes, letting us know our little blonde angel is awake.

"I've got it," I jump up, leaving Tahlia laughing to herself.

I walk into her nursery, finding Elsie talking loudly to her hanging mobile. She notices me over the side of her cot and she kicks her feet. I smile at her messy short hair from the night's sleep. It's grown patchy and in the cutest mullet style. It's damn adorable.

"How's my baby feeling?" I coo as I pick her up and lay her down on the changing room table. I take her out of her sleeper and change her diaper.

Elsie's eyes are a darker green, and they remind me so much of her mom. She's a gentle and quiet soul. Not like other babies. Well, I only have Ethan to compare to, but he's now two years old, with the funniest temperament. He's like a little Mike, with the same scowl set between his brows. It's hilarious.

Except when I tickle her, she becomes loud. I rub her ribs gently to tickle and the sound out of her mouth has me smiling brightly down at her. I love her laugh as much as I love her mom's.

"Are you ready to go stay at gramps and grams for the night?" I ask.

Elsie smiles happily with no care in the world. Her rosy cheeks from her laughing make me want to cuddle her.

I swoop her up in my arms, and it's funny how much I'm wrapped around her little finger, and she doesn't even know it. Her mom owns me and she does too.

After hanging out with my whole family and leaving Elsie there, I drive Tahlia and me home. Parking the car, we step out and make our way to the door. I'm ready to spend some time alone with her before our second baby arrives.

"Sorry, what did you say?" She blinks rapidly, meeting my gaze.

"Are you okay?" I ask louder.

Her face softens. "Yeah, just tired."

"Too tired for that shoulder massage?" I ask her. Having my hands on her is always a risk, because I get visions of touching her intimately. Stroking her breasts and down to her sweetness between her thighs. I shake my head, needing to clear the dirty thoughts before an erection tents my pants.

"Never," she says back with a half-amused smile.

"I thought so." I wink, happy she is lighter now.

I open the door, and she brushes past me.

"I'll go put my sweats on," she calls out over her shoulder, practically racing through the house and skipping every second step.

The door closes behind me, and I flick the lock. Her dressed up is one thing, but there's something uber-sexy about Tahlia dressed down. Her natural freckles, tousled messy hair, and sweats are my kryptonite.

Moving through the house, I flick on the TV and scroll to find our show. I've been forced to watch with her, but it's not half bad. I'm just keeping that secret to myself.

Otherwise, after this season, she may expect me to endure more. The reason I watch it is to be with her.

I pause the show and walk into the kitchen. Her light footsteps sound down the stairs, and as I finish grabbing us a bottle of water, I smile to myself as she's clearly looking for the remote. I hit play and her face lifts. Her eyes meet mine. I come to a halt in front of her. She straightens and grabs the bottle from my outstretched hand.

"Thanks," she says and takes a seat, unscrewing the lid and taking a sip.

I lower my bottle to the coffee table and lay my hands on her shoulders. Her body jumps a little with shock from my sudden touch. I move my thumbs in deep, sweeping movements.

As she eases back, I watch her eyes flutter closed, and I can't help but move my lips to her ear. "You're missing the show."

She grumbles and waves me off. Her shampoo hits me at full force, and I bite back a groan.

"Does this feel good?" I ask, my voice deep with arousal.

"Yes," she says as she eases farther into my touch.

"Good. Now just relax."

She takes a big intake of breath, and she tries to open her eyes. But fails.

I grin and move my hands to either side of her neck. Stroking up and down and finding her pulse. I love how hard and fast it goes underneath me. The rhythm matches my own. As I draw my touch in harder and slower, a whimper escapes her lips. My sole focus is on her and to make her feel good.

Her breathing picks up as she mumbles, "You really are a doctor, aren't you?"

Chuckling from above her, I tease, "Didn't believe me before?"

Her eyes snap open. "I did, I just...I've never been your patient before."

My hands freeze. I'm unable to massage for the moment. Thinking of her as my patient wouldn't be good. "I don't want you as my patient. Ever."

I curse at my tone. It's too clipped; I sound almost angry. And I instantly regret it. It's just the dread of a loved one getting ill scares me. "I didn't mean to be rude to you, but the patients I treat are not healthy. And I can't bear—" I swallow past the lump in my throat from my thoughts.

She tries to turn, and it snaps me back to reality. My hands hold her still so she can't turn around and see the pain I know that's etched into my face. I return to the massage, trying to distract her.

"Sorry," she whispers.

"Don't be sorry."

She opens her mouth to add something, but when she closes it, I'm kind of relieved.

Tahlia and my kids are my whole universe. I don't want to imagine anything ever happening to them.

She stays silent as my fingers dig into her knots and ease the tension that's built.

"Your hands are seriously magic, Doc."

"Magic?" I repeat, chuckling at her analogy.

I shake my head. "And you calling me Doc?" I smirk.

"Can I call you that?" She looks away, returning to watch the TV.

I lean down to whisper, and it comes out huskier than I mean for it to. I blame her intoxicating scent for being inches away from her skin.

"You can call me anything you want. I love all the nick-names you give me."

She nods her head, but I can't read her expression. My mouth doesn't move from her ear. My finger twitches to touch her, and on instinct, I do. Moving my finger along the front of her neck, I stroke it delicately, feeling her pulse ricochet up and then her swallow.

And I imagine her swallowing me, my dick coming to life just from the imagery. It's one hell of a vision I wouldn't mind having for real right now. But I don't want to ruin this sweet moment.

"All right, Doc," she whispers hoarsely, licking her lips, and my dick twitches at the sight.

I can't help but lean in and kiss her temple slowly before pulling back.

I don't know what's coming over me. I'd like to think I know exactly what I'm doing, yet my body isn't syncing with my brain. But she didn't say to stop it, so I inch closer.

She turns and her lust-filled eyes drink me in. I want to say fuck the massage and haul her upstairs to our bedroom.

My eyes drop down to her pouty pink lips, and they are wet from her just licking them. Teasing and taunting me some more. She's letting out these cute pants, and I want to just lean in and kiss her.

I clear my throat and pull away, leaning my forehead on the back of her head. My eyes slam shut tight, and I'm telling myself I'm doing the right thing. Let myself enjoy the peace of us doing something so mundane and then ravish her in our bed later.

When I'm finally off the ledge of kissing her, I slide her silky blonde hair to one side and return to giving her a massage. She hasn't moved or said a word. Only our heavy breaths can be heard. I don't even know if she's paying any attention to the show. I know I'm not. I'm still focused on every inch of her and how I'm struggling to rein myself in. Being sexually frustrated will make later so much better.

We continue until the episode ends, and she yawns. I stop massaging but keep my hands on her. I'm not ready to remove them; I feel closer to her like this.

"I think it's bedtime," I growl, knowing I can't hold on a second longer. I need my wife now.

I hear a cute gasp, and then her giggle. God, the sound is like music to my ears, soft, sweet, and so her.

"Ladies first."

That wins me a snort. "That's so kind of you."

She rolls her eyes at me with a smirk, and gets off the sofa, before turning to take the stairs.

I follow her until we're upstairs then I smack her ass. "Hey. No teasing."

She stares for a second, completely baffled, and I don't even know what came over me. But she's giving me a look I know so well.

"Did you want more of that, honey?"

We stare at each other. I'm drowning with desire. The chemistry is thicker up here than it was downstairs, and it causes me to sweat. I run a hand through my hair as I stare back at her. Her alluring eyes are bringing me closer.

When we are toe to toe, her sexy pants leaving her mouth are back. The sound through those parted pink lips is so sexy, and I just want those lips screaming out my name. Fucking hell, this woman is a force to be reckoned with. As I stand, taking in her begging eyes, her mouth parts, giving me a glimpse of her tongue. Without another thought, I lick my lips and dip my head down and capture her mouth. When I pull back for air, I watch as her eyes flutter, matching the beat in my chest.

"Yes. I want more," she breathes.

I bend down and lift her up, walking her into our bedroom. I need to take her now.

The End.

The Christmas Agreement

Resisting Chase

Saffron and Secrets Novella

Chicago Billionaire Doctors

Doctor Taylor

Doctor I DO

Doctor Gray

ACKNOWLEDGEMENTS

There are always so many people to thank, but I'll try to remember all the people who helped with this story.

I'd first like to thank my husband and kids. They are the most supportive people in the world. I wouldn't be able to continue without your love and understanding. I love you.

Next are my friends and family. I've been lucky to find people who read, love my stories, and even ask for more. (Even if you're biased I love you and it encourages me.)

To my beautiful betas: Amy, Kirstie, Nadelle, Sarah, Lara and Dee. Thanks for reading this book and putting up with me. There was a lot of stress to make it right for readers who wanted this story. In the end, I love how Alex and Tahlia's story turned out and I know it had a lot to do with your words and support.

To the team who helped polish the book, Word Emporium, NaughtyGirlNiceEdits, Lilypadlit, Wildheart Graphics, and Wild Love Designs. Thank you I'd be lost without you all.

Most importantly thank you, to you, my reader. Thanks for reading this love story and loving it as much as me.

About Sharon Woods

Sharon Woods is an author of Contemporary Romance. She loves writing steamy billionaire love stories with a happy ever after.

Born and living in Melbourne, Australia. With her high school sweetheart husband and two children.

http://www.sharonwoodsauthor.com